"Lynn Cahoon has hit the golden trifecta—
Murder, intrigue, and a really hot handyman.
Better get your flashlight handy, *A Story To Kill* will
keep you reading all night."
—**Laura Bradford**, author of the Amish Mysteries

TOURIST TRAP MYSTERIES

"Lynn Cahoon's popular Tourist Trap series is set
all around the charming coastal town of South
Cove, California, but the heroine Jill Gardner
owns a delightful bookstore/coffee shop so a lot
of the scenes take place there. This is one of my
go-to cozy mystery series, bookish or not, and I'm
always eager to get my hands on the next book!"
—*Hope By the Book*

"Murder, dirty politics, pirate lore, and a hot police detective: *Guidebook to Murder* has it all! A cozy
lover's dream come true."
—**Susan McBride**, author of The Debutante
Dropout Mysteries

"This was a good read and I love the author's
style, which was warm and friendly . . . I can't wait
to read the next book in this wonderfully appeal-
ing series."
—**Dru's Book Musings**

"I am happy to admit that some of my expectations were met while other aspects of the story exceeded my own imagination . . . This mystery novel was light, fun, and kept me thoroughly engaged. I only wish it was longer."
—*The Young Folks*

"*If The Shoe Kills* is entertaining and I would be happy to visit Jill and the residents of South Cove again."
—*MysteryPlease.com*

"In *If the Shoe Kills*, author Lynn Cahoon gave me exactly what I wanted. She crafted a well told small town murder that kept me guessing who the murderer was until the end. I will definitely have to take a trip back to South Cove and maybe even visit tales of Jill Gardner's past in the previous two Tourist Trap Mystery books. I do love a holiday mystery! And with this book, so will you."
—*ArtBooksCoffee.com*

"I would recommend *If the Shoe Kills* if you are looking for a well written cozy mystery."
—*Mysteries, Etc.*

"This novella is short and easily read in an hour or two with interesting angst and dynamics between mothers and daughters and mothers and sons . . . I enjoyed the first-person narrative."
—*Kings River Life Magazine* on *Mother's Day Mayhem*

Four
Charming
Spells

LYNN
CAHOON

Kensington Publishing Corp.
www.kensingtonbooks.com

All Kensington titles, imprints, and distributed lines are available at special quantity discounts for bulk purchases for sales promotion, premiums, fund-raising, educational, or institutional use.

Special book excerpts or customized printings can also be created to fit specific needs. For details, write or phone the office of the Kensington Sales Manager: Attn.: Sales Department. Kensington Publishing Corp., 119 West 40th Street, New York, NY 10018. Phone: 1-800-221-2647.

The K and Teapot logo is a trademark of Kensington Publishing Corp.

First Printing: April 2023
ISBN: 978-1-4967-4078-6

ISBN: 978-1-4967-4081-6 (ebook)

10 9 8 7 6 5 4 3 2 1

Printed in the United States of America

To my mother-in-law, Virginia Cahoon—thanks for believing in me.

CHAPTER 1

The Lodge in Magic Springs was the go-to place for most of the town's events. Weddings, anniversary celebrations, birthday parties, the meeting rooms in the historic lodge had seen it all. But today, Mia Malone and her crew from Mia's Morsels, the new catering, cooking school, dinner delivery, and now event planning business, was catering a more solemn event. Theresa Ann Holly's funeral had been at ten this morning graveside; now the coven was holding a wake to celebrate the life and the passing of one of their members. James, the catering director over at the Lodge, had sent the coven social committee to Mia when the Lodge had already been booked for a large celebrity wedding this weekend.

Mia appreciated the referral, but the coven's requirements for the food were a little odd, even for Magic Springs. And they'd asked for a discount because Theresa didn't have family to pitch in for the expense. As she watched another box of champagne being brought out from the kitchen, Mia hoped the discounted rate would at least cover her costs. Next time, she'd build in the extra charges for the coven's special requirements plus some extra before she took off the discount.

"You look like you're ready for this to be over." Christina Adams stood next to Mia and watched the group. "I have to say, for a coven event, it's pretty mild."

"What were you expecting? A lot of chanting and spell casting?" Mia watched as a man who'd been watching his phone for the last twenty minutes raised his hands in a cheer. "That one's too busy watching the baseball game."

"I thought I heard him mumbling about a bad ump call." Christina chuckled. "All the food's out and the last trays are being passed around. The food around the floral arrangement hasn't been touched. Is there a reason?"

Mia nodded, looking at the expensive caviar and cheeses sitting on the table. "That table is for the deceased coven members. Apparently, it's tradition for the newly departed to put on a feast not only for the ones she left behind but the ones who went before. It's bad luck to eat from that table."

Christina's eyes widened. "Like the you'll-die kind of bad luck, or the general seven years' curse?"

Mia laughed, keeping the sound low. "I believe it's the general seven years' kind. But you'd have to ask Grans. I don't know a lot of the rules, especially around the funeral traditions. I wish she would have warned me before I said yes to catering this thing."

"I would have thought that Mary Alice would be here. We didn't do the ghost table for Adele's party, or maybe I've just forgotten it? It's been a while." Adele had been a friend of Grans's who had passed on a few years earlier. She'd also been Mia's Morsels's first catering client. They'd planned a birthday party for her but turned it into a wake when Adele was found dead. Christina glanced around the room and pointed out one of the guests. "That woman looks like she swallowed the canary, as my mom would say. Isn't it rude to be happy at a funeral?"

"Not quite an appropriate emotion, that's for sure." Mia smiled as she saw Abigail Majors crossing the room toward them. Abigail and her husband had started Majors Grocery in Magic Springs many years before. Now, the store was run by their son, Trent, who also happened to be Mia's boyfriend. "Abigail, so good to see a friendly face."

"Yeah, these things can be intense," Abigail gave them both a hug. Christina was dating Levi, another one of Abigail's sons. "I'm really glad I wasn't part of the planning for this event, even though I'm excited to be part of the Mia's Morsels team. Ginny Willis can be a bit of a stickler for tradition. I see she made you do an ancestors table. I thought that went out of style fifty years ago."

"I thought she was making it up when she told me it was mandatory. Of course, that was after I'd finalized the bid and we'd signed the contract. Believe me, I'll be jacking up the prices of any coven event I do in the future. This one isn't turning out to be very profitable." Mia nodded to the woman Christina had pointed out. "Do you know who our Sally Sunshine is over at that table?"

"Karen Elliot?" Abigail stifled a laugh. "I've never heard anyone call Karen happy."

"Well, she looks happy today. Did she know Theresa?" Mia was taking an instant dislike to the woman who was now watching the other mourners with interest.

"Not that I know of. Theresa was kind of a hermit. She didn't attend coven events. Or have any family to speak of. That's the reason Ginny had to step in and do the wake. Most of the time, the family takes care of this send-off. I'm sure Ginny was doing everything by the book, just in case she's questioned about it. She's had some issues as the social chair." Abigail waved at a man over by the fireplace. "I'm being summoned. I'll see you next week, right?"

"I'm looking forward to finalizing your contract with Mia's Morsels. For a lot of reasons, not just your heavenly cakes." Mia watched as Abigail moved across the room, greeting people as she passed the tables.

"Abigail knows a lot of people in Magic Springs, at least around the coven. That should bring in more business when she joins the team. Hey, who's that?" Christina pointed out a man standing by the door to the room. "He looks like he's ready to sprint as soon as anyone notices him."

"Or he's waiting so he's not the first one to leave." Mia shook her head. "I have no clue who he is. Of course, there's lot of people here I don't know. Bethanie Miller, your bestie, is over by the bar, getting another glass of wine."

"Bethanie and I aren't quite friends anymore. Not since she pulled that last stunt with Levi. I don't know if she was jealous of me having a boyfriend or of me being with Levi, but either way, I don't need that kind of negativity in my life. I can get that at home. Not our place—I mean my mom's house." Christina looked up at Mia. "Are you ready for tomorrow?"

"Moving your stuff or talking to your mom?" Mia knew Mother Adams wasn't the friendliest person, even to her only daughter.

"Talking to Mom. And maybe an appearance from Isaac. I heard from him last night. He wanted to verify what time we'd be at the house to get my things. You'd think I was moving out of a hotel or an apartment the way they're treating me, not my childhood home." Christina blinked, and Mia realized she was on the verge of crying.

"They'll figure out how to deal with you having a brain sooner or later." Mia gave her a hug. "Let's go check out what we need to do to clean up in the kitchen. I'm tired of watching these people eat and ignore the fact this woman died. I don't think anyone is here to mourn; it feels like a mandatory meeting."

Christina nodded and headed toward the staff-only door, but Mia felt a hand on her arm and she turned to see Mahogany Medford standing next to her. "Christina, I'll be there in a moment."

"Sorry to bother you. I know you're working, but I just wanted to talk to you about Theresa's death." Mahogany took in the room as she spoke. "It's just like Mom."

"I know it must remind you of your mother's wake. It hasn't been very long since you had to do this yourself." Mia felt bad for the woman. She'd come home to bury her mom, but there were some questions on how Mrs. Medford had died. "Did the coven help with the wake for your mother?"

Mahogany shook her head. "Mrs. Willis, she said since I came back, I was responsible for the funeral planning. And the costs. Mom had some savings, so it wasn't a hardship, but Mrs. Willis seemed really put out that I even existed. The first time I called her, she hung up on me."

"That's weird." Mia watched as Ginny Willis stood and went over to get another glass of wine. At least the woman hadn't talked Mia into including an open bar in the contract. Besides the two cases of champagne, the alcohol costs were on the attendees. "She's been pretty involved in setting up this wake. Maybe she had a lot of the work done for your mom's event too."

"Maybe. That sounds like the woman. Once she realized I was the next of kin, she sent me a list of what needed to be included in this send-off. The way she talked about the wake, it was more like a welcoming party than a traditional funeral." Mahogany took a tissue out of her bag. "Have you learned anything about my mom's death yet?"

Mia shook her head. "My grandmother, Mary Alice Carpenter, is working on finding a spell that could have masked your mom's true age. She was planning on being here, but she came down with a cold or something. She didn't want to spread it around."

"Well, come by the house on Wednesday and we can talk some more. I know you have things to do here." Mahogany paused and pointed to the man at the door. "I wonder why Jerimiah's here."

"You know him?" It was the same man Christina had pointed out earlier, who was ready to bolt at any minute.

Mahogany nodded. "He was at my mom's wake.

He said he knew her from when she lived in Twin. He leads a small coven there."

"Maybe he's just here as a courtesy, then." Mia relaxed a little about the man. "Intercoven relationships are very important to keep connections, especially because there are so few of us around Idaho."

"That's probably it." Mahogany waved at another woman across the room. "I've got to go mingle. Maybe I can find out something about Mom's death while I'm at it."

Mia watched Mahogany disappear into the crowd. People were starting to leave and the mysterious Jeremiah had now left as well. This must have been just a courtesy visit, then. She turned back to the kitchen to escape the room. It wasn't a feeling of sadness that Mia felt permeating the crowd; it was worse. It was a feeling of indifference. Like Theresa's death wasn't affecting any of them. Except for maybe Mahogany, and that was just because she'd lost her mother so recently.

Theresa Ann Holly was being sent off to another life today. And it seemed like no one in this life even cared. If Mahogany Medford hadn't come home to bury her mother, she would have been sent off with a lifeless event like this. It wasn't fair, but Mia could only control one thing today, and that was the food at the wake.

Everything else wasn't on her list.

CHAPTER 2

As Mia watched out the passenger-side window, Trent Majors drove the van through Boise and toward the foothills. Mia loved this part of Boise. The area between the Boise River and the Foothills just seemed cozy. The houses were all bright and shiny, but that might have been the sunlight coming from the way too blue sky that day. Flowers bloomed in beds around the houses. And the weather was what her mom would call soft. Just warm enough to go without a jacket, but not blazing hot like the temperature got in August.

The Adams family home was near the foothills that curved around the upscale North Boise neighborhood. If you kept going up Harrison, the street they were currently on, they would end up at Bogus Basin, the one ski resort within thirty minutes of the capital city. Harrison was one of the old neighborhoods where the original Boise founders had built homes away from the city center and their work. Now they were too close to the growing city for comfort, still the old Boise families kept their homes while the new rich who moved from California built mini-mansions in the small towns surrounding the city. If Boise had families with old money, this area and the houses on Warm Springs Avenue was where you'd find it.

Trent and Mia were following a small moving van. Trent's brother, Levi Majors, was driving the van and Christina served as the navigator. A few weeks ago, Christina had been asked by her mother to collect her belongings from the family home because she wasn't living there. They were in Boise to help Christina fulfill her mother's request. And to hopefully keep the woman from making Christina cry.

Mia hated Mother Adams. Not just because the woman had been a thorn in Mia's side when she was engaged to Isaac, the favored son. No, Mother Adams had proven her inability to even pretend to be a nice person with her treatment of her only daughter, Christina. The girl had been told she wasn't worthy for way too long. And this demand just put the nail in the coffin as far as Mia went.

"You're quiet," Trent commented, turning down the stereo. "Is this going to be a problem?"

"You mean am I going to tell Mother Adams what a horrible person she is and curse her to having bad hair days for the rest of her life?" Mia watched a woman pushing a baby stroller down the sidewalk. Her husband—or Mia assumed it was her husband—had a goldendoodle on a leash next to her. The perfect Boise family.

"Something like that. I'm not sure there is a bad hair day curse, at least not in our family grimoire." He chuckled as he stopped at a crosswalk so the family Mia had been watching could cross the street.

"I'm sure the Miller family has one. You can't tell me that Bethanie Miller went through high school and college without using the spell at least once. You know the girl doesn't like anyone to out-shine her." Mia pointed ahead of them. "The house is on the right in the middle of the next block. We should be able to pull in the front drive-way. It does a half circle and then kicks back onto the road. Easy in, easy out."

"Seriously, you're okay with seeing Christina's mom, right?" Trent let his foot off the brake and slowly eased to where the moving van was already turning into the driveway. "You have a history with Isaac."

"History. And she probably held a party the day after I broke off the engagement. I wasn't good enough for her perfect boy. And now I know that he wasn't good enough for me." She took Trent's hand and squeezed it. "I like my new man so much more. Although if she's cruel to Christina, I might have a few choice words for the old bat."

"You're always sticking up for the underdog." Trent followed the van and parked a few feet be-hind it, giving them room to fill the back with the boxes and furniture they were retrieving. "One of the reasons I love you. Let's go get this done so we can get out of here. I'd rather not get in a fight with your ex-boyfriend."

"Just don't react to anything he says. Isaac can be a little bit of a pill. I'm sure he's not happy to have to monitor Christina's moving out process." Mia smiled as she got out of the van and met up with Christina. "We might as well bring boxes in with us on the first run. You know this is going to be hard."

"I can do it." Christina put her arm around Mia and gave her a hug. "I've got my friends by my side. I can do anything."

They grabbed several boxes, as did Trent and Levi, and then they moved toward the front door. It flew open before they reached it.

Isaac Adams stepped out onto the landing. He wore a suit that screamed high end and he glared at Christina. "What on earth are you doing?"

"Isaac, we talked about this. Mom asked me to come move my stuff out. She knows I'm coming." Christina started up the stairs. "By the way, it's great to see you too. I've been fine, thanks for asking."

"I know you're moving things out today. That's why I'm here. Mother asked me to help." Isaac pointed to the vehicles. "Why didn't you come up the alley to the servants' entrance?"

Christina narrowed her eyes at her brother. "Because I'm not a servant! I used to live here, just like you. And how on earth are you supposed to help wearing that suit? Or are you sure you're just here to make sure I don't take the silverware?"

Isaac's face flushed red as Christina revealed what must have been the real reason his mother had asked him to supervise the move. "Don't be silly. I came directly from the office. I just haven't had time to change yet."

"So you have another outfit to change into from your closet in your room that you haven't lived in for what, ten, twenty years? And yet I've been gone for less than two years and I'm being kicked out." Christina's eyes were shiny, but she held it together. "Never mind, I'm not here to argue. I just want my stuff. I'm taking my bedroom furniture with me, so you probably should call Mom to make sure she knows. I'd hate to be arrested on my way out of town for stealing."

"Christina, it's not like that . . ." Isaac started, but his sister didn't wait for an answer. She went through the front door.

Mia hurried after her, as did Trent and Levi. "Nice to see you again, Isaac. I see you haven't changed a bit. Still your mom's errand boy."

"Mia and others," Isaac sighed as he held the door open for the group, "welcome to the Adams family home. I'll change and be right with you to help move the furniture."

A woman stood near the stairs and Mia heard her call out to Christina, but Christina didn't stop. That must be the new fiancée. Mia nodded to the woman and hurried after Christina. It was better not to engage with the enemy. She called to Trent and Levi. "Her room's on the second floor; follow me."

When they were all standing around in the bedroom, Mia went over to where Christina was trying to put together a box. She handed her some tape and held the box straight so Christina could secure the bottom. "I thought that went well."

Christina finally looked up at her and started laughing. She turned the box over and moved to her dresser. "I should have realized Mom would put Isaac on guard duty. Let's make boxes and get the dressers emptied so Trent and Levi can get the furniture out of here."

They worked in silence for a bit, then Levi

opened the doors to Christina's closet. "Seriously? Who has this many clothes?"

"I do." Christina laughed. "And I'm taking all of them. With the events Mia has us lined up for the next six months, I'm going to need some party dresses."

"Well, I'll go down and get more boxes as well as a dolly," Trent offered. Then he pointed to the desk chair. "Levi, pick that up and come with me. This is going to take several trips and I want us to be as efficient as possible."

"The elevator is in the first alcove on the right." Christina smiled as she saw the relief on the men's faces. "Seriously, you thought you were going to have to move this down those stairs?"

A voice came from the doorway. Isaac stood there in a polo shirt and what looked like new jeans. "The larger pieces, like the bed and dresser, we can use the larger, staff elevator at the end of the hall. I have men ready to help if you can show us how you want the van packed."

"That would be useful." Trent nodded, glancing at Christina. "The dresser's ready, as is the bed. We'll put those in first. If someone could clear out the desk and the vanity now, we'll get those pieces in the second trip. And the bookcase. I'd like to get all the furniture in the van, then we can stack boxes."

"Whatever." Christina grabbed a box and headed to the desk.

Mia followed but stopped at the bookcase. "Thanks for helping, Isaac."

"I asked Mother not to do this, but you know how she can be." He glanced at Christina, who had her earbuds in and was pretending to listen to music. "She thought threatening this would bring her home."

"Christina has her own mind. And she's safe with me, you don't have to worry. She's an amazing party planner. And not a bad chef." Mia smiled over at the girl, who was trying hard to ignore everything that was going on around her. "I'm not going to let anything bad happen to her, I promise."

He nodded. "Thanks, Mia. I could always count on you to keep Christina's best interests in mind, even after we split up."

"I care for her too," Mia said, watching Christina pack the items without looking at what she was putting in the box.

Isaac stared at Mia for a long minute, and just as it was beginning to become uncomfortable, he turned and grabbed a box. "We'd better get this done. Mother is having a dinner party tonight and the staff will be needed to set up the dining room."

The four of them decided to stop at Jake's for an early dinner before driving back to Magic Springs. Gathered around the table, the group looked exhausted. Mia set down her menu. "Alternate plan suggestion: Should we grab a couple of hotel rooms for the night and drive back tomorrow?"

Christina picked up her coffee. "As long as I have a lot of this, I'll be fine. We'll grab some snacks and drinks when we fill up by the freeway."

"I'm good. I've got to work in the morning, so I need to be back by eight anyway. And I sleep better in my own bed." Levi grinned at Christina. "Especially since all my muscles are going to be screaming tomorrow from carrying so many boxes of shoes."

Christina shrugged. "I used to like shoes. I'm sorry I made you take everything, but it's my stuff. I didn't want to have to make decisions on what to give away and what to keep on the fly. I'd rather do that later, when I have time to think, and not just react."

"That's smart. Don't worry about it. You aren't the first person we've moved and I'm sure you won't be the last. Besides, Isaac's 'staff' did a lot of the heavy lifting. Thank him for me when you talk to him next." Trent studied the menu. "I'm having a steak. I checked in the kitchen for some water before we left the house. Those poor people attending your mom's dinner party are having quail. It just doesn't have enough meat on the bone for me. Give me a medium rare T-bone anytime."

"Neanderthal," Mia teased and leaned into his shoulder. "I hope you're at least having a salad with that to cut the fat. I didn't know they had local trout on the menu. I know what I'm having."

"I bring you fresh caught trout every time Dad comes back from a fishing trip." Trent pointed to her menu. "You should have the fried shrimp instead."

"Seriously? I love trout. You can't get this just anywhere, and I don't have to cook here." Mia gave Christina a nudge with her shoulder. "What are you having, princess?"

"I guess I'm not a princess anymore. Guys, I'm sorry Isaac was there. Although I think he was better than Mom being there, watching our every move. I don't even like the silverware." Christina rubbed her arms.

"Don't worry about it. Your mom made a play for your attention, you acted like an adult. I'm proud of you." Mia took her sweatshirt off the back of the chair where she'd slipped it off when they'd entered the restaurant. She handed it to Christina. "Let's just put it behind us and enjoy this meal that Trent's buying."

"Oh, dude, if you're buying, I'm having the porterhouse." Levi grinned at his brother. "I need the protein."

The group followed Mia's advice and for the rest of the meal, they chatted about upcoming events and the addition of the men's mother to the staff roster of Mia's Morsels. The topic came up over dessert as they shared four different desserts. Mia had a bite of the flourless chocolate cake and said, "I need to see if Abigail can do this in a portable way so we can add it to the delivery menu. It's amazing."

"Dad's already having a fit about her doing wedding cakes for you. Now you're going to see if she can work on the delivery service?" Levi took a bite of the apple pie with cinnamon ice cream and then passed the plate to Christina. "He's grumbling that he'll never get fed."

"He was out of town the week of the wedding," Mia countered. "He didn't even know she made those cakes. Besides, Abigail loves working in my kitchen."

"I think that's what he's afraid of. It's been just the two of them for years since they retired from the store. He's forgotten that Mom might want a life too." Trent passed the key lime pie to his brother. And took the chocolate lava cake from Mia.

"No one should ever have to give up what they love for who they love." Christina passed Mia the apple crumble with caramel sauce. "My mom wanted to be a fashion designer, but when she married Dad, she had to stay home and run his house. Dinner parties, charity work, and raising kids. Or watching the nanny raise us. I think Mom got more time with Isaac than she did with me because Dad's business was just starting to expand. When I came along, she just dropped me in the nanny's arms and went back to party planning. I always wonder who she would have been if she'd been allowed to follow her dreams."

Mia hadn't heard about Mother Adams and her fashion design dream. "Well, that explains a lot."

"Yeah, like why you have so many shoes. You were her personal Barbie Doll." Levi turned to Christina. "I hope you don't expect me to supply the Barbie Corvette and the Barbie Dreamhouse. And just to let you know, I draw the line at changing my name to Ken."

"You're already Ken in my head. EMT Ken. There's a reason I love you. Barbie loves her hero dolls," Christina teased back. She took a bite of the apple pie. "As for the Corvette and the Dreamhouse, don't worry about those. I'll buy my own."

The sun had set by the time they reached Magic Springs. Levi parked the moving van in the parking lot of the schoolhouse Mia had remodeled into Mia's Morsels, at least on the bottom floor. The third floor held her apartment, a storage area, and a library stuffed with old school desks and miscellaneous items she was just beginning to clear out so it could be useful. The second floor was filled with classrooms, and Mia had no idea what she was going to do there. Yet. It would come to her. Today, some of the empty classrooms were becoming Christina's storage center.

Levi handed her the moving van keys and she dropped them into her tote. He gave Christina a hug and a kiss. "I'm heading home. My alarm is going to go off really early."

"Maybe you'll have an easy day." Trent gave his brother a bro hug and nodded to the house. He still had the van keys, which had Mia's house key on it. "I'm going to walk through the school to make sure there aren't any changes since we left. Then you guys can come in. Levi, can you hold a minute until I clear it?"

"No problem, bro," Levi leaned against his car as Trent jogged up to the front door to walk through the building.

"Do you think this is necessary?" Christina adjusted the tote strap over her shoulder. "I'm beat and just want to sink into my bathtub for a while."

Mia thought about what she'd been told about the wards on the house. They were there for a reason. And she thought she'd found out why. The ones who built the school might not have relocated an old cemetery that was right near the building site. She hadn't been able to get anyone to verify her suspicions, but Trent had walked the grounds.

His reaction had been enough for her to believe the stories. And she trusted him to at least know if there were any spirits running around the old school. She and Christina were there alone a lot of the time, so she needed to know they were safe.

She nodded to Christina. "This will just take a minute. Better safe than sorry."

A scream echoed from the third floor. Mia took off, yelling back at Christina and Levi, "Stay here."

Chapter 3

Mia had crossed the entryway when she saw a figure coming down the stairs. She flipped on the foyer lights and saw Trent grab the banister "Trent, what was that? Are you okay?"

"Besides the fact that you blinded me with those lights, I'm good. I ran into your grandmother in the hallway upstairs and about gave her a heart attack. She'd been reading in the library." He hurried down the stairs and popped his head out the doorway. He called out to his brother, who was sitting in his Jeep, waiting. "Levi, it's fine. You can go."

Mia realized she'd seen her grandmother's car in the parking lot when they'd pulled in, but she hadn't let it sink in that she had company. She hurried over and gave him a hug. "Sorry, I didn't realize she was here."

"She's just leaving. I'm going to join her and head home now too. I think I've had enough excitement for the day. I'll bring over a crew from the store tomorrow night and we'll unpack the moving truck and take it back to the rental lot." Trent squeezed her and leaned in to kiss her. "Just leave one of the classrooms empty for her stuff. Do you need me to bring over a lock?"

"I think it's a smart idea. Sometimes we have visitors." She kissed him back, leaning into the safety net she felt every time he touched her. She sighed, then let him go. She watched as he walked to the parking lot and got into his truck. She'd gotten a good one this time. Christina came inside and yawned. Before she could start up the stairway, Mia said, "Grans is upstairs in the library. I think Trent gave her a fright."

Christina laughed as she headed up the stairs. "I didn't think anything scared your grandmother."

"Me neither. I'll be right up." Mia locked the door, watching Levi and Trent's vehicles leave the parking lot through the side window. She left the lights on, moving through the foyer to the gathering room, checking locks as she walked through. The classroom and her office were still locked, but the kitchen was unlocked. Grans must have come in to get a dinner to warm up in the apartment kitchen. She walked inside, checking the locks. When she reached the side door, the doorknob was ice-cold. She checked and it was still locked. Nothing had gotten in, but it was obvious that something had tried. She hurried out of the kitchen, locking the inside door as she left.

When she got back to the front door, it stood open. She glanced outside and saw Grans's car leaving the parking lot. Mr. Darcy, Mia's cat, sat on the front step, watching the car drive away. Or maybe it was Dorian who was watching Grans leave. Mr. Darcy was currently sharing his body with Grans's former boyfriend, Dorian. The spell her grandmother had been casting to get information from Dorian about who had killed him had backfired when Mr. Darcy had jumped on the table. Grans blamed Mr. Darcy, but Mia thought her grandmother should have cast the spell in a room with a closed door. Either way, the cat now had two souls fighting for control. Or they were getting along, sometimes she couldn't tell. Mia picked the cat up and went back inside

Turning off the lights and relocking the front door, she looked around at what she could see of the first floor. Everything looked normal from where she stood, yet she felt like she was still missing something.

She just didn't know what.

Early Monday morning, Mia was working in her office, finalizing the delivery orders that had come in the week before. Typically, she did this and the shopping on the weekend, but because they'd spent the day before moving Christina's stuff, the work hadn't gotten done. That was the bad thing about owning your own business. If you took off a day, no one was there to pick up the pieces. Not like when she was director of catering in Boise, where she'd had a full staff to fill in and take care of the missing tasks. But, on the other hand, she'd rarely taken off a day there either. Here in Magic Springs, she had a flow to her week. One week might be busier than the next due to catering events or cooking classes, but she was the one to make those decisions. Not her boss.

Unless you called her pocketbook, Boss. Mia glanced down at the calendar she kept on her desk. She needed to schedule a time to update her financials this week. But today would be a long day of cooking in the kitchen. Tomorrow was deliveries. And Wednesday, she, Christina, and Abigail were meeting Mahogany Medford at her house to see what they could find out about her mother's recent death.

Somehow, Mia's Morsels had not only become a meal delivery, catering company, wedding planner, and cooking school, now Mia was seen as the local mystery whisperer. She solved things that the police department couldn't or didn't want to handle. Like she needed one more job to add to-do items to her list. She'd tried to convince Mahogany that her involvement in the prior murders had been accidental. That Mark Baldwin, the local police chief, had been the one to solve the cases.

Mahogany had laughed in Mia's face. "I know better than that. The coven is even saying that your magic is supporting you in this investigation addiction you seem to have. All I know is I wouldn't be asking for your help with this unless it wasn't urgent."

Mia had agreed to look into Mrs. Medford's death. "I'm an idiot," Mia said to the empty room. She ordered the food she still needed, which was supposed to be delivered by noon. Mia had made a big order from the food service company on Thursday, so this order would just fill in the holes.

Then she went into the kitchen and started making apple crumbles for the delivery boxes.

Christina arrived with two cups of coffee right at nine. By that time, Mia had finished the dessert baking and was starting on the entrées. She smelled the coffee as Christina came through the door. "Bless the Goddess. Thank you. I ran out a while ago, but I didn't want to stop to brew a pot."

"I'll do it before I get started. My arms feel like they're going to fall off. Maybe I do have a few too many shoes." Christina set the cup in front of Mia, then she pulled up a stool. "I wanted to thank you again. You didn't have to use up your one day off moving me."

"I did have to do it. We're friends. Besides, I can't stand it when Mother Adams picks on you. You're worth so much more than that. I told Isaac all the time that we should have just kidnapped you and raised you as our own." She set down the chef knife and put the onions she'd been chopping into a bowl. Then she went to wash the chopping block for the next ingredient along with her hands. After that was done, she picked up the coffee and pulled a stool up next to Christina.

"And now you have me with you, twenty-four seven without having to deal with my stupid brother." Christina sipped her coffee. "I should be asking you how you're doing. It couldn't have been easy seeing Isaac with the new girl."

"It's not hard, actually. I was mad at him for what he did. But I'm so much happier now, I can't stay mad. She's going to find out what type of man he is, just like I did." Mia set down her cup. "I know he's your brother, but he's quite the tool."

"I'm not going to argue that." Christina glanced at her watch. "Do you think we'll be done cooking by five? Levi called me just a bit ago and said Trent's bringing a bunch of guys to unload the truck then."

"We should be." Mia counted out the timing on the rest of the items. "As long as our restock order gets here before noon. Otherwise, we won't have enough chicken for the Parmesan. I had fifteen more orders come in since Friday."

"Have you given any more thought to hiring someone?" Christina held up a hand. "I'm not lobbying for Bethanie. Your grandmother and Abigail talked me out of that idea, but you may want to get someone on now, before summer hits in full. You know the houses are going to start filling up and we're going to be swimming in orders."

Mia nodded. "You're right, we do need more help. I'll email the recruiter tomorrow morning when I go back to my office."

"I'll let my summer class know who you go through and tell them to use my name as a reference. There might be someone you would like." Distracted, she stared at the door next to the laundry area.

Mia turned to see what she was watching. "What?"

Christina shook her head and stood, pushing the stool back. "It's nothing. I just keep almost seeing something out of the corner of my eye, you know? Then I turn to look and nothing's there. Weird, right?"

Mia watched the door area a while longer. It was the same door that had felt like ice the night before. She stood and handed Christina her prep list. "Lots of weird things happen here at the school. Just make sure you don't follow anything you don't know is actually human."

"That's creepy. And are witches human?" Christina looked up from the list, a hint of fear in her eyes.

"Of course we are." Mia smiled to try to ease some of the tension. "I'm talking ghosts and such. And maybe werewolves. Unless we know them. I just need you to know that all ghosts aren't sweethearts like Dorothy. Some do mean us harm. I've been reading some books Grans found in Adele's library. Apparently, Magic Springs has a history of some weird stuff. And not all of it surrounded the coven." Mia had been obsessed with reading up on the history of the paranormal, at least as it came to witches. Some of the books were based on the common misconceptions that the writer had about the other world, but some were actually helpful. Maybe she should cull out a few for Christina to read as a human living in a witchy world.

"Three years ago, I thought witches, werewolves, and ghosts only existed in fairy tales and books. Now, my world view has been expanded. I'm pretty sure I'll run into a big-eyed alien next." Christina went to the pantry and pulled out some tomatoes and chickpeas. "Hey, when are we meeting Mahogany? Wednesday or Thursday?"

"Wednesday at her house. I need to call Grans to see if she's coming. I'm pretty sure there's not a 'magic' cause to Mrs. Medford's death, but I wonder if there were any spells cast lately around the house." Mia started searing the chicken. "Oh, and we have a small wedding to plan for later this month, so Thursday we're meeting with the bride and groom."

"Cool. I've been hoping for another wedding. I've got some ideas I've been working on." Christina continued to talk about the wedding planning notebooks she'd been putting together. Every once in a while, she'd pause and turn her head toward the laundry area, but she didn't say anything.

Mia needed to get an expert in the house to check out the ghosts. And the cemetery. Abigail had been looking for someone in her contacts with the coven. Mia would give her a call this evening. One, to put her on alert for the wedding cakes she'd be responsible for, and two, to see what she'd found out about any ghost specialists. Ghost hunters? With Christina starting to see at least the traces of the ghosts, Mia didn't have much time until they'd break through her assistant's mental barriers against all things paranormal.

They finished up the cooking and packaging right at four thirty. A record for the number of dinners they'd produced. She counted the containers again as she put them in the oversize fridge where they'd stay until tomorrow, when they'd pack everything up in travel cooler bags and start the deliveries. Once they were all put away, and the kitchen was cleaned and back in order, Christina kicked off her shoes and looked at the clock.

"I know we're going to start moving boxes again at five, but can I run upstairs and shower? I smell like chicken and garlic." She peeled off the apron she'd put on that morning and tossed it into the laundry basket by the washer. "I never realized how many muscles I used just cooking until I came to work with you."

"That and the stairs keep us from putting on weight from all the tastings we have to do in a week." Mia took off her own apron and went over to the basket. Laundry was a Friday thing, if they didn't have a weekend event. She judged from the basket that it could wait. She looked out the back window to the trash bins and froze. A man stood there, watching her.

"Are you ready to go upstairs? I don't want to leave you alone down here," Christina said.

Mia turned her head to make sure Christina wasn't nearby, and when she turned back, the man was gone. Vanished. She went over to check the locks again. Mia had taken the trash out to the bins earlier, when they were starting to package everything. She'd locked the door herself, but it didn't hurt to check again. She turned back and smiled at Christina, who was watching her. "I'm ready. I just need to check this other door and shut off the lights. I think we'll order delivery tonight rather than cooking. Pizza and salad good?"

Christina was still finishing freshening up, but Mia had jumped into the shower and out quickly. Then she'd dressed in jeans and an old tee, putting on tennis shoes and going downstairs to wait for Trent to arrive.

Right when the grandfather clock struck five, three vehicles pulled into her parking lot. Trent, Levi, and four other men—who Trent introduced, though Mia quickly forgot their names—met her by the moving van. She handed Trent the keys and he got the first load going and headed to the elevator to go to the second floor. Mia rarely used it because it had been built for moving boxes and furniture up and down.

"There's a big difference between your elevator and the one at the Adams estate," Trent said later as they stacked the boxes that had been brought up into what the sign on the door said was the English room. She'd chosen it to store Christina's belongings because from what she could see, it didn't have a secret passageway leading to the outside, but of course, with this building, you never knew. The others were on their way back down to grab another load.

"What?" Mia turned to him, her face red from the heat in the room coming from the sun shining in through the uncovered windows.

"I knew you weren't listening. What has you bothered? You're not rethinking having Christina store her stuff here, are you?" Trent handed her a bottle of water. "Drink this before you collapse. I take it you cooked all day?"

"You worked all day too. So don't be freaking out about me doing too much," Mia snapped, but then she sighed as she opened the water and took a long drink. Then another. She recapped the bottle. "Sorry, I *was* distracted. We had a ghost visitor in the driveway this afternoon. And Christina is starting to catch glimpses of our ghosts."

"Not Dorothy, I take it. The others?" Trent opened another water bottle and drank the entire thing.

"Yeah, the not-so-friendly Caspers." Mia ran her hand over a white-and-gold carousel horse statue that had been in Christina's perfect girl room at her house. "Maybe the school isn't the safest place for her?"

"I think you're overthinking this. The wards have held for years. And the graveyard was there a year ago; we just didn't know about it. Now that we do, it ups the creep factor, I agree, but I don't think either Christina or you, for that matter, are in danger. If you were, I'd tell you to leave." Trent stood next to her, leaning his shoulder into hers. "You're not putting her in any danger here, except for being more open-minded about the world and all of its residents. You've given her a gift by sharing our world with her. Not just the cooking one, but here in Magic Springs. And she's going to benefit from knowing there's more than just what she can see or hear. And after seeing where she grew up, I think she needs a little reality added into her world."

"You're saying it's better to live with the knowledge that the paranormal exists than be a rich jerk like Isaac?" Mia blinked at the idea.

"Exactly." Trent smiled at her. Then the door opened and they watched as Christina came into the room with another box.

"A couple more loads and we should have that truck empty. But we're down to the heavy stuff I can't help with." She set down the box and nodded to Trent. "Levi wants you to come look at the bookcase. He's not sure it will fit in the elevator."

"Well, if it doesn't, you'd better find a place in the living room because we're not hauling that thing up a flight of stairs." Trent slapped Mia's leg and whispered, "Stop worrying about her. She'll be fine."

Christina watched him leave, then went over to help Mia move the last few boxes out of the open space so there would be plenty of room for the furniture. "What were you two talking about?"

"You," Mia said, then grinned as Christina's eyes widened.

"He's mad about the amount of stuff I have, isn't he?" Christina guessed the topic.

Mia shook her head. "Nope, we were just wondering how you came out so amazing after living as an Adams for most of your life."

Christina grinned, then pulled a cobweb out of Mia's hair. "You have to remember, you were almost an Adams yourself. You would have been my sister and had to go to all those dinner parties Mom likes to throw."

"Yeah, I dodged the bullet there." Mia nodded to the final boxes. "Let's get this done so we can veg for the rest of the night."

CHAPTER 4

Tuesday, they didn't start deliveries until after ten, just so they didn't wake any still-asleep customers. So while Christina caught up on some sleep, Mia was downstairs in the office, setting up the next month's menu plan. She had motion alarms and cameras in the parking lot and at the front door, so she saw Abigail's SUV pull in. She went to the door to greet the matriarch of the Majors family.

"Oh, you're waiting for me." Abigail adjusted her purse over her arm. "I don't mean to bother you; I know you have deliveries today. I just wanted to talk about what you think my schedule for the month might be. Thomas is getting a little antsy about me starting a new career and wants to take me on a cruise. I told him I'd have to check my schedule."

"Anytime you need to go, you can just tell me you won't be here. And today's probably better than tomorrow anyway because we're going to

Mahogany's then." Mia held the door open for Abigail to come inside. The sun had just crested the mountains and was bathing the valley in a soft light. She paused for a minute to let the view soak in. She took in a deep breath of clean pine-scented air and remembered how lucky she was to live in this mountain community. "Do you want some coffee? I've got a pot going in the office."

"Sounds heavenly. I left home before my second cup." Abigail waited for her to close and lock the front door. "Honestly, I like having a little control over my world. Thomas has been the only one with commitments for way too long. He's gotten spoiled having me around all the time waiting to grace me with his presence. It's good for him."

Mia didn't comment on that, but she agreed with Abigail. It wasn't good for relationships to be one-sided. Even if she got married, her job, her business would be important to her. Just as her family life would be. Women didn't have to give up everything just to be married. When they reached the office, she grabbed a cup. "Black, right?"

"As black as sin." Abigail giggled as she sat down, and then she pulled out her day planner. "So, what does our month look like, boss?"

Mia set down the coffee in front of Abigail, then closed the office door. She took down a three-month whiteboard calendar and brought it with her as she moved to sit next to Abigail. "I keep this on the door, so if you have a time you won't be able to work, you can put it on the calendar. I'll work around you. And when I get a booking, I'll put it on the calendar. That way we can plan around the big events. I'm emailing the employment agency today to see if I can get someone part-time to help with the catering events and maybe even deliveries. I think we've hit a max that Christina and I can do on our own."

"I'll let my friends know you're looking." She wrote down a note in her planner. "What agency do you use?"

They went through the schedule for the next three months and Abigail wrote down the days when she either needed to do a cake or some other type of dessert. She tapped her pen on the note about the wedding. "Do we have a date for that?"

"They want to be married by the end of June, but it depends on what they're willing to give up to make that date and how creative we can be. We may not be able to get them in anywhere, even if we do the ceremony outside and the reception at a local restaurant. I'll know more on Thursday."

"Just call me or text or email. Whatever is easiest." Abigail tucked her planner into her tote. "Sorry, I'm freaking out a little about this job. I think it's the first time I've worked for someone else since high school."

"I could just consider you a contractor if that would help. You'll be doing things that meet the criteria. That way I'm not your boss, you're just doing a project for me." Mia frowned. This was the part of running a business that she hated. The legal employee stuff. "Either way, there's no health insurance or retirement plan. You'll just have to invoice me for the cakes and stuff. I'd still buy all the materials for you, so you wouldn't have to worry about fronting that money."

"Thomas asked me how we were setting up the money part and I told him I didn't know. He said being a contractor would probably work better for your business structure. He handles our taxes and stuff, so let's just do it that way." She pulled a folder out of her tote. "Here's the form he said I'd have to fill out."

Mia glanced at the document, and Mr. Majors had been correct. It was the form she needed. "Okay, then, I guess we're done for the day. Unless you need something else."

"I wanted to update you on my progress about the cemetery. Which is no progress at all. I keep hitting brick walls. No one wants to talk about the school except to say how lucky we all were that you bought it instead of selling it to John Louis. He would have torn down the school, broken the wards, and then what would have happened?" She waited for Mia to respond.

"Which means everyone knew about the cemetery, but no one wants to talk about it."

Abigail nodded. "It's like they're confirming their knowledge by not talking about it. It's assumed. From the looks on people's faces when I'm asking them, they don't want to even admit the cemetery ever existed."

"What about you? Had you heard about it?" Abigail and her family had lived in Magic Springs for years.

Abigail shook her head. "As a kid, we told ghosts stories about the school. Even when we were in school here. It just had that feel. But if a teacher caught us talking about ghosts, we were in trouble. So we stopped exploring and kept inside the playground fence. I think they were hiding things even back then."

"And there's nothing like telling a kid there's

something dangerous to get them looking into the situation."

Abigail nodded. "The teachers were clever that way. They said the problem was we were scaring the younger kids, not that we might be inviting trouble. It was all laughed off. But as I remember, we were moved to the other side of the playground right after that. They'd put in new equipment and turned that side into a mini football field. They only let the players there to practice. No one else was allowed on that side of the yard. They said we'd ruin the grass for the field."

"Look over here, nothing in this hand at all . . ." Mia mumbled. Then she looked at Abigail. "You don't know anyone who used to teach here, do you?"

She pulled out her planner again. "I'll make a note to go through my last yearbook. We all got them, not just in high school like the public schools do. I'll let you know if I find anything."

"Okay, then, I guess I'd better go check on Christina and get the delivery started. It's going to be a long day." She stood and opened the office door. Christina was sitting on the couch, looking at her phone. "Oh, there you are. You could have come in."

"I figured you guys might have some work things to talk about." She stood and gave Abigail a hug. "Are you still coming with us to Mrs. Medford's tomorrow?"

"You're kidding, right? I've been trying to get into that house for years. Hetty Medford was pretty private. She was a member of the coven but never attended any events. At least as far as I knew. I guess I thought she was older too. Maybe people thought that because she stayed to herself?"

"Maybe, but it doesn't explain why someone in their fifties was said to have died of old age." Mia shook her head. "Something's going on with her death. Mahogany's right. It's weird."

"Weird? It's Magic Springs. You of all people know that weird is normal here." Christina nodded to the kitchen. "I'm going to start loading up the van. I've already backed it up to the back door. See you tomorrow, Abigail."

"We should do lunch tomorrow after the meeting. Should I pick up Mary Alice before I come to get you?" Abigail's phone rang and she looked at the display, then put it in her pocket. "I don't mind driving."

"That would be awesome, but I haven't checked with Grans to see if she's feeling up to going. She was so sick last week, she didn't even want me to come in when I dropped off a box of dinners for her."

Abigail paused. "You should have called me. I could have gone over and sat with her. She must be going stir-crazy at home all alone."

"She said she thought she was contagious and told me to stay away. I figured you'd get the same response. But she said she was feeling better yesterday when I called her." Mr. Darcy was weaving in between her legs as they stood at the front door. She leaned down and picked him up. "Did you sneak out when Christina came down?"

The cat winked at her, and Mia knew she wasn't talking to her feline; instead, it was Dorian, the witch whose soul was stuck inside Mr. Darcy. Dorian used his magic to open doors and get down the treats. She knew it wasn't the upscale restaurant fare he was used to, but Mr. Darcy didn't mine.

Abigail reached out and stroked Mr. Darcy's head. "What a lovely black cat. Familiars are so special, aren't they?"

"Yes, they are." Mia opened the door and held it as Abigail left. When she'd locked the door after her, she set Dorian down. "You really need to stop using magic to get what you want. People are going to talk."

"About what?" Christina stood in the kitchen doorway. "Who are you talking to?"

"Mr. Darcy or, actually, Dorian. He's downstairs again." She shooed the cat upstairs, but he ignored her and went running down the hallway. She stared after him, but then turned and met Christina. "I really need to find out where he's getting out."

"Dorian took over the planning, so there might not be a real place. Dorian might be making a doorway for himself." Christina held up a paper bag. "Are we taking this one too?"

"I hadn't thought about that." Mia looked at it and shook her head. "That's for Mahogany. I told her I'd bring over a sample of our desserts tomorrow to see if she wants to order some from us for her tea shop."

"Mr. Majors isn't going to be happy if that means Abigail will be working more hours." Christina tucked the bag back into the oversize fridge.

"I think Abigail can handle him. Besides, I think she does what she wants." Mia moved to the freezer.

"Already packed. I think I've got everything."

She picked up the clipboard and the packing list Mia had made early that morning. She pointed to the list. "Check, check, and check."

"Then let's get this show on the road." Mia shut and locked the kitchen door. She'd already shut the front and her purse sat on the kitchen cabinet. It was time to drop off the dinners they'd worked so hard on yesterday.

As she drove, Christina chatted about school and Levi. Sometimes Mia didn't want to know what she heard, but she knew Christina didn't have a lot of close friends. Especially those she could talk with about the weirder sides of dating a witch and working for Mia. "Levi told me the other day why his dad isn't happy that Abigail is coming to work with us."

"Okay, so spill. Why?" Mia had gotten that feeling from Abigail too, but she hadn't wanted to pry.

Christina pulled into the first house where they were dropping a delivery and turned off the engine. She met Mia at the back and went to put together the package as Mia called out the order. When Mia had come back from the delivery with next week's order in hand, she met Christina in the front of the van.

"Levi says his dad has always been the one to do things in their retirement. He hunts all the time. And he's in all these fishing tournaments. I guess Abigail went once, but she was bored out of her mind. So his dad thought she'd just stay home and do crafts. When she told him she was going to bake wedding cakes for you, Levi said he popped a gasket."

"I don't understand why that's a problem, especially if he's gone a lot. Doesn't he want Abigail to have a life too?" Mia programmed the next address into her phone. "I'm sure not going to be the housewife-of-the-fifties type if Trent and I get married."

"Ha, you actually said it." Christina pulled out into traffic.

Mia turned her attention from the next order to watch Christina drive. "Actually said what?"

"That you're thinking about marriage with Trent. I hoped my brother hadn't ruined your trust in men." Christina turned down the next street following the AI's voice from Mia's phone. "Anyway, I'm the same way. Besides, Trent and Levi are on Abigail's side in this too. I think Mr. Majors just forgot that Abigail didn't have to be sitting and waiting for him to come home. Like one of those robot wives in that old movie."

"*The Stepford Wives*," Mia pointed to the house on the right. "We're here. This is a new customer, so make sure we throw in one of the cheesecake brownie packets and the welcome letter."

Mia double-checked the bag, just to make sure their first order with Mia's Morsels was correct, and then went to meet the Banks family. When she came back, she keyed in the next address and put on her seat belt.

The road they were on would be the same one they'd take to go visit Mahogany tomorrow. Mia didn't come into this part of town often. Most of the houses were owned by longtime residents who didn't see a need to buy dinner to be delivered. They cooked for themselves. Mia watched out the window and wondered how she could get more orders in this neighborhood. Maybe going door-to-door with a small giveaway meal? Or a dessert?

They drove by the Medford house. It looked empty. Mahogany must be at the teahouse today, working. One of the good things about living over the business home of Mia's Morsels was that she could pop upstairs anytime and do something like run laundry or watch a show if she was bored. The bad thing was that the work was always there, waiting for her to come down and spend a couple of hours doing her accounting or something else. At least Mahogany had a clear division between home and work.

A division Mia wished more and more that she had as well. Instead, she'd chosen to buy the school, warts and all. She was just going to have to deal with the baggage with which it came. Like the ghosts trying to break in. Or the heater that didn't always want to work.

"You're lost in thought today," Christina said as they finished up the next delivery. "Are you worried about visiting with Mahogany tomorrow?"

"Maybe. For some reason I've got this reputation around town that says I can solve any mystery. I think I've just been lucky to figure out what was going on before Baldwin did in the past. Or at least figured out the magic side of the mystery because he's not a believer." Mia keyed the next address in the phone and the AI voice directed them to go back down the way they'd come. "I need to get a program that will schedule all our stops with the least amount of backtracking. I wonder what that will cost. Probably more than the gas I'd save."

"I can't help with the rumors around your superpowers in mystery solving, but I can route us on Monday night; then we'll at least have a plan." Christina slowed down the car as they came over the hill and in sight of the Medford house. "Uh-oh. There's a bunch of police cars at Mahogany's. Should we stop?"

Mia leaned forward. She saw Mark Baldwin, Magic Spring's police chief, getting out of his car just ahead. "Pull up next to Baldwin there. Maybe he'll tell me what happened."

"Or arrest me for slowing down to look at a crime scene," Christina muttered.

Mia smiled as she rolled down the window and stuck her head out to get Baldwin's attention before he walked over to the house. It was true that Christina had been the main suspect—at least in Baldwin's eyes—for all sorts of minor crimes when she was the new Goth girl in town. But now Christina had cycled out of her Goth stage and Baldwin had admitted he just liked teasing her. Mia called out, trying to get his attention. "Baldwin. Hey, Mark?"

He turned and scanned the street. Mia recognized the frown on his face as he walked toward the van and her open window. "You have a knack of showing up at the wrong place and the wrong time. Can I ask why you're on this side of town today?"

Mia held up the clipboard and pointed to the last delivery address. "Just dropped off dinners here. What's going on at Mahogany's? Is she okay?"

"I haven't talked to the homeowner yet. A neighbor called in seeing a suspicious car at the house and then an open door when she walked her dog a few minutes ago. Ms. Medford is on her way home from her teahouse." He peered over at Christina. "And if you don't want to be questioned about the break-in, you should go finish your deliveries. Sarah said you're stopping by my house today."

Mia pointed to an address farther down the list. "Yep. I think you'll like this week's menu items."

"Sarah hasn't been feeling well lately. She's pushing herself too hard since losing the baby last year. And she'd kill me if she knew I said that. You know Sarah, she wants to do it all." He waved a hand at an officer who called his name. "Anyway, I need to get going. And because this is a possible crime scene, so do you two."

"Yes sir," Christina said as she put the van in Drive. She looked at Mia. "Ready?"

"Sure. Nice to see you, Mark. I hope Sarah feels better." Mia made a note on her delivery schedule as they pulled away. "Remind me tomorrow to grab some of Gran's chicken soup from the freezer before we leave to see Mahogany. We'll drop it off at the Baldwins'. I have a feeling Sarah could use some."

"She's probably just sick from hanging out with him all the time." Christina drove slowly away, keeping her speed right at the posted limit. "Did you hear him threaten me?"

"He was just teasing. He likes to see if you'll react." Mia drew a box around Sarah's name. Something was bothering her about Baldwin's statement. She would take two quarts of the soup over, not just one.

As they approached the next house, she put Sarah Baldwin out of her mind and checked the list for the next delivery. But before she got out of the van, she made a second note on her list to call Mahogany that evening. Hopefully, nothing had happened at the house, but if it had, Mahogany might not want them dropping in tomorrow. She heard Christina call out to her, and she opened the door. Worry about tomorrow when it comes, Grans always said. But she'd been hit with two waves of energy as she'd talked to Baldwin. One about his wife and the other about Mahogany.

Whatever was happening, her powers were telling her it wasn't good.

CHAPTER 5

Abigail pulled into the parking lot exactly at ten. Which gave them enough time to make a detour to drop off the soup with Sarah Baldwin before meeting Mahogany. When Mia had called last night, Mahogany had told her she'd explain about the police visit when they got there. Mia checked the basket she'd made up for Sarah: two quarts of the soup, a loaf of bread, and two dozen cookies, all different varieties. Hopefully something would catch her attention. When they'd delivered the meals yesterday, Sarah had looked pale and Mia was sure she'd lost weight. And the woman didn't have much weight to lose.

Mia covered the basket with a gingham napkin and tucked a menu for additional meals into the basket. The freezers at Mia's Morsels always had a supply of foods that someone could take home and heat up in the oven, in addition to the weekly delivery service. Something in Mia's gut told her that the Baldwins might be needing those easy meals soon.

"Christina, they're here," Mia called up the stairs. The door to the apartment was open, so she knew she could hear her.

Christina came down the stairs, with Mr. Darcy on her heels. "Sorry, I was looking for my tennis shoe. It was in the hall bathroom. Do you think Mr. Darcy is messing with me?"

"I'd blame Dorian. I found the television remote in the kitchen on the window seat yesterday. Unless you put it there." She pointed to the black cat that was now sitting on the fourth step, watching them. "You be good. We're going to be back after lunch."

A meow was her only answer, but Mia could see the twinkle in Mr. Darcy's eye. Dorian had some running around to do. She didn't know where the cat took off to, but he always came home, so she just hoped Dorian was smart enough not to get his new body run over in his wanderings.

"Fine, just be home before dark." Mia opened the door for Christina. "Are you ready?"

"Let's go." Christina nodded to the basket. "Is that for Mrs. Baldwin? I was supposed to remind you."

"Thanks, and yes. This is for Sarah." She met Christina's gaze and realized that they were both worried about Sarah Baldwin.

Christina nodded and held up a notebook. "I've got a new notebook so I can take notes as Mahogany is talking. I find I think better when I'm writing things down. And I can see holes in what I know that way too."

"That's a good idea." Mia locked the door after Christina stepped outside. The morning was a bit chilly, but it would warm up quickly. There was no reason to grab a jacket. By noon, it would be too hot for one, and they'd be home before the evening cool hit the mountain valley. Dressing for June in Idaho was an ongoing challenge.

Abigail stood outside her SUV and met them on the sidewalk, giving each of them a hug. "I was just coming to let you know we're here."

"I was downstairs and saw you come in on the security camera." Mia nodded to the back hatch. "Mind if we stop at the Baldwins' first? I need to drop off a few things to Sarah."

"Not a problem." Abigail hurried to the back and opened the door. A jacket, a backpack, and some hiking boots were back there and she pushed them to the side. "Sorry, I'm going on a short hike after lunch. I need to see if the huckleberries have started setting yet."

"I'd love some huckleberries. Let me know if you have any to sell. I have a syrup recipe I've been itching to try." Mia set the basket in the back and closed the door. "Did you pick up Grans?"

"She's in the front."

The tone of Abigail's voice had changed and Mia turned to look at her, but she hurried to the front and climbed into the vehicle without saying anything else. Mia followed Abigail and because Christina had gotten in behind Grans, she took the other side. After she heard her seatbelt click, she leaned back and turned to greet her grandmother. A squeak came out of her mouth as she viewed the woman in the front seat.

She was at least twenty years younger, and if Mia hadn't known it was her grandmother, she would have thought her mother was visiting from Boise.

Abigail had turned to watch her reaction. Then she met gazes with Grans. "I told you she'd take it well."

"Grans? What on earth did you do?" Mia couldn't look away. Grans's skin was plump and the lines that had been so visible were now almost gone. Her hair was a dark brown rather than the blond/gray she'd been sporting for the last ten years.

"I want to know too, but I didn't want to ask," Christina whispered to Mia.

"I can hear you both. My hearing is much better now and I don't seem to need my glasses anymore." Mary Alice Carpenter turned in her seat to address Mia. "It's not that bad. I was playing with a spell that I thought might be the answer to getting Dorian to go on to his next stop and leave your poor cat alone. But I must have misread the warnings. Sometimes they use Latin in the older spells and that makes it difficult, especially when a word could have two meanings. So, ta-da, I've shaved a few years off my body age."

Mia couldn't believe it. "Are you staying this way? What if someone sees you?"

"Mia, dear, this is Magic Springs. Most of the women here have had a lift or two. Many didn't understand why I let myself age in the first place." She turned to Abigail. "Support me on this, will you?"

Abigail shook her head. "There's a big difference in keeping yourself free from the signs of aging and turning back the clock. I've never seen something this dramatic actually work."

"Well, maybe it will wear off, then. I waited a couple of weeks and tried my best to reverse the spell, but I'm afraid you're stuck with me this way for at least a while."

"Don't get me wrong, you look great, but this is going to take some getting used to." Mia blew out a breath. "You look like Mom."

"Don't remind me. I'm sure your mother will have a cow when she finally decides to visit. However, since that doesn't happen often, we might have a year or so for this to wear off before I have to deal with her reaction." She leaned over and tried to see what was in the back. "Is the basket for Mahogany?"

"No, we're dropping it off with Sarah Baldwin. She's under the weather." Mia tucked her purse next to her.

"Hey, didn't Mahogany say her mom was younger than everyone thought? Could she have done a spell like this that made Mahogany think she was younger than she was?" Christina was still staring at Grans.

"Highly unlikely. For that to work, she would have had to do the spell when Mahogany was a child; then everyone around her would have known her as younger too." Grans pursed her lips together, a clear sign she was thinking.

Mia turned to Christina. "That's a good idea, though. Maybe it was a spell, but maybe it wasn't a younger spell; maybe someone aged Mrs. Medford. That could have happened after Mahogany left for college. Put both of these ideas into the notebook."

"You're keeping a notebook?" Grans rolled her eyes. "Can we be any more cliché?"

Christina's face turned red, but Grans couldn't see her reaction.

"It's a good idea. Keeping all the notes in one area." Mia countered the dig with a smile aimed at Christina. "Besides, it's cliché because it works."

"If you say so." Grans turned and watched out the window. "You should turn on the next road. It will take you directly to the house without hitting any lights or being on the main road."

Mia met Christina's gaze. This wasn't like Grans at all. This version had a lot of opinions, whether or not you wanted to hear them. Abigail didn't say anything, but she followed Grans's direction.

When they stopped at the Baldwins', Mia jumped out. "I'll be right back."

As she got the basket out of the back, she heard Grans telling Abigail that she needed to keep up on cleaning the carpet in her car or it would start to smell. Mia groaned. Being with this new, updated version of her grandmother was going to be torture. As she walked over to knock on the door, she wondered if this was how her grandmother had been when she was younger or if it was a side effect of the spell. Either way, she needed to fix it before she couldn't stand to be in her grandmother's presence.

Before she could knock on the door, Mark Baldwin opened the front door. "Good morning, Mia. What can I help you with?"

She pushed the basket into his arms. "Nothing. I was just dropping this off. There's soup in there. I hope Sarah feels better soon."

"Thank you, but you didn't need to do this— we're fine." He moved the basket back toward her.

"Nope, it's delivered. Sorry, no take backs." She turned to go back down the stairs to the sidewalk.

"Well, thanks, then. Hey, is your mom in town?" He waved toward Grans, who waved back, with a lot less enthusiasm. "I haven't seen her forever."

"Actually, we're on our way somewhere; otherwise, I'm sure she'd love to get caught up. Besides, there are frozen items in there. If you don't want to eat everything today, I suggest you get them in your freezer now." Mia hurried over to the SUV and climbed inside. "This new you is going to be a problem. Mark thought you were Mom."

"Well, maybe she'll be my alter ego. That way I don't have to stay hidden in the house until this disappears." Grans yawned and leaned on the door. "If it ever does."

Grans was still asleep when they got to the Medford house. Mia looked at Abigail. "Maybe we should let her sleep. She's not quite herself."

"She's horrible," Christina added.

Mia nodded. "She's different, but maybe it's just a phase she's working through. Like the terrible twos?"

"Possible. I'll do some research tonight to see what I can find out about these types of spells. She said she got it out of Adele's grimoire. Maybe that's affecting the implementation." Abigail glanced back at the car. "Oh, she's waking up. I guess we're too late in running and hiding from her."

Mia almost laughed, but the look on Grans's face made it seem impossible. She wasn't happy about being left in the car. She leaned over to Abigail as Grans climbed out of the SUV and slammed the door shut. "Next time, yell 'run' earlier. We might actually make it."

Christina giggled, then about swallowed her tongue when Grans turned her angry gaze toward her. She headed up the sidewalk and onto the porch. "I'll see if Mahogany is home."

When Grans joined them, she pointed to the stairs. "Shall we?"

The house was on the edge of the forest that ran through the mountains that bordered Magic Springs. The yard was mostly dirt and rocks with several planter beds around the house. Mia noticed several herbal plants that the Medfords must have used in their tea blends as well as a few flowers to add a pop of color. This close to the woods, you didn't know what would grow and what the deer would eat. Another reason Mia had decided to put a privacy fence between the schoolyard and the greenbelt that ran behind her house. A fence wouldn't keep out a determined deer, but it might deter some.

When Mia's foot hit the first step, she could feel the spell. It was still active, even though its focus had been dead for weeks. Grans didn't feel it, but Mia could tell Abigail did when she shuddered. She paused, looking around to see if she could find the spell's weaving, but it was tightly wound. "Well, we found the appearance spell. Now we just have to figure out if Mrs. Medford cast it."

"She didn't," Abigail said as she stared at the intriguing design on the house. She turned back toward Mia. "If Hetty Medford had cast the spell, it would have died with her. This spell's owner is very much alive. And male, if I can feel correctly."

"That's a guess. You shouldn't guess on spells." Grans narrowed her eyes toward Abigail. "Don't they teach you that in charms classes?"

"Mary Alice, we haven't had a magic academy for decades. It's been all home-taught since the school closed." Abigail started to say something else, but Mia put a hand on her arm.

She studied her grandmother, who now looked confused at the information Abigail had just given her. Knowledge she should have known. "Maybe we should reschedule this."

The door opened and Mahogany Medford stepped out on the porch. She stepped around and hugged every last one of them. "I'm so glad you're here. I need to talk to someone or I'm going to scream. That Baldwin man is an imbecile."

"Tell me about it," Christina muttered.

Mia stepped forward, waving the others to follow. "Let's get inside. There're a few things going on that I'd rather not be out in the open discussing."

"Okay, then, way to be even more mysterious than I am. I thought I was the only drama queen in town. Or at least that's what the good police chief told me when I explained that my mother had been murdered." Mahogany held open the door and waved them inside. "Can I get anyone something to drink?"

"I'd love a glass of wine," Grans said. "Or a shot of bourbon."

Mahogany blinked. "It's only ten in the morning."

"She's just kidding." Mia took her grandmother's arm. "Coffee would be lovely."

"Go ahead and have a seat in the parlor. My mom always called the room that." Mahogany motioned to a doorway to their left. "I'll grab some coffees and be right back."

Abigail stepped closer to her. "Let me help."

As they disappeared, Mia moved into the parlor. The room was filled with what appeared to be antiques. The chairs had those carved wooden legs that looked like they'd break as soon as you sat on one. She gingerly sat down. "Well, this is nice."

"A little stuffy to me." Grans sniffed as she sat primly on the chair next to Mia. "It could use a total remodel. Including that fireplace. I'm sure it lets in cold air during the winter."

"What is wrong with you today? Besides the new look? You're snippy and mean. Is this from the spell?" Mia asked, looking out the door to make sure Mahogany and Abigail weren't on their way back.

"I don't know what you're talking about. I'm completely the same as I was before." Grans sit up a little straighter. She pointed at Christina. "You're slouching. Sit up straight, missy, or no one will ever extend an offer of marriage. Not even that ski bum Levi."

"Yeah, like what you just said. You would never say something that mean." Mia paused as she thought about it. "At least not to Christina's face. Maybe your social appropriateness filter got damaged in the spell."

Her grandmother sniffed. "If you think I'm that rude, maybe I should wait in the car."

"Just don't talk to Mahogany. I need your expertise here. Can you feel the spell in here?" Mia didn't want to anger her grandmother. On the other hand, she didn't want her to say something to Mahogany that would get them tossed out of the house.

"Actually, no. I can feel the edges of it, but it's apparent the maker intended for the spell to cover the resident when they left the house. Has it had any effect on Mahogany? Maybe you should ask to see her driver's license picture to see if the spell has aged her here in Magic Springs." Grans looked around the room. "Although if all the rooms are decorated like this, I'm sure she feels older just living here."

"Okay, then, thank you for the information and please limit your comments until we get back into the car." Mia waited for her grandmother to nod, then turned to Christina. "As our resident non-magical expert, have you noticed anything since we've been here?"

Mia saw Christina look over at Mary Alice and nod. "No. I mean other than the changes in Grans?"

"Oh, well." Christina paused and looked around the room. She took a deep breath, then cocked her head to one side. "Nothing visual, but there's a tiny hum going on in here. There's no electronics, but it could be from the lights."

Mia looked up, but there were no lights in the ceiling. Floor lamps sat in two corners of the room. She stood, crossing over to turn the lights off. "Do you still hear a hum?"

Christina nodded. "Yes, so it isn't the lights."

"It could be the spell," Grans said, leaning forward. "Something powerful enough to change Hetty's appearance, well, it might emit a slight sound, especially if it's been in existence for years."

Mia turned the lights back on and returned to her chair. "Christina, write down the hum and anything else we said about the spell on the house. I think when we get home, we need to do some research into this type of magic."

"Adele's library will probably be more suitable for your work. I'll see what I can find this afternoon when you drop me off. It will take my mind off this." Mary Alice made an up-and-down movement encompassing her body. "I'll be more conscious about the words I use. I hadn't noticed any change, but again, I haven't been out of the house since this happened."

Mia noticed her grandmother was trying to control her outbursts, so the change had to be from the spell. "Thanks. I appreciate you trying."

"You always were more appreciative than your mother. That girl would argue that the sky was any other color but blue just because I made a comment." Mary Alice bit her lip. "Sorry, maybe I *will* try to limit what I say right now."

Abigail and Mahogany came back into the room, each carrying a tray. One had five cups of coffee and cream and sugar containers. The other, an assortment of tea cakes and pastry treats. Abigail set the treat tray on the coffee table, then Mahogany handed off cups to each person, with the cream and sugar bowls going onto the coffee table as well.

"There we go. I was working on a few recipes last night. I always bake when I'm troubled. After finding out someone tried to break in, I have to say, I was troubled." Mahogany sat on the love seat and took a sip of her coffee.

"I'm sorry about the break-in. Did Baldwin find anything?" Mia set her cup down on the table.

Mahogany shook her head. "He thinks they were spooked when the neighbor walked by with her dog. I'm not sure I believe that."

"Why is that?" Mia asked, picking up one of the sandwiches.

Mahogany sighed and set down her coffee. "Because they moved the furniture in this room. Everything was in a different place. It looked kind of like where I had it, but I could see rings in the rugs where the furniture used to sit. Someone came into the house, moved the furniture, then moved it back where they thought it had been."

CHAPTER 6

"What did Baldwin say when you pointed that out?" Mia watched as Christina wrote notes in the book she had on her lap.

Mahogany shook her head. "Like I said, he thinks the guy was scared off by the neighbor and her dog. I didn't find the evidence the furniture was moved until after he left. I took pictures and sent them to his phone, but he texted back that it was probably the cleaning lady who moved the furniture. He seems to always be looking for the easiest answer."

"That's Baldwin. He looks for horses before unicorns. I'm surprised he didn't tell you that I probably broke in and was stealing from your fridge," Christina mumbled.

Mia gave Christina a look. "Baldwin's not that bad. Mahogany, what about his answer—is that even possible?"

Mahogany shook her head. "I don't have a clean-

ing service. I do my own cleaning. It helps me unwind after a day at the tea shop."

"Okay, so we have a few things going on. One,
we have the discrepancy in your mom's actual age
and the age everyone thought she was." Mia held
up one finger.

"Which has to be because of the spell we felt on
the house. Thank you, Captain Obvious." Grans
bit into a cookie. "These would be better with
chocolate."

"They're pecan sandies; they aren't supposed to
have chocolate in them." Abigail patted Mary
Alice's leg. "Go on, Mia, I'd like to hear you break
this down."

"Thanks." Mia held up a second finger. "Two,
we have someone looking for something in the
house. Grans, Abigail, if there was a cloaking type
of aging spell on the house, would there be something holding it here? Something the witch that
cast the spell needed back?"

"I've been looking into this type of spell."
Abigail set down her cup. "I haven't found any
spells that are tied to an item, but it's not unusual.
If the spell was aimed at Hetty to age her, her
death could have been an accident. Or the plan all
along."

"So the spell ages someone so long that the
body reacts as if it was that age?" Christina frowned,
focusing on writing down as much as possible.

"It's not possible," Grans muttered. "The spell I
found was an age reversal. I haven't found any evidence of one that actually aged the corporal body.
It's all a glamour, even this. My body is the same
age I was two weeks ago. I just look different to the

people who look at me. My mirror image didn't change until I'd done the spell three times."

"Mary Alice, you didn't!" Abigail's hands flew to her mouth to cover her gasp. "Once, to check the spell, I get, but three times? You know you might have made this permanent."

The woman who no longer looked like Mia's grandmother set down her cup and fluffed out her hair. She looked down at herself and ran her hands over her shoulders and down her body to her legs and back up. "Yeah, but what a way to go out of this life."

Abigail dropped Mia and Christina back at the school. Mia paused at the driver's door and Abigail rolled down the window. She called over to her grandmother, "I wish you'd stay here until we get this sorted out."

"Muffy likes being home. Mr. Darcy and Dorian tend to freak him out. If something starts to go bad, I'll pack my stuff and move over, but I'd rather spend my time with Adele's books to see if I can help Mahogany. You know, if we don't reverse the spell, she won't be able to live in that house much longer. I saw some gray on her temples today that I'm sure wasn't there when we met her at the teahouse."

Mia nodded. She'd seen the changes in Mahogany over the last few weeks as well. "I agree, we don't have much time. Abigail, maybe you could reach out to some friends in the coven? Discreetly. I don't want the fact that we're looking into this to get back to the killer."

"I've got some contacts I can talk to." Abigail glanced over at Mary Alice. "You could come stay with me. Thomas told me this morning he's taking a group on a backwoods fishing trip. He'll be gone for a few days."

"Muffy and I like our house. And the problem still stands. Adele's books are the best chance at finding a reversal spell." Her gaze went to the third floor and the windows of the old school library. "Unless it's in there. I didn't find anything at the library this weekend while you all were in Boise."

"That's why you were here Sunday? You didn't even stop to say anything. You just left." Mia hadn't realized what her grandmother had been doing.

"Trent had already seen me and I had to adjust his memory. If you all had seen this, I don't think I could have changed everyone's memory at once," Grans explained like Mia was a child. "Anyway, I'm tired and want to put my feet up. Abigail, can you take me home now? Please?"

"Sure thing," Abigail turned back to Mia. "I'll call you if I find anything. Maybe we should meet up this weekend. Do you have an event?"

"Just the meeting on the wedding Thursday. And a small conference dinner on Friday. They're small business accountants, so the lodge thought we might be more in their price range for a dinner. I think James is just throwing me a bone because he wanted the weekend off."

"It's a gig. Let me know if you want a cake or dessert. I think better when I'm baking." Abigail waited for Mia's answer.

"Yes, we have fifty diners, so whatever you want

to make. I didn't ask you before because Thomas was home and we hadn't formalized our agreement." Mia could feel her shoulders relaxing. She'd planned on making some sort of crumble, just so it was fast. Having Abigail take this on made her Friday a whole lot less stressful.

"Then it's done. I'll call when I have an idea for the dessert. Can you email me the menu?"

Christina held up her phone. "I already did. I've been playing with a place card for each diner that has what we made and our website, just in case they want to hire us again."

"Smart idea," Abigail said.

"Oh my Goddess, can we go already? Or do you want to continue to pat each other on the back some more?" Grans grumbled from the passenger seat.

Abigail said goodbye and Christina and Mia watched the SUV as it pulled out of the lot.

"Your grandmother is . . ." Christina started.

"I'm not sure how you were going to end that statement, but remember, she listens in a lot. She's different right now, that's for sure, but maybe it's just a stage. Maybe we'll get the Grans we love back sooner rather than later." Mia went to unlock the front door and sent a plea up to the Goddess for that exact request. She needed her grandmother here and this snippy woman gone for good.

Mia had some work to do to get ready for tomorrow's appointment, and because this was the part of the catering business that had caught Christina's attention for a future business, she asked her to come into the office to help her work out a plan. They needed at least a shell to be able to walk the couple through the choices that needed to be made to put this wedding on in the next few months.

"You look up ten possible event sites that can handle fifty to two hundred and fifty attendees, at least for a reception. I'd like to have wedding venues as well, so if they aren't attached to a human church, we can suggest some appropriate Wiccan sites. I've got the name of at least one person who could do the ceremony for them, but I bet I'm going to need a few more, especially for short-notice events like this." Mia was writing down notes in her notebook as she spoke. She'd transcribe them later into a digital file, but for now she needed to brainstorm. And she worked best creating with pen and ink. "I've printed out the vendors we used for our last wedding, but I'm sure we'll have to be creative on this one."

"Creative is the fun part of the job." Christina pulled out her laptop and started searching. She didn't look up, but when she saw Mia settle in her chair, she asked, "Do you think we'll be able to help Mahogany? Will the spell age her as well?"

Mia set down her pen. Sometimes she forgot that Christina hadn't been raised in a world where witches existed outside of books and fairy tales. "Look, I'm sure she's going to be fine. If you'd rather sit this investigation out, I'd understand."

"What, no." This time Christina did meet Mia's gaze. "I want to be part of this. I'm just concerned about Mahogany. She looks older than that person we met at her shop. Or am I imagining that?"

Mia shook her head. "You're not imagining anything. I saw it too. I'm glad you noticed it. You're becoming more advanced in your people-reading skills. A critical component of being a great caterer.

Anyone can slap a plate of food in front of your guests. But a good caterer will make dinner a theme and make it all about the event or the client. Just by noticing the clues."

"Especially in wedding planning, right? That's such a stressful time for both the bride and the groom and the family. If we can step in and handle the little things that pop up, they can worry about the big ones, like getting the ring sized." She looked over at Mia, whose mouth was hanging open a bit. "Sorry, I've been researching the job. Our professor says never go into a job before you know how it's going to affect you or your choices. I enjoyed working on the last wedding much more than being a bridesmaid in it."

"Let's just hope this event goes better," Mia said as she opened her wedding planning file.

They worked together for several hours before Christina closed her laptop. "I just sent you a list of twelve event sites with a checklist on if they cater or not, if they have a chapel or not, and if we can bring in stuff. I've also listed off the ones that provide the linens and the costs for all of them. Some of them have graduated costs based on the number of guests. I guess for the chair rental?"

"Probably." Mia focused on her computer and opened the document. "Perfect. I see you also added websites and a description of the place. I think I'll print this off for tomorrow's meeting. Well done."

"I'm glad my classes are making me more useful." Christina stretched and her stomach growled. "Time for lunch? Or do you want to work longer?"

"I can finish this up this afternoon after we eat.

Grab a few meals out of the kitchen and we'll heat them up in the stove upstairs. I'd like to sit at the table to eat for at least one meal this week."

"You're such a homebody, no wonder Trent's in love with you. You remind him of his mother." Christina set her laptop on her chair. "Do you want anything specific?"

"Mexican, I think. If we have some dinners. Or whatever is oldest in the fridge; we need to rotate the supply to keep everything fresh for the customers." She pulled out a folder she'd had made for Mia's Morsels and then added a wedding sticker that had room to write the last names of the bride and groom. It felt more personal that way, and Mia hoped it would bring her some more business through referrals. She scanned her email as she waited and was surprised to see one from Baldwin. She opened the email, reading through the letter. First was a thank-you for the soup. It was making Sarah feel better. And the second was a question about coming in to talk to him regarding Mahogany and her claims. The email implied the woman was loco, but he was trying to give her the benefit of the doubt.

Mia opened her phone and found Baldwin's number. He was on her favorites list. Mostly because she needed to call him that often, not because they were friends. She dialed the number and then set back to wait. Baldwin answered on the second ring.

"Mia, I've been thinking about you." His booming voice echoed in her ear and made Christina smile as she came back into the room.

"Really? Don't let Sarah hear you say that. Not

even a flu bug would keep her in bed and not on the streets looking for me to kick some butt." Mia almost laughed as Christina mimed putting her finger down her throat. "So, what's up, Baldwin? Why did you want to talk to me?"

"Mahogany Medford is driving me crazy. She's convinced someone killed her mother and that they covered it up. She's even accused me of being in on the plan." Baldwin paused. "I was thinking that maybe you two are friends? I mean, because you stopped by her house yesterday. Any chance you could call her and let her know that Magic Springs isn't out to get her?"

"Actually, I've talked to Mahogany about her mom and there is something weird about how she died. Was there an autopsy?" This was the opening Mia had been hoping for. Maybe Baldwin could give her some answers to start figuring out what really happened to Hetty Medford.

"Of course we did an autopsy. Every unattended death gets looked at, but Mia, the woman was elderly." Mia could hear Baldwin shuffling files on his desk. "Here it is. I got it back a few days ago, but with Sarah being under the weather, I haven't had a chance to review it."

"Can you look at it for me? And just forget about what you think you know about Hetty Medford?" Mia knew there was a fine line with Baldwin. One, he didn't believe in magic, so she couldn't come straight out and tell him there was a spell on the house. And two, he didn't like her messing in his investigations. But she smiled as she waited for his answer; he had asked her to get involved this time.

"Hold on. I'm not sure what you think I'll find,

but I have to read it anyway. Do you want me to call you back?"

"I'll hold for a few minutes." Mia wanted to be there when he started to question what he knew.

"Okay, then, I have to warn you, I'm a slow reader." He chuckled, and then the other side of the line went quiet.

Mia put the phone on Speaker, then started working on the wedding book ideas. It didn't take long before she heard something from Baldwin. "Did you find something?"

"No, I'm just wondering if Rory got the files mixed up. This woman seems to be in her late fifties–early sixties according to the report." Baldwin sighed. "This kind of mix up has been happening a lot since they moved over to the new county building last fall. They have a new system that can't seem to keep files straight. They print out the files and courier them over. This must be a different case. I'll get ahold of them and have them send the right file. Then I'll call you back, if you promise to talk to your friend."

"I promise, as soon as you've read Hetty's autopsy report, I'll call Mahogany." She hung up the phone and looked over at Christina. "So, we know one more thing."

"What's that?" Christina looked up from the laptop, where she'd been working on a form they could use to make sure they asked all the right questions for the wedding planning.

"The spell isn't strong enough to go outside of Magic Springs. The new county building is out on the highway going into Sun Valley. The coroner saw the body as it actually was, not the glamour spell." She picked up her phone and texted her grandmother the information. "I don't know if that fact is important but Grans will."

Christina glanced at her watch. "Lunch will be ready in fifteen minutes. Do you want to go over this interview guide to see if I've missed anything while we wait?"

Mia nodded. "Print it out and we'll go through it. We'll test it out tomorrow and see if we need anything else. I think this is going to be really helpful."

"Well, most of the planning was done on the other wedding, so I thought we needed something to start fresh with. And you need to add any magical requirements or questions I wouldn't know to ask about." Christina looked at the form. "Maybe we could do an addendum that would cover special weddings. That way, we have both on file and we can just print one or the other."

The two of them quickly finalized the form and then Mia made four copies and put it in the wedding folder for tomorrow's meeting. Baldwin still hadn't called back when they went upstairs to eat lunch.

Mia set the phone by her as they sat down to the table to eat. "Okay, so you're off the rest of the day. I need you for the meeting with the new client at ten, then you're free until Friday, when we need to get the food ready for the event. We're cooking at the lodge, so we need to have everything prepped and packed by three so we can get over there and set up. Abigail's doing the dessert, so that's off our plate."

"Remind me, we're off Saturday and Sunday this week, right?" Christina set the steaming plates of chicken enchiladas on the table along with a salad she must have made when she put the entrée into the oven. "Levi wanted to know. He's planning something, but he won't tell me. He likes his surprises, that one."

Mia smiled as she dished up some salad. "You deserve a weekend of pampering. It's been busy around here."

"I'm really glad I only took one class this summer. It's intense but fun, you know?" Christina chatted about the science class she was taking. "I have class tonight and then I can fit my labs in anytime during the week. So I'll go tomorrow afternoon. Levi's letting me borrow the Jeep. I really needed to pick up one of Mom's extra cars when I moved out. But I didn't think a vehicle would be on the table as being 'mine.'"

"Maybe you should think about buying a car. You don't have rent cost now; it might be a good time to get a cheap car and get it paid off before you graduate." Mia tasted the enchiladas. They'd frozen well, which was always a question, at least in her mind. She wanted her customers to love her food. She charged more for her frozen dinners than the ones people could get at the local grocery store, but they weren't filled with sodium and fake ingredients. Everything she put into a dish, she could spell.

CHAPTER 7

After lunch, Mia was downstairs working in the office. She needed to finish up this month's finances, especially after the wake, where she was sure she'd lost money. At least she'd know what to charge for a magical wake versus a human one the next time she was asked for a quote. No wonder Ginny Willis jumped at her proposal. Mia had thought it was just because of the short time frame. Instead, Ginny knew Mia was undercharging. Mia was still steamed. She muttered, "It would have been nice of her to mention the ancestor table costs."

An alarm sounded, causing Mia to look up at the camera feed. A young woman stood on the steps. She looked up into the camera and waved. Probably someone coming by to pick up some meals. Mia pressed down on the Speaker button. "Hold on a minute, I'll be right there."

She didn't mind having people drop by, but if this had been a cooking day, taking time to help a shopper pick out meals might take too much time. She needed to make a new sign saying she was only open for drop-ins at certain times and on certain days. Or hire someone. She would send an email to the hiring agency as soon as she got this woman taken care of and sent on her way. She flung open the door.

"Hello, I'm Mia Malone. How can I help you today?"

The young woman who stood there had long blond hair and blue eyes. She looked like the Sun Valley type who spent their days on the mountain, skiing in the winter and on the lake in the summer. She smiled and held out her hand. "Nice to meet you, Mia. I'm Hailey Berger. I heard you're looking for some help around here. I have experience working for a catering company in Washington State. I moved here a few months ago and have been trying to find something in my field forever."

"Nice to meet you, Hailey." Mia held open the door. "Come on in and let's talk. I was just about to send an email to my service about the job. How did you find out about it?"

"A friend heard it from a friend. You know how small towns are." Hailey walked into the foyer and gasped. "It's so beautiful in here. I can't believe this was an old schoolhouse. I never saw it before you started remodeling, but I've heard you've done a lot of work on the building."

Mia glanced around the meeting room, which she'd painted a sunny yellow to invite people into the space. "It's been a labor of love. Not that there aren't issues trying to bring an old building up to code, but I fell in love with it as soon as my grandmother told me it was up for sale. What kind of catering company did you work for?"

"We did a bit of everything. Small family business. They did weddings, birthday parties, the works. Nothing huge, and not usually anything black tie or fancy like that." She followed Mia into her office. "We were up in the Tri-Cities area."

"So, northeastern Washington, not Seattle." Mia nodded as she listened. "Were you front or back of house?"

"Both. I worked in the kitchen doing food prep, then I also was a server when they wanted tray service. Doing both gave me almost full-time hours. You know how it is in a small town. Are you looking for one or the other?" Hailey set her purse on the other visitor chair and sat down as Mia did.

"I need both. We're kind of fluid right now in our job descriptions. Everyone does everything, so having experience in both areas is a bonus in my eyes. Can I get you some coffee? Or water?"

"Water would be great. I tend to drink my coffee in the morning before I leave the house." Hailey had great posture. Grans would love her, Mia thought as she grabbed two bottles of water out of her minifridge. The woman was dressed in nice black pants and a business-casual shirt. Not too overwhelming, but a floral with a pop of color. Her blond hair was pulled back into a pony at the nape of her neck. She looked professional but approachable.

Mia handed her the water bottle, wondering if Abigail had mentioned the job to her contacts. "Do you have a résumé?"

Hailey set down the water and pulled a folder out of her purse. "A résumé and a list of my references. I was with Walla Walla Catering for ten years, and my other jobs were more fast food, so I added a few personal references of people I've worked with here. I've been volunteering with the children's home in Twin Falls since I moved. And I worked a few shifts at the soup kitchen. I hate seeing people struggle with making sure they have a hot meal."

Now Mia was almost certain Hailey must have come from one of Abigail's mentions of the job. Abigail did a lot of volunteer work in the area. And Majors Grocery Store as well as the family was one of the supporters for the food kitchen that fed people in the Twin area. There'd been talk about setting one up here in Magic Springs, but the city council had nixed the idea. Instead, they supported the food bank that worked with the local schools to make sure kids had meals. She scanned the paper and set it down. Hailey seemed to be a perfect candidate for the job. Now she just needed to know if she would fit in with the team.

"Tell me about your work at the soup kitchen. What did you like about it?' Mia started with an easy question, one that would get Hailey talking about herself and her life.

Hailey talked about her love of cooking as well as the joy that service to others had given her. Mia thought the woman sounded sincere in her answers. Bethanie Miller, Christina's former friend, would never be able to fake this part of the interview, even if she'd been expecting the question.

Working for a food bank or soup kitchen because you wanted brownie points on your permanent record was totally different from doing it to help other people. When she was a catering direc-

tor, Mia and her crew had worked the kitchen at
the Boise Rescue Mission once a month. She knew
which people on her staff hated going there but
went along because they thought it looked good.
Those people didn't last in her crew. Not because
they didn't have a generous heart, but instead, it
showed a lack of being able to be an effective team
member. She hadn't expected the charity work to
be such a good test of a solid employee, but over
the years, it had shown to be effective in most
cases.

By the end of the interview, Mia was ready to invite Hailey onto her team, but she'd learned better
than to just jump. She needed to call references
first, then she'd make an offer. She put Hailey's résumé and reference sheet aside and stood, indicating the end of the interview. "Thank you so much
for coming in. I'll look over everything and give
you a call in the next week or so."

She took the hint, standing and holding out her
hand to shake Mia's. "Thank you so much for your
time. If you think I'd be a good match for your
team, I'd love to work here with you."

Mia smiled and walked her to the front. "It was
really nice to meet you."

When she'd left and Mia had relocked the front
door, she went back into her office. Yes, Hailey
Berger seemed to be the perfect candidate. But
something about that word, "perfect," was bothering Mia. She set the résumé aside and went back to
work on her accounting. She'd call the references
tomorrow, after she'd thought about the interview
some more. Sometimes it took a while for Mia to
realize what was bothering her. It wasn't red flags

and alarms going off, just a tingle of something. She'd figure it out.

It was five before she remembered that she'd never heard back from Baldwin. Her accounting was done and she had folders set up for tomorrow's meeting. She picked up the phone and dialed his cell. No answer. So she called the police station. "Hey, can I talk to Mark Baldwin?"

"I'm sorry, the chief has left for the day. Can someone else help you?" a male voice informed her in a tone that said he didn't appreciate Mia's use of Mark's name rather than his title.

"No, I'll call tomorrow or try him on his cell." Mia threw that in just to let the guy know that she actually knew Mark as more than just the police chief. It was petty, but the guy was giving off bad vibes. She hung up and wrote herself a note to call him in the morning. As she did, she sent a prayer up to the Goddess for Sarah's health. Whatever was going on with Mark's wife clearly had him upset and worried. Normally, Mia would call Grans and talk this out with her, but well, yeah, Grans wasn't herself.

Instead, she walked through the kitchen again, checking locks and looking out the window to make sure no apparition was hanging out by her trash can. Maybe she should have asked Hailey about her feelings regarding all things supernatural. Especially if the school was under attack by angry ghosts. But she hadn't felt any magic on the woman and most humans didn't see ghosts. Christina was already aware of the work they did with Magic Springs's special residents. Maybe Mia could ease the new girl into the special world they lived in after Mia figured out if she was even a good fit for the team.

Being a small business owner came with a large to-do list. Being one who was also a kitchen witch in a town with an active local coven made hiring a bit more complicated. Most people in Magic Springs knew about the special people who lived there. But some, like Baldwin, chose to ignore the magic side of the area. Mia just needed a way to identify who was who, especially if they were going to be part of the team.

Her phone rang right after she'd made her way upstairs to find Mr. Darcy lounging on her couch watching *Judge Judy*. She picked up the remote and turned down the volume as she answered the call. Dorian gave her a dirty look. "Hey Trent, what's going on?"

"Are you busy? It sounds like you're in a meeting or something?"

She moved to the kitchen and heard the television volume go back up a couple of notches. "No. Mr. Darcy and Dorian are just watching their favorite show."

"*Pets on Parade?* Or *America's Funniest Home Videos?*" Trent chuckled.

Mia got a bottle of wine out of the fridge and poured herself a glass. It might be a long night. "No, they like the judge shows. I think Dorian was a lawyer in his past life. It reminds him of being in court. He also loves *Law and Order.*"

"Your cat has good taste."

Mia sipped her wine. "We both know it's not Mr. Darcy making the entertainment choices. I think he'd rather sleep than watch television. But with

Dorian stuck inside, he doesn't have much of a choice. What are you doing?"

"Seeing if you want to meet me at the Lodge for dinner." Trent paused. "We missed date night last weekend and I hear you're busy on Friday. Dad's got me going with him to some sort of hunting convention this weekend, so I'll be out of town until late Sunday."

"Dinner sounds good. Can you pick me up? That way I can finish this glass of wine and maybe have another during my bath." She kicked off her shoes under the kitchen table.

"Long day?" Trent asked.

Mia rolled her shoulders. Her day hadn't been that crazy. What was bothering her? "Maybe. It just feels like it's been crazy busy lately. Maybe because we moved Christina on Sunday."

"Well, I'm feeling the same way, so I'm thinking you're on to something. Maybe we need to plan dinner out tomorrow night too. Just so you can get out of the house for a few hours this week."

Trent was amazing. He wanted to take care of her. But she'd jumped into the relationship with Isaac too quickly and stayed too long. This time, she was taking it slow. "I probably need to do some planning for next week Thursday. And having you gone this weekend means I can go hang out in the library to see if our resident ghost knows anything about the cemetery. I really need to make sure she's friendly."

"Maybe your grandmother has met her. She was in the library Sunday when we got home from Boise." Trent reminded her.

"Maybe." Mia thought it was more likely that her

grandmother was researching ways to reverse her antiaging spell than checking in on the ghost Mia had discovered in the library. But Trent didn't know that story unless his mom had told him. "Anyway, dinner would be amazing. I'll get dressed."

"Don't go crazy on me, I'm wearing my work clothes." Trent paused. "Is there something you're not telling me?"

Mia smiled as she thought about Trent. "Always. See you in a few minutes?"

The hostess sat them at a window table where they could see the ski mountain. Even in the summer, the lights from the ski runs lit up the night sky. The resort had hiking and biking trails down the mountain for their summer guests. If she skied, Mia would take the time to hike down the trails just to orientate herself to the mountain terrain without the snow. She turned to Trent, who was still reading the menu under the dim candlelight that danced around the room. "We should hike down the mountain sometime this summer."

"I didn't know you enjoyed hiking." He set the menu aside and looked out at the mountain. "There are a lot of different trails we could follow. Of course, it's mostly all downhill, so it can be a little tricky."

"I like being outside in nature. I worked all the time when I lived in Boise. What's the good in being your own boss if you don't take time off to enjoy life?" She took out her phone. "I'm booked next weekend, but could we do it next week on Wednesday?"

"I like a girl who implements her dreams." He

took his own phone out of his pocket. "I don't have any meetings on Wednesday, so yes, I can play hooky."

"Seriously, you work as much as I do. I think they can spare you for a morning." She blocked out the day with a short description. Hiking with Trent. "I'll even buy dinner that night here at the Lodge."

"I'm thinking we might want to head over to the hot springs and soak for a while to recover from the hike. You know this isn't just a nature walk, right?" He tucked his phone away and watched her.

"A soak would be great. Maybe after dinner, though? That way when I get home, I can just crawl into bed and go to sleep. We have an event that weekend that I'll be working on starting on Thursday." She rolled her shoulders. "This makes me happy. I have an actual nonwork event scheduled. That's pretty rare for me. I put the goal on my new year's resolutions list, but I've been less than diligent on making it happen."

"It's the small-business owner thing. You need to carve out Mia time during the day and the week so you're on top of your game. Maybe a morning run or even a swim. The folks have a pool at the house that you could use anytime." He paused as their waiter came up to get their order. "Mom adores you."

"And I've made an enemy of your father." Mia turned back to the view. "I wanted to install a pool at the schoolhouse. Now, I'm scared to do any digging. Who knows what we'll find?"

"Speaking of your hidden cemetery, I finally got ahold of Silas Miller. He admitted that the builders may not have taken care of all of the cemetery, just the area where they were building. And of course, they took out the gravestones. He's sending me the records he has on the project, but the original builder is long gone. Silas thinks he's one of the last living souls who worked on the project."

"If you don't count Brody McMann. I'm going to have to go visit our favorite werewolf to see if he has any records of the build."

"Brody? Why?"

Mia took out her phone and found the picture. She handed it over to Trent. "That's Brody in the picture, right? If not, it's some relative. How long do werewolves live? He doesn't look like he's aged at all."

He handed her back the phone. "Actually, I'm not sure. From what I've read and the history of the local pack, maybe one hundred to two hundred years? Although the internet makes them almost immortal and living two thousand years or more."

Mia blinked at the information. "So, if we go with the two hundred years, this could really be Brody and he should have some knowledge about building the school and what happened to the cemetery."

Their wine came and they stopped talking for a minute while the waiter poured the Riesling. When he'd left, Trent took a sip before he answered.

"I think that picture is more than likely Brody, but you're not going up to his compound alone. If you want to go, I'll drive you."

She glanced out at the mountain. "We're going

to have to put off our hike and go on Wednesday, right?"

He grimaced. "Maybe. Or we put it off for another week or two. I can't take off another day next week until the weekend, and you just said you had a catering job. I could go by myself next weekend. Well, not alone; I'd take Levi with me."

"I've already got you working with Silas on the school's history. I need to go so I can possibly tell the lie if he says one." She made a note on her phone. "I'll call to see if we can get an appointment with Brody. He may be out of town anyway."

Trent grimaced as their food came and Mia put her phone away. "We can't get that lucky."

CHAPTER 8

"Are we ready for the meeting with May Hornbuckle and Henry Lasher?" Mia asked Christina over coffee the next morning. "They're coming at eleven. We'll meet in the living room. We'll need drinks and treats."

"I'm baking some cookies this morning." Christina opened her notebook to her to-do list. "I've got our packets ready and sitting on the table downstairs. All we need are the treats and some drinks. I'll make fresh coffee at ten forty-five."

"You've got this down." Mia stood and grabbed her own list. "I loaded up the websites on my laptop for all the wedding sites we're suggesting who have room for next month. It's not ten, but we have a nice selection. I'm going to steer them toward an indoor event because you never know what the weather is going to be."

"We had snow last June. It didn't stay long, but it was snow." Christina took a bite of her muffin.

"Abigail sent over some photos of different cakes she's done so we can show them some of her past work. That way, they can decide if they want something specific."

"I'm thinking they mostly want to be married, sooner rather than later. The amenities are important, but not the crucial factor. Please tell me you have the next three weekends free."

Christina nodded. "I told Levi that as soon as I knew when I would have a free weekend, I'd let him know. He wants to do a road trip to the Oregon coast. He says we've been cooped up too long."

"Sounds like a fun trip. Do you need extra days?" Mia tapped her pen. "Oh, I almost forgot, I think I might have found another person. I need to do reference checks today, but she's worked in catering before in Walla Walla and she sounds perfect. I really liked her too."

"That's great," Christina looked up from her to-do list. "Anyone I know?"

"I'm not sure where she found out about the job. I'm thinking she must have heard from one of Abigail's friends. Her name is Hailey Berger. Ring any bells?" Mia added "call references" to her to-do list. "If everything checks out, I'll see if she can be here on Friday. That way we can see how she works in a catering position, and then she'll be on the schedule Monday to Tuesday for the deliveries. If we like her, you and she might just take over Tuesday deliveries."

"You're not excited about driving all over Magic Springs every week?" Christina teased. "I sent out an email to my school group, but that name doesn't ring any bells. She must be someone Abigail knows, or someone that one of her friends knows. I've got mixed feelings about adding another person to our team. We work so well together."

"It will be fine. You'll always be my favorite," Mia joked. "Anyway, this is just a trial, and we both know we need to add someone if we're going to expand. Abigail doesn't want to come on for a full-time gig. And her husband really doesn't want her to work that much."

"True." Christina sighed. "Maybe you need to give me a title, like heir apparent or VP in charge of events so this new person knows they have to listen to me."

"I'll think about that." Mia stood to get more coffee. "As long as it's not queen of the universe, because you know that's my title. Now, let's go over today's meeting again to make sure we're on the same page."

After breakfast, Mia went down to her office to call the references, but first, she called Mark to see if he'd read the autopsy report. He picked up on the first ring. "Hi, Mark, how's Sarah?"

"She seems to be feeling a little better. At least that's what she says. Can I stop by to pick up more of that soup? It seems to be the only thing she can keep down." Mark Baldwin sounded tired and more than just worried about his wife.

"Of course, I'll be here all day. Trent and I might go grab some dinner tonight, but mostly I'm here until we head to the Lodge for the dinner I'm catering on Friday." She scribbled a note to pull out the soup and add some of the cookies that Christina was making. "Have you verified the autopsy report?"

"Yes, I have. And it wasn't a mistake. Apparently, Hetty Medford was a healthy woman in her late fifties who happened to die. I have someone pulling her birth records to see where the mix-up happened. My notes from the case show her to be significantly older. I guess Mahogany Medford wasn't just pulling my leg on this." Mark Baldwin didn't sound happy that he had to admit he was wrong.

"I think something weird is going on with Hetty's death. Could it have been a poison that just made her look older externally?" Mia didn't want to say "potion" or "spell" because Baldwin didn't believe in any of that, but a poison—that was a real possibility, at least in the practical law officer's eyes.

"You may be on to something. I'll ask the coroner to check her tox screen again. He was naturally interested in the case, as he and his tests put Hetty in her late fifties. Which matches Mahogany's description." He sighed loudly. "I really don't need one of these woo-woo cases on my plate right now. But it's clear that the woman didn't die of old age like the original report, so now I have to find out what really happened. It's my job. Maybe some of that radiation came up from Arco. You know, they test nuclear bombs there at the site. If we got a good northwest wind, it could bring that crap this way."

"And hit only one of our residents?"

"She did live out of the main area of town. It's possible."

But highly improbable, which both Mia and Baldwin knew. But Baldwin was looking for a real-world answer to the woman's death. Mia knew there was at least one spell that was placed on Hetty. Maybe more than one. She needed to call Grans. "What was the cause of death?"

"Asphyxiation. The tox screens will show us if there were any chemical causes. The report doesn't show any physical bruising on her neck." He paused. "Look, Sarah's calling, I need to talk to her. Sorry, I'll be over later this afternoon to pick up the soup."

"Tell her I hope she's feeling better," Mia said, but then she realized that Baldwin had hung up. She called her grandmother, but she didn't answer. Mia left a message. "Hey, can you see if there are any spells that look like asphyxiation? Apparently, that was Hetty's cause of death. Call me. I'd like to know how you're doing."

She hung up the phone and then wondered if she should have asked about the ghost in the library. She'd call later this week. And it would give her another reason to reach out.

A knock sounded on her door. "Come in."

Christina poked her head in and put a plate of several cookies on Mia's desk. "Check these out. If you think I should make something else, I will. These are Mexican wedding cookies according to the recipe, but the cook at my house always called them snowballs. I loved them, but they can be a little messy. Should I make something else?"

"You're kidding, right?" Mia bit into one of the cookies and groaned. "These are perfect. Can you package up a batch for Sarah Baldwin, along with three quarts of the chicken soup? And check our stores. If she continues just eating soup, we'll need to make more."

"Is she still sick? That bites." Christina took one of the cookies and ate it. Brushing the powdered sugar from her face, she asked, "You don't think she's allergic to her husband, do you? If I was married to someone like Baldwin, I'd be sick all the time."

Mia laughed and then ate another cookie. "Every hat has a head. Besides, Sarah loves Baldwin. She might want him to be more than just a small-town police chief, but she supports him in everything he does. She ran the police ball to raise money for the food bank last spring. I don't think her illness has anything to do with her marriage."

"Okay, don't believe me, but I'll be saying 'I told you so' if they break up and she gets better." Christina looked at her watch. "We've got an hour before May and Henry show up. I'll make a second batch of cookies. You can send any extras home with Trent for an after-dinner treat."

"Did I mention we're going to dinner tonight? It's been so busy, I must have forgotten." Mia wiped her hands and opened her computer file on the new wedding plan.

"No, Levi told me this morning. I guess he called Trent to see if he'd go to the rock gym tonight, but he was busy." Christina grinned. "Which means I get dinner out tonight too. Thanks!"

"Where are you going?"

"He wants to try a new place in Twin. And I talked him into stopping at Shoshone Falls first. I hear the water is running crazy this year." She paused at the doorway. "I'll shoot some pictures and send them your way."

"If I wasn't worried about the weather, I'd suggest that May and Henry have the ceremony there. The waterfall emits a lot of power. It's good luck for a ceremony. At least, that's what the books are telling me. I've done a lot of reading on magic wedding ceremonies since our last one, and we probably need to talk about what they want as far as that goes as well." Mia went to the bookshelf behind her desk and pulled out a book. "I got this from the bookstore's magic section. Apparently, it's the go-to magic planning book for weddings for the last three years. If you have questions, let me know."

"This is so rad. I love working for you." Christina opened the book and scanned a few pages. "Funny, there's a lot of things we do in nonmagic ceremonies that mirror these, except there's reasoning behind these rituals."

"Exactly. The reason behind the ritual is the important part." Mia sighed and picked up Hailey's résumé. "And this conversation is the exact reason that Miss Berger might not work out. How do I explain to a nonmagic person why we're reviewing a book of spells before planning a wedding?"

"Maybe she already knows about Magic Springs. She lives here. There aren't a lot of people who live here who don't believe in the existence of witches." Christina's watch started beeping. "Sorry, my cookies are ready to come out of the oven. We'll chat later, but I'm sure it's going to be just fine. I was."

Mia watched her assistant leave the office and nodded. "Exactly. You were, but you are extraordinary. How do I find anyone else to replace you?"

There was no one to answer her question, so she returned to the wedding file and started reviewing what they had already developed. All they needed from the happy couple was a direction, a decision on the venue, and a date. And the wedding planning would be on. Which was another reason she needed to hire someone else. She glanced at the clock. She had a little while before she would be needed for the wedding planning. Time to check some references.

By the time she'd called all of Hailey's references and gotten glowing recommendations, the engaged couple was at the door. She didn't have time to think about Hailey anymore, but she tucked the file into her tote. She'd ask Trent if he knew Hailey or any of her local references. She could always count on him being a voice of reason. And his logic allowed her to make an informed decision. She grabbed the folders and went out to the living room to greet her new clients.

May and Henry were an older couple. May appeared to be in her late forties and Henry a little older. Both were professionals. May was a counselor and Henry taught high school history. Both were fun and excited to get on with their lives together.

"Henry was married before but lost his wife to cancer over ten years ago now," May was explaining. "I've always been married to my work. I worked with a movie studio for years in Hollywood, working with actors in getting ready for their parts. So when people started moving to Sun Valley, I would come up and do house calls. I reconnected with Henry at a local fundraiser for at-risk youth in the area. We clicked immediately, and before you know it, I'm buying a house up here and moving my practice."

"She still goes on set with some of the movies," Henry said, pride showing on his face for his soon-to-be new wife's established career. "I told her we could live in California."

"And lose this beauty? I love the beach, but there is something special about this place. It's magical." She looked between Christina and Mia. "I was told you were familiar with our special needs for the ceremony?"

"Familiar, but I'd rather you be specific on what exactly you want so I don't miss anything. I have a minister who can do the ceremony if he doesn't have a conflict." Mia nodded to the folders. "Let's see what we already have on the list and then you can add or subtract as we need. First up, let's look at venues in the Magic Springs area. I'm assuming you want to stay in town?"

"Definitely," the couple said together, and then they laughed.

"This is a great start, then." Mia held up the venue sheet. "We have several choices listed out with an estimate of costs for the wedding and/or reception. I'd suggest we focus on indoor venues unless you want to put off the wedding until later in July or August."

"No, inside is fine," May said as the couple locked their gazes. "We want to be married as soon as possible. Do you have availability next week?"

"The weekend after is our first available slot, and we have several venues that also have time available. We need to make a quick decision, though, if we want to get our first choice." Mia went through the venues, showing the websites that Christina had already loaded on a tablet the couple could review. When they'd gone through the pros and cons, Mia nodded to Christina. "Why don't we give the two of you some time to think about it and we'll get some refreshments?"

With the drink choice list in hand, Christina and Mia met up in the kitchen. Mia opened a cabinet and set items on a nearby table. "Let's set up a tray. We can watch them on the monitor there. When they set the tablet down, we should go back into the room."

"They're a really nice couple, don't you think?" Christina went to pour coffee and to grab sparkling water for her and Mia. The cookies were already on a pretty plate.

Mia added napkins and a single daisy to the tray to make it special. She glanced over and saw a fuzzy outline in the door window. The ghosts were getting closer. She started to walk over, but Christina grabbed her arm. "What?"

"Look, they set the tablet down. I think they made a decision."

Mia blinked, then glanced at her watch. They had been there less than five minutes. These two knew exactly what they wanted. "That was fast. Let's go see where we're doing a wedding."

"This is fun!" Christina picked up the tray and moved out of the kitchen.

Mia paused at the door to look back at the window. Nothing was there. She took a breath and then set a smile on her face. The school was going to give her a heart attack.

"So, it looks like you've picked a venue," Mia said as she sat down at the table. She pulled the tablet closer to her side of the table. "What's our lucky winner?"

May and Henry shared a look, then May answered my question. "None of them."

"So you want a venue outside of Magic Springs?" Mia opened the tablet and the next set of websites. She handed the tablet back to May. "We actually anticipated that, so here's some in Twin that would be appropriate."

May waved off the tablet. "You're misunderstanding. We want the wedding to be here, in Magic Springs."

"So you want an outdoor site? I really can't recommend it, or at least not without a backup plan."

"Sorry, what May's trying to say is we'd like to rent the school for the wedding. If it's nice, we'll do the ceremony and reception out in the backyard area. If not, you have a gym behind those doors, correct?" He pointed to the doors that led into what had been the school's gym.

"Yes, but are you sure? I know we can get places with more natural beauty in the area." Mia had rented out the school for a reunion last year and had wound up kicking people out of one of the upstairs classrooms, where they were trying to spell cast. And then a dead body had shown up on the second floor the next day. All in all, for a first run of the school as an event-hosting site, it had failed miserably.

"We both have families who went to school here. I was raised in California, but my mom went to school here, as did Henry's entire family. It has meaning to us, much more than the Lodge or the local Methodist church. I know it wasn't one of the choices, but I really want you to think about it. It would mean a lot to both of us and our families." May leaned forward, trying to add as much authority to her words as possible. "Please, Mia, we'd appreciate it."

Mia thought about the ghosts who were now literally knocking on the back door and prayed the wards would stay up at least until after the wedding. Although if there was a wedding guest list that included a ton of magical people, maybe having the wards fall at that time would at least give her the firepower to put them back up. It would ruin the wedding, but the school wards would be fixed.

"I'm not sure the school is really where you want to celebrate your joining," Mia began to explain, but both May and Henry shook their heads.

"It's exactly where we want to start our new life together. The view of the Sawtooth mountain range from your backyard would make memorable wedding pictures. We want memories of a ceremony where we can celebrate who we are, as individuals and as a new couple as part of our community. A lot of places don't have any magical history. The school—it's filled with history, good and bad. Just like life is." May glanced around at the room. "The décor is perfect, and hopefully we'll have a nice day and can move the entire event out in that backyard of yours. Maybe by the herb garden."

"I've been having some issues with the wards and the history of the school." Mia didn't want to blurt out that the wedding could be interrupted by a cemetery full of angry ghosts, but they needed to know at least some of the problem.

"My great-uncle, Alphonso Lasher, helped build this place. If we can get him over to shore up your wards next week, would that make you feel more comfortable?" Henry asked as he squeezed May's hand. "I told you my family has history with the school."

Mia studied the two. It was clear that they'd made their mind up long before they'd walked in for the appointment that day. Maybe they'd been afraid that to ask up front would be an easy "no." Now that she had put some time and effort into the planning stages, they were counting on her saying yes. She leaned back in her chair. "If your great-uncle comes and says it's safe for you to have the wedding here in two weeks, you've got a venue. If not, we're going to be scrambling."

"If he says no, we'll get married wherever you find us a place. No arguments on size, area, or even its appropriateness for a coven-sponsored wedding. I'll even say yes to a fast-food restaurant's ball room." May bounced a little in her chair.

"It seems to mean a lot to you, so yes, have your uncle call me to set up a time to meet. I do deliveries on Tuesday and I'm out of town on Wednesday, so our days are limited. If he doesn't reach me by Friday, we'll go with plan B." Mia met Christina's gaze and shrugged. Sometimes, the client was always right. Even when they weren't. "So let's talk about the guest list. Do you know how many people you want to invite?"

CHAPTER 9

After May and Henry left, Christina helped Mia clean up the refreshments and the dishes for the meeting. "This is going to be hard to pull together in two weeks, no matter where the event actually happens. It will be easier here, but you're worried about the ghosts in the yard, right?"

Mia nodded and ate the last cookie before Christina could nab it. "If the wards fall during the ceremony, the wedding could be ruined. Think of the hotel scene in *Ghostbusters*. Or even worse."

"They can't say you didn't warn them. You said everything but plague and pestilence on their houses to stop them from seeing the school as the perfect venue. On the bright side, you may be able to get it fixed and you won't have to worry anymore." Christina glanced at her watch. "We've got to get moving. Did you say Baldwin is coming over?"

"He said he'd be here after work, but I'm expecting him anytime. He's worried about Sarah. I'm sure he's shortening his time in the office while she's not feeling well." She looked up as the monitor beeped and showed Baldwin's truck coming up the drive. "Speak of the devil."

"The basket is on the counter there with the cookies and the quarts are in the front of the freezer. We have about five left, so we should make some more on Tuesday, if not sooner." Christina washed the tray and put it on a towel to dry. "And I'm heading upstairs. A day I don't have to talk to our favorite police chief is a good day for me."

"I can't believe you're still scared of him." Mia laughed as she took three quarts from the freezer and settled them into the basket. She added a loaf of bread she'd baked on Monday to go with the basket and headed to the front door to meet Mark.

He'd just knocked when she reached the foyer. She set the basket down on the table and opened the door. "Hey, Mark, how's Sarah?"

"I think a little better, but she might just be telling me that because I tried to take her to the emergency room last night. The only thing she can keep down is your soup. I appreciate you keeping us stocked up." Mark Baldwin ran his hand over his face. He looked ragged. "I'm sorry about not getting back to you on the Medford case. I'm still doing some digging. I hate to admit I dropped the ball on this, but it looks like your friend may be right."

"Well, you just take care of Sarah. The case will wait." Mia wanted to say the case had waited for six months, so there wasn't a hurry now. But she didn't want to kick him while he was clearly hurting about his wife. "I'm making up a new batch of soup next week. Let me know if you want me to drop some off at the house on Tuesday. And maybe this week's dinner for you? You need to eat as well. I put some cookies in the basket too."

He smiled as he took the basket from her. "You've been very helpful, Mia. Thank you."

"We're a community, Mark. All of us here in Magic Springs. You should know that by now." She watched as he returned to his truck, carefully setting the basket on the passenger-side floor of the truck. She sent up a prayer to the Goddess for Sarah, and in response, she heard Gloria, the kitchen witch doll she kept in the apartment kitchen, giggle.

She closed the door and looked up the stairs toward her third-floor apartment. "What exactly do you know that I don't, Miss Gloria?"

This time only silence met her question. That was the thing about familiars and connections to the Goddess. They didn't always respond, at least not on your schedule. Gloria had been her familiar since Mia could remember. Mia's mother had declined the magic mantle from Grans soon after Mia was born, so Mia had been raised to take the power. She really hadn't wanted to deal with it, until she moved to Magic Springs. Now she let Grans train her, mostly because she believed in the tradition. Besides, a little world peace spelling couldn't hurt.

Mia pushed the notion away and decided to go make some lunch. Trent was coming to take her to dinner again tonight. She didn't want to eat too late or not eat at all and look like she was starving when they finally got to the restaurant.

Mia grabbed her notebook, where she had Hailey's résumé and the folder for May and Henry's wedding and headed upstairs. She wanted to divide out the planning part with Christina. And she needed to call Hailey. Mia was going to give Hailey a trial run, hopefully she'd be able to work tomorrow.

By the time Trent showed up, she'd set up Hailey to be at the school tomorrow at eight and had assigned a lot of the planning tasks for the wedding to Christina. She'd let her know if Mia needed to step in and help. And she'd texted Abigail, letting her know that they'd need a wedding cake and the date of the event. She asked her to handle setting up a cake testing in the next week and let her know it was okay to use the school for the meeting. When Trent came up to the front door, Mia buzzed him in. She was waiting for him at her apartment door. She gave him a long kiss, then held the door open. "Are you ready to go, or do we have some time to talk before we leave?"

"Uh-oh, what did I do now?" He came into the apartment, closing the door just before Mr. Darcy bolted out.

"Nothing. It was me. Do you want a soda?" She studied her face. "Or coffee? You look wiped out."

"Coffee would be great." He sank into a kitchen chair. "I'm trying to get everything set up at the store before I take off with my dad this weekend."

"We could have canceled tonight, you know."

Mia made him a cup using her one-cup machine. "And we still can. I can whip up something for dinner here."

"No, we're going out. But unfortunately, that means we're not being adventurous. How bad are you going to hate me if I take you to the Lodge again tonight?"

"I've got a big day tomorrow anyway. The Lodge is fine. But my offer to cook still stands." Mia got herself a soda. She'd already consumed more coffee than she tended to drink in twenty-four hours, if not forty-eight. Unless she was on a two-day event.

"Okay, so if it's not dinner, what's on your mind?" He sipped his coffee.

"I scheduled a wedding here in two weeks." She let the words hang as the caffeine kicked in.

Trent's eyes widened. "Are you sure that's a good idea? We don't know if the wards are going to hold."

"It comes with a visit from one of the school's builders." She went on to tell him about Henry's great-uncle and how she'd explained the issue with the couple. "Anyway, Henry thinks his uncle can shore up the wards. If that happens, we may not have an issue."

"But we still have to move the bodies if there are some left in the cemetery," Trent reminded her.

"I know, but having the wards reset may give us the time to be able to do that with a funeral director. I'm not sure what we need to do to move the bodies. And, worse, what it might cost." She saw Trent's eyes flash. "I'm not saying not to do it at all. I know this has been hidden for years. I want to do it right, not just rushed to protect the school."

Trent sipped his coffee. "I still don't think it's a good idea to hold a wedding here. If the wards don't hold, the entire coven will be able to point the blame to us."

"Actually, I had them sign a form holding us harmless on all physical and nonphysical matters that could happen because we woke something up with their ceremony." She rolled her shoulders. "It's not ideal, but this way we don't have to take off Wednesday and go ask Brody what he knows. You realize he'll never be direct with us. Unless he thinks it's in his best interests."

"You don't know if you can trust this great-uncle of Henry's either," Trent countered.

She took a sip of her soda. When she set down the can, she stared directly at Trent. "He has a vested interest in telling me the truth. If he doesn't, the wedding won't happen here, and we'll have to get the coven involved."

He finished his coffee and stood. "Okay, just send me a text on when this wedding is happening. I want to be here for the fireworks. Let's go to dinner before I fall asleep on you."

The Lodge was quiet for a Thursday night. According to the waitress, some of the convention people had shown up early for tomorrow's event, so there were a lot of room-service orders happening.

Mia sipped her wine as she looked around the empty dining room. "We're early for dinner. Maybe it will pick up later."

"I'm sure they're doing okay." Trent set aside the menu. "Mom came into the store today to get ingredients for the dessert she's serving tomorrow."

"She left a message that she'll be in the kitchen tomorrow at eight. I'm hoping she can help me judge my new employee too." Mia decided on her order. "You'd think since I was just here I'd know what I wanted to eat. But everything looks good. I can never decide if I want to go with an old favorite or try something new and risk being disappointed."

Trent smiled as he sipped his wine. "Eating out with you is always an adventure. I'll never look at food the same way after meeting you."

"I'm not sure that's a compliment," Mia laughed as the waitress returned to get their order. Mia ordered the trout. It was her go-to meal. Trent went with the bison burger. A local farmer had started raising buffalo last year and the Lodge had just begun to serve their meat. After the waitress had left the table, Mia turned back to Trent. "You don't know a Hailey Berger, do you?"

He shook his head, but Mia could see the thoughts running through his eyes. "Doesn't ring a bell. Is that your new employee?"

"Yes. She says she's from eastern Washington and has catering experience." Mia ran a finger around her wineglass.

"You don't sound very convinced of her résumé. Did you call her references?" Trent waved at a passing guest. "That's Caleb Spellman. He comes in a lot for fishing trips with my dad."

"See, that's why I asked you about Hailey. You know everyone." Mia wondered how long Hailey had been in town. "I called her references and they were glowing. There's just something I'm not

finding in her. I guess we'll have a trial by fire tomorrow, and if she gets through a catering gig, I
should know everything I need to know."

"I'll ask around if you want. Is she staying with
someone? I suspect she's not living out of the
Lodge, especially if she's been here for a while.
And Magic Springs isn't known for its cheap hous-
ing."

"True. Which is why Christina's staying with me.
I can't afford to pay her what she'd need to rent a
condo here in town. And I'd hate it if she had to
live in Twin and drive the mountain roads home
after a late catering gig."

"Mother Mia," Trent teased. "Well, let's hope
this Hailey has a place to stay or I might be having
to help turn one of the second-floor classrooms
into a bedroom."

A woman in a black cocktail dress and a man in
a suit entered the restaurant, following the hostess. Mia leaned closer to Trent. "Isn't that Ginny
Willis? She still hasn't paid the balance on the
catering bill. Maybe I should visit her table."

"You're going to bring up business on a dinner
date?" Trent watched the couple as the hostess sat
them across the room.

As Ginny sat down, she met Mia's gaze and nodded.

"You think it's a date?" Mia broke eye contact
and studied the man with Ginny. "Do you know
who that guy is?"

"One of the coven leaders. Malcolm McBride.
He took over a spot after the whole Dorian thing
happened and there were two empty spots. I guess
it could be a coven meeting, but they're awful

dressed up for just a meeting. And sitting pretty close together."

"Oh, I saw him at the Holly funeral. He was going through the picture album at the back of the room. He took a couple of the pictures. He must have been close friends with Theresa to be in her album." Mia paused as their meals arrived. The smell from her parmesan-crusted trout made her stomach growl. "I guess I'm hungrier than I thought."

"Did you work all day or stop for lunch? Even a small serving of fruit and cheese will keep you going. I'm hooked on a protein bar at afternoon break. My stomach knows when it's three on the dot because I'm instantly hungry." He took a bite of his burger. "I think you don't get enough protein during the day."

"Probably true. But I love to bake, especially breakfast items like muffins and pastries. Sugar is my wake-up call." She took a bite of the fish; it was amazing.

"Well, your metabolism is going to start craving that protein. Anyway, I forgot that Ginny was in charge of the Holly estate. I wonder where all that money's going."

"There was a sizable estate?" Mia focused on her meal, not wanting to even look up as she talked. "If I'd known that, I wouldn't have let Ginny talk me into a discount on the catering."

"Ginny probably just wants to look good for the coven. If my guess is right, the estate will probably go to the coven coffers. The leadership is very appreciative of estate gifts. My folks get calls every year from the foundation, asking to be put in their will. Dad was on the coven board for a few years, so he knows how much money they have stockpiled, and he's not leaving the coven anything. He's concerned that the leadership is skimming." Trent took a bite of his potato. "I love how James has the kitchen cover these with rock salt before they're baked. It makes them so tasty."

"But a normal coven member wouldn't know that, so they leave their estate either to the kids or, if they don't have family, to the coven." Mia thought about Adele. She'd left her money to her grandson, but he'd died several years before, so Mia's grandmother had received the money Adele hadn't designated to go to charity. "I can see how that might add up over time, especially here. There's a lot of wealth in this area."

"Yes, ma'am." Trent glanced over at Ginny and Maxwell, who'd just ordered a bottle of wine. "And a lot of people around who love to spend money. Especially cash that isn't theirs."

When Mia got home, she felt even more tired, but with an event tomorrow, she knew she wouldn't be able to sleep if she lay down now. Instead, she drew a bath and lit some candles in the bathroom. She brewed a cup of herbal tea and took a book and a notebook and pen into the bathroom with her. The prior resident of the apartment had remodeled the bathroom with a large claw-foot tub, and with the right amount of bubble bath, the water was heaven. She set everything on the tray that fit across the tub and sank into its warmth. Instantly, the muscles in her neck and back started releasing. She started reading the book, but every few minutes a question would pop into her mind about the event. Or the paperwork needed for hiring Hailey. Or how on earth she'd figure out who had actually killed Hetty Medford. Or the fact that she needed to call Ginny Willis to follow up on the missing payment.

She wrote down all the questions and notes on the paper and, after she did, returned to her book. By the time the water had cooled, she was in the middle of the story and her eyes were drooping. And she had a full page of things to check on for tomorrow's event or things she needed to do for the business.

She came out into the kitchen in a large terry-cloth robe that Isaac had bought her on their trip to Chicago. The old hotel had been magnificent in the day and had provided them with robes to sit around the room in. She'd fallen in love with hers and, in a rare moment of generosity, Isaac had packed it in her suitcase, telling the hotel to put it on their bill. The trip had been one of the last they'd taken together. Now Mia wondered if, even then, he'd been cheating.

She set the tea kettle back on to heat up and sat at the table, adding the notes she'd made in the tub to her official to-do list for the morning.

Christina walked into the kitchen from the living room. "Can't sleep?"

"One more cup of this and I'm going to be out like a baby. Or like me on a non-pre-event night." Mia pushed away her to-do list. "Why are you still up?"

"Just working on some homework. I have to

keep up because it's a condensed summer schedule." She dropped into one of the chairs. "And, I have to admit, I'm a little nervous about adding someone to our team tomorrow."

"You can't mean Abigail. Is this because she's Levi's mom?" Magic Springs was small. Which meant that anyone they worked with probably knew someone who knew at least one of them.

"No, I adore Abigail. And she's fun." Christina sighed. "This is going to sound stupid, especially because I've been telling you to hire someone else, but what if you like this new girl more than me?"

"They could be less of a pain than you are. And maybe like to work earlier than you do," Mia teased Christina. "But you have to know you're not just an employee. You're family."

"No, I *would have been* family if you'd married Isaac," Christina pointed out.

Mia stood when the teakettle started whistling. "No, you're still family, even though I didn't make the mistake of marrying your brother. Do you want some tea?"

Christina stood and grabbed a cup from the cabinet. "I would love to have some tea with you. Thank you for easing my freak-out."

"My pleasure." Mia poured hot water into both cups and then turned off the stove. "I'm still wondering who sent Hailey our way. I asked Trent if he knew her and he doesn't."

"Neither does Levi," Cristina added as she chose Earl Grey as her tea blend. "Maybe Abigail knows who told Hailey about the job. She didn't come from any of my school friends; I've already asked."

"If Abigail doesn't know, we'll just go to the

horse's mouth and ask Hailey tomorrow." Mia checked her tea. "So, tell me about this science class. I suspect it's mandatory for graduation?"

Mia decided she wasn't going to let any of her worries follow her to her bedroom. Maybe, if she tried clearing her mind before she went to sleep, she'd get a full eight hours. That definitely would be a miracle on a night before a catering event.

CHAPTER 10

Mia was up too early the next morning, so she made a breakfast strata. The early morning meal was becoming a bit of a tradition. She would have made cinnamon rolls, but Trent's warning about needing more protein in her diet hadn't fallen on dcaf ears. She posted a picture of the fresh-out-of-the-oven treat on her Instagram page for the business. A few moments later, her phone buzzed with a text.

Looks good, have enough for me? I'll bring the orange juice. Need anything else?

She read Trent's text and smiled. Then she checked her fridge and texted her answer back. **See you when you get here.**

She checked her hair in the mirror and decided to pull it back in a clip, but she'd hold off on the makeup. Trent knew what she looked like. Makeup was mandatory for meetings and dates, but when she was cooking, like today, she'd leave it off until right before the event started. Christina had put together a travel makeup kit for her that she kept in the catering van. It had been Christina who'd first told her she needed to look the part of owner, not staff, when she oversaw an event. Mia had to admit it did boost her confidence a bit when she freshened up right before service. And on-site bookings had increased after she started implementing the change.

Mia had years of experience in catering, but Isaac had done most of the bookings. He'd told her she was the heart of the department and he was the face. Which really meant she'd done all the work. He was great at the schmoozing. Christina had come from the same Adams family finishing school in dealing with the rich. It was one of the talents she brought to the business. The secret code of the rich and famous. Christina was her translator.

Trent must have already been at the store when he'd seen her post because he showed up sooner than she'd expected. She started a cup of coffee for him and went downstairs to let him in. When she opened the door, the surprise on his face was clear.

"I figured you'd just buzz me in." He moved a hand behind his back and held out the orange juice. "Here."

"Thanks. I figured I might as well start my step count for the day." She held up her watch. "Last catering job, I got almost twenty thousand steps. I'm trying to break that goal today. I'm so glad I'm off Saturday and Sunday. My feet are going to be screaming after today."

He followed her in and up the stairs. "I can smell the strata from here. Sausage?"

"Yep, and potatoes, onions, peppers, and eggs. I still need to look it up, but I'm thinking it has a lot of protein. If not, I'm planning on a turkey sandwich for lunch." She opened the apartment door and headed to the kitchen, where she grabbed his cup of coffee from the machine. "Here you go."

"And here you go." He moved his hand from behind his back and held out a bouquet of daisies. "I hope you like them."

She took the flowers and breathed in their scent. "They're lovely. But what's the occasion? Did I forget something? Can't be first date, right?"

He grabbed a vase from under the sink and filled it with water. "No special occasion. I just know how you get on catering days and wanted you to have a spot of joy before you started your grueling day."

"That's so sweet of you." She arranged the flowers in the vase and moved them to the side of the table. "They're pretty."

"So are you." He leaned over and kissed her.

A sound came from the hallway. Christina moved into the kitchen and headed to the coffee pot. "Gross. Get a room."

"Or I could just kick you out and have an entire apartment to myself," Mia said as she picked up her coffee.

"Sure, threaten me before coffee. I won't remember this in a few minutes, you know that, right?" Christina sat at the table and pointed to the flowers. "Nice move, dude."

"Thank you for your approval." Trent nodded to the casserole. "Do you want to do the honors or should I?"

"I'll serve. Christina, are you hungry?" Mia asked.

"Yep. I thought I might make lunch for the team today. Abigail's going to be here, right?" Christina lay her head on the table as she spoke.

"That's nice of you." Mia set a plate in front of Trent and went back to make Christina's.

Christina raised her head as Mia brought over their plates. "Thanks. I thought about it last night. I think it will be a good time to get to know our newest member. And figure out if she's going to fit in."

Trent snorted. "I love a thoughtful gesture with an ulterior motive."

"Dude, no one knows anything about her." Christina grinned as she loaded her fork with food. "Besides, I really do want her to work out. Now that Bethanie's heading out of town, I need someone else to hang out with that's not Levi."

"I totally understand that. My brother can be a handful." Trent took a bite. "This is freaking awesome, Mia. I can't believe your best work is done in the wee hours of the morning."

"Thanks, I think." Mia stood. "I almost forgot. We have orange juice too."

Christina opened the bottle as Mia set down the glasses. "I'm not saying Levi's not fun to hang out with. I just meant when he's working and when I need a girl to go to the nail salon with me, or on a girls' night out."

"He'll be happy to hear that clarification." Trent sipped some juice. "Hey, James called last night. He saw us at the restaurant but then got tied up in the kitchen. We were gone when he got it settled. Anyway, he mentioned Ginny being there again. I guess she's been out and about with several guys lately. Last week it was Jerimiah."

"The coven leader from Twin?" Mia remembered seeing him at the wake.

Trent nodded. "I guess Miss Ginny has a thing for men with power. Anyway, I wanted to mention it to you, just in case she starts throwing around names to get you to cut more off that bill she owes you."

"You're such a sweetheart," Mia responded.

"Me? You're the prize. You cook, you let me come over for an impromptu breakfast for the cost of a bottle of orange juice. And you hired my mother." He eyed her. "Are you sure you don't have a place in your work crew for Dad too? He seems to be a bit lost now that Mom's working."

"She's not even working full time. Tell him to take a chill pill." Mia laughed at Trent's expression. "Okay, maybe not that exact phrasing, but maybe when you're on this weekend away, you could talk to him and bring him into the twenty-first century, where even married women hold jobs."

"Now don't get all crazy over here. You know Dad's kind of a traditionalist." Trent stood with his plate. "Okay if I get seconds?"

"Please, or we'll have it for breakfast for days." Mia shook her head. "I never can figure out how to cook for just a few people."

"Good thing you're a caterer." Trent sat down with a full plate and the conversation changed over to the plans for the day. The front doorbell rang and Trent pointed to the display. "Mom's here. And it looks like she brought Dad to carry in her stuff. I'll go let them in. Okay if they come up for a bit before I send them to the kitchen? I'm not sure you've ever met my dad."

Mia swallowed; she hadn't met the patriarch of the Majors family yet.

Christina looked at her funny. "Really? I figured you'd already met Thomas. He's a good guy. Not like his sons."

Trent playfully tousled Christina's hair on the way out of the kitchen. "Watch it, kiddo, I haven't been giving you the full Majors kid treatment yet. But if you keep up with the teasing, all bets are off."

"Whatever. I'm not scared of you." Christina waited for him to leave the apartment. "Uh-oh, I think I just called his bluff. Tell him I didn't mean it, okay?"

"You have to fight your own battles. I've told you this many times, and besides, Trent is a lot less scary than Isaac. You can take him." Mia glanced around the kitchen. It looked pretty clean, but she stood and started rinsing off the pans she'd cooked with that morning and then realized she couldn't finish them in the time it took for Trent's parents to walk up three flights. She stacked them and put them into the oven. Out of sight. She rinsed the sink and cleared the cabinets.

"Oh my Goddess. You're nervous." Christina started to laugh.

Mia looked at the spray bottle of cleaning fluid and the rag in her hand. Then she tucked them under the sink. "I am not. Why would I be nervous? It's just Abigail."

"And Trent's dad, who you haven't met yet. Don't worry about him, he's a softy. Besides, he won't do anything stupid in front of Abigail. He loves that woman." Christina stood and made another cup of coffee. "And you're in cute pajamas anyway."

Mia's eyes widened as she looked down at the flannel pajamas she wore with heavy socks and pink slippers. "Crap, I didn't think about what I was wearing."

The door opened and Trent called out, "We're here."

Mia ran her hands over her hair, resetting her clip and praying she didn't look as crazed as she probably did.

"Take a breath; it will be fine." Christina started more coffee for the newcomers. "Trent loves you, that's all that matters."

Mia hoped Christina's words were true because she wasn't making the best first impression. She smiled at the trio coming into the kitchen. "Good morning. Can I interest anyone in some sausage and potato strata? Maybe coffee or orange juice?"

"I'd love a plate and coffee, please." Abigail came up first and gave Mia a hug. With her arm still around Mia, she turned to Thomas. "And this, my dear, is the lovely and talented Mia Malone. You really should try her food. It's amazing. And you already know Christina."

Thomas stood next to his son. He was a little shorter than Trent, but in all other ways, the apple didn't fall far from the tree. They had the same smile, the same kind eyes, and the same hair, even though the older Majors had more salt and pepper sprinkled in. He held out his hand. "Mia, it's good to finally meet the woman who has captivated my son and my wife's attention and time."

"Now, be nice. Thank you, dear." Abigail took

the coffee cup from Christina. "Can you stay for a few minutes and at least eat something?"

"I'm meeting a new client at the Lodge. I'll eat there. Christina, good to see you again. And it's really nice to meet you, Mia. I hope next time we can spend some time getting to know each other." Thomas glanced at his watch. "But not today. I need to go if I'm not going to be late. Trent, you can see that your mother's things get in the kitchen. That box is heavy."

"I'm not an invalid and it's not that heavy." Abigail ran a hand down her husband's arm. "I'll call you if I need a ride home. Otherwise, I'll see you tonight when I get done."

He leaned over and kissed her. "Have fun and come home safe."

"See you soon." Abigail hugged her husband, then sat down at the table. "I'd love some strata, Mia."

"'Bye," Mia called after the retreating man and then turned to make a plate for Abigail. Her face felt hot. She took a breath to calm herself. "Thanks for coming in early, Abigail."

"No trouble. Thomas wanted to meet you and he worries about me carrying anything heavier than my purse. I have no idea why." Abigail took the plate Mia handed her. "Smells divine."

"Thanks." Mia sat just as a loud crash came from the oven. She groaned.

"Are you baking something else?" Trent stood to open the oven door, but Mia grabbed his arm.

"Don't open that."

He looked at her and then at the empty sink, understanding. He nodded and turned to his mother. "Would you like a glass of orange juice to go with that?"

After they finished breakfast, Abigail and Christina headed down to the kitchen. Trent and Mia cleaned up the dishes.

"When does your new employee arrive?" Trent asked as he pulled the pans out of the oven where Mia had stashed them.

"Nine. I have a few minutes. Your dad seems nice." Mia filled the sink with hot, soapy water.

"I can't believe you hadn't met him yet. It seems like every time we stopped by the house, he's been out." Trent stacked the dishes and cups from the table onto the counter. "The table's clean; do you want me to dry?"

"If you have time. I'd like to get these done and on with my day." Mia felt a cold draft in the kitchen. She looked around but didn't see anyone materialize. "Did you feel that?"

Trent nodded. "It's coming from the direction of the library. I'm not sure you taking a field trip in there this weekend without someone being with you is a good idea."

"I'll take someone with me." Mia turned back to the dishes and started washing.

"Christina isn't trained. Talk to my mom or your grandmother. Maybe they can go with you and help you reach the entity." He picked up a towel and started drying.

"She's a little girl," Mia reminded him.

"She took the shape of a little girl. Or if she is, that doesn't mean there isn't someone else with her," Trent pointed out.

"Fair, but at this point, all we can do is deal with

what we know. And if the wards are what keeps others from getting in, that might be the reason she can't get out. I know your mom doesn't think the ghost is the girl who's rumored to have died here, but she's someone. And maybe she knows more about the wards than we do." Mia slipped the dishes in the water. There was something comforting about washing dishes by hand.

"I think you're being overly optimistic, but still, promise me you'll wait until I get back or take someone with magic with you." He didn't take the plate she handed him until she met his gaze. "Please?"

She pushed the plate toward him. "I promise. Now, let's get these done before I have to meet my new employee."

Hailey Berger showed up exactly at nine. She was dressed to cook. She wore clean jeans and a blue T-shirt. On her feet were comfortable shoes. Black, so if she needed to be in uniform, she already had her shoes. Mia was impressed. The choice of clothing told her that she had worked in a kitchen before. Mia opened the door farther. "Come on in. We've already started in the kitchen. I've got some forms for you to complete; then we can see what you can do. The event we're catering is small. Twenty-five plates. But I like the fact it's only one meal. It will be a nice entry point for you to check out if you like working with us."

"I'm sure it will be fine." Hailey followed Mia into the foyer. She pointed to Mr. Darcy, who was curled on the couch, watching the new arrival with interest. "What a lovely cat. Is he your mascot?"

Mia laughed at the look Mr. Darcy gave Hailey. "Kind of, but he's more family than anything else.

Hailey reached out a hand to pet the cat, but Mr. Darcy raised up on his haunches and hissed, then ran upstairs. Hailey blinked, then dropped her hand. "I guess I didn't make a good impression."

Mia had never seen Mr. Darcy act like that, but maybe it was Dorian who was reacting. She set the thought aside and pointed to a door at the end of the room. "The first door leads to a classroom. I teach demonstration lessons a few times a month. I'd like to have the students do a real cook in the classroom, but that's on the wish list, right after the air-conditioner upgrade. The second door leads to the kitchen where we'll be cooking today. And this," Mia opened a door and waved Hailey inside, "this is my office. Like I said, I have a few forms for you to complete. Would you like some coffee while you do it?"

"I'd love some. Black is fine." Hailey sat in the visitor chair and looked around the office. "I take it the whiteboard lists the events you have scheduled for the next month?"

"Exactly. Since you and Abigail joined our team, I needed a place where I could list off all the events we have going. And it's also where you put your days off so I know if we can pull off an event like the wedding in two weeks." Mia pointed to the weekend where May and Henry had decided to get married at the school. "I really hope you can work that weekend because we're going to be slammed. It's a small wedding, but still."

"May Hornbuckle? She's getting married?" Shock echoed in Hailey's voice.

Mia handed Hailey the clipboard where she'd put all the employment forms and a pen. "You know May? She's so sweet."

"I guess I didn't think at her age she'd be marrying." Hailey took the clipboard and shook her head. "Now, that sounded worse than I'd expected. I guess Cupid can fling his arrow at any time, right?"

Mia was just about to ask how Hailey knew May, but the door to the office opened and Christina poked her head in. "Hey, sorry to bother you guys, but I need some help with this recipe. It doesn't seem like enough to feed twenty-five people."

"Yeah, we'll need to convert it. Sorry, I thought I mentioned that." She turned to Hailey. "Hailey, this is Christina, my right hand and roommate."

"Hi, Hailey, I was almost Mia's new sister-in-law, but that seems like a lifetime ago." Christina waved from the doorway.

"Nice to meet you," Hailey said, looking a little overwhelmed with the information.

Mia saw the look. "Why don't you complete those forms, then set them on my desk? After that, come join us in the kitchen and we'll get this day started."

Mia and Christina went into the kitchen, where Mia walked Christina through the process of converting a recipe. When she'd finished, Hailey still hadn't appeared in the kitchen. She excused herself and went out to see if she was having problems with the forms. When she left the kitchen, she heard Hailey talking. She must have taken a phone call. She turned back to give her some privacy when she thought she heard May's name.

Confused, she stepped closer to the doorway and listened.

"Look, I don't know where you got the information on that one, but you need to take her off the list. Yes, I'm sure. I'm looking at the schedule right now." Hailey turned the corner and almost ran into Mia. "Sorry, Mom, I've got to go. I'll talk with you tonight."

Mia held up her hands. "I'm sorry to interrupt. I was just checking to see if you were stuck on the paperwork."

"No, it's done and on your desk." Hailey turned off her phone and tucked it into the back pocket of her jeans. "I forgot to turn it off when I left the house. My mom calls every morning. She likes to know that I'm okay."

"That's nice. I talk to my grandmother a lot. My mom? Not so much. She has a busy life in Boise. Are your folks here?" Mia opened the door to the kitchen.

"They live in Washington." Hailey nodded to the kitchen. "So, what are we cooking today?"

Chapter 11

Mahogany Medford pulled her SUV into the school parking lot. Mia and Christina were out in the van, loading up the food to go to the Lodge, where they'd be finishing the cooking and serving. Mahogany climbed out of her car and went over to the van, where Mia was adjusting trays. "Looks like I caught you at a bad time."

"We've got an event tonight at the Lodge. But we're almost done here; I can take a break. What's going on?"

"Baldwin is stonewalling me. I called him earlier this week and he said he needed to check on some things. Now, it's complete silence." Mahogany leaned on the truck. "I'm so tired of being the only one who cares that my mom is dead."

"You're not alone. Not anymore. I talked to Mark this week and he's looking into the autopsy. Whatever spell was on the house and on your mom, it has a distance limit. It didn't transfer with her to the county morgue."

Mahogany stood upright. "Are you telling me he believes me?"

"It's getting closer. Mark believes in facts. So now we just need to know more about how your mom died." Mia noticed the streak of gray in Mahogany's hair. "Maybe you should stay somewhere besides the house. You're looking like the spell is affecting you."

Mahogany reached up and pushed her hair behind her ear. "I saw the gray this morning. I'm going to get a room at the Lodge for a few nights. Did your grandmother or Abigail find a counter-curse for the house yet?"

"Not that I've heard." Mia realized she hadn't heard from her grandmother since the day they visited Mahogany. "I'll reach out tomorrow first thing. I need her help with something else anyway."

"Okay, I'll check back in a few days." She pulled a book out of her purse as her phone buzzed. "If it helps at all, that's my mom's last planner. Maybe there's something in there that you can see. I've been through it several times and it feels like something's there, but I can't see it. Sorry, I need to get this."

Mia tucked the book into her tote and then put it in the front of the van. Christina came up with a tote and nodded a greeting to Mahogany.

"This is the last one. Abigail's going to meet us there with dessert at about five. She's talking to Mr. Majors on the phone. She says she'll pack up the dessert and take it home unless you want to give her a key or meet her here later."

Mia held up a set of keys. "Give her these. Then lock up the kitchen from the front. This will get her into the kitchen through the back door. Is Mr. Darcy in the apartment?"

"He was a few minutes ago when I went through and locked everything up." Christina looked over at Mahogany, who was still on the phone. Then she lowered her voice. "But you know him."

Mia glanced at the school. Her cat did have a mind of his own. And now, with Dorian inside, he had powers to do whatever he wanted, including raiding the treat jar and leaving the house whenever he felt like it. She really needed to press Grans to fix the spell and let Dorian's spirit go into the great beyond. Mia had a feeling Grans was stalling, not wanting to lose Dorian forever. But that wasn't her cat's fault. "Okay, as soon as you're back from dropping off the keys and I've finished talking to Mahogany, we'll get going. I'm looking forward to this dinner. We haven't cooked at the Lodge for a while."

"You just like how James helps out and sends his guys to help serve," Christina teased. "Catering at the Lodge is a whole lot easier than doing it off-site."

"James wants the Lodge to look good. So he helps out." Mia rolled her shoulders and then remembered. "Hey, where's Hailey?"

"She took a quick break. I think she needed to call someone. She walked over to the greenbelt. She'll be back in a few minutes." Christina pointed over to the backyard, where the town trail system met the school's property. "There she is. I think she's going to fit in, don't you?"

Mia had been impressed with the woman's skill in the kitchen. And she jumped into the conversation easily. She didn't boast or take over like some did, and she was thoughtful and asked all the right questions. At least in Mia's mind. "I'm glad you think so. I was going to ask you how you thought she was doing."

"She's got prep down to a science. She showed me a different way to pack up the veggies that should keep them fresh as we transport. I think she's going to work out." Christina dangled the keys. "Looks like Mahogany wants to talk to you again. I'll go give these to Abigail and lock up. I'll send Hailey over. I don't know if she just wants to follow us in her car or not."

With that, Christina jogged over to the kitchen door where Hailey met her. Mia turned her attention back to Mahogany. "I told you that Mark's wife wasn't feeling well, right?"

"You did. And I don't mean to be a pest, but if the spell is still on the house in a few days, I'm going to have to start sleeping at the shop until we get this figured out. I can't afford to stay at the Lodge long. And . . ." she paused, taking a breath, "if Mom was murdered, I want to know that whoever did it is rotting in jail."

"I can't promise that, but let's just see if we can track the spell. Maybe I need to talk to the coven leadership too." Mia leaned against the van, thinking about Ginny Willis.

"Believe me, I've tried. For a bit, that woman didn't even want to believe I was Mom's daughter. She said Mom hadn't registered any children to the coven. I guess that's a thing. But I didn't want to join or have anything to do with her magic side, so she didn't register me." She glanced at her phone. "I've got to get to the shop. We're having supply issues. Can't run a tea shop unless you have tea, right?"

"I'll talk to you in a few days." Mia waved and shut the back of the van after visually checking for the bins they'd finished packing a few minutes before. Then she climbed into the van to wait. While she was there, she called her grandmother. The call went to voice mail. Again. She left a message this time. "Hey, Grans, just checking in to see if everything's going well. I'll try again tomorrow. I need your help with something."

Abigail would be home alone tomorrow too because her husband and Trent were going off on some hunting convention. She could ask Abigail to pick up Grans and come over first thing, then she'd make lunch for them as they talked through Mahogany's issues, as well as the house wards. She needed to kill one bird with two stones this weekend. She had way too much on her plate.

Christina climbed in on her side, waving at Hailey, who was getting into her car. "She says she'll meet us at the Lodge in about fifteen minutes. She has to run home first."

"Sounds good," Mia glanced over at the blond girl who had been by her side as she built the business. "I'm glad we found a new member for our team."

"Me too." Christina locked her seat belt and leaned back. "You're going to get so much work now that we've expanded our capability, I can feel it."

"I hope the Goddess agrees," Mia pulled the van out of the parking lot. "I've been looking at buying a new van before this one dies on the side of the road."

When they got to the Lodge, James had his staff bring in all the bins for the dinner. He led Mia and Christina to a small section of the kitchen away from the main part. "You guys can set up here. I need to just give you the keys to the kitchen, you're here almost as much as I am nowadays." James set down the bin he'd taken from Mia when she came inside on the counter. "This group is very nice. They had morning coffee and treats at ten and then an ice cream bar at three, just before they ended today's session. Tonight's dinner is an award banquet and then they have a half-day session tomorrow before they leave for home. Very coordinated and efficient."

Mia nodded. The organizers had gone through the same schedule when they'd talked a few months before to set up the menu. "I wish all my events were this well run."

"If they were, they wouldn't need people like us to help out." He watched as Christina headed back to the van. "Do you mind stepping into my office for a minute?"

"Sure." Mia followed him, and when he closed the door behind them, she sat down in a chair. "Okay, what's up?"

"I just wanted to let you know that the Lodge is thinking about hiring a catering director." He sat on his chair and watched her.

"You think it's going to take business from us." Mia followed up on his statement.

"I know it will take your business. Like this event. But that's not why I'm telling you this. I think you should apply for the job." He pushed some paperwork toward her. "There's the folder with the salary range. If I were you, I'd ask for twice what you were making in Boise. There's a location bonus you need to take into consideration. There's not a lot of people who want to work out in the boonies."

Mia didn't pick up the folder. "James, I have a business. If I lose a few clients, that will be okay."

"Mia, this expansion will tank your catering business, not just in Magic Springs but Sun Valley too. You need to take this job." James pushed the folder closer. "At least take a look at it. I'm serious, I'm worried about you. This new hotel manager wants all the events that are held here to be one hundred percent serviced by the hotel. I won't be able to send work your way after this person gets hired."

Mia picked up the folder and tucked it under her arm. "I'll look at it. Right now, I have an event to cater."

"I'm sorry to be the one to tell you," James said as she was leaving his office. "Let me know if you're going to apply. I'd love to work with you."

Mia felt the tears trying to fight their way out of her eyes, but she willed them away. She wasn't giving up on Mia's Morsels this quickly. Maybe she'd need to make some contacts with the Sun Valley hotels. The larger one already had a catering director. Mia had met her at a conference a few years ago. But maybe her hotel wouldn't be such sticklers about farming out some of the smaller events.

Or maybe she'd have to expand a different part of the business. Like the cooking school, or maybe even event planning. Whatever it was, she was going to do it. She hadn't come this far to go back to working for someone else again.

Christina looked up from where she'd been explaining the setup process to Hailey. She frowned as she watched Mia come across the kitchen. "Uh-oh, what's wrong?"

Mia shook her head as she tucked the folder into her tote. Then she tied on her apron. "Nothing that can't be handled tomorrow or later. Today's all about making this event memorable for our client."

"Repeat customers are the best. The place I worked for in Walla Walla had been catering this one family reunion for twenty years. It started feeling like we were part of the family, not just providing the food," Hailey chatted as she worked on the prep work Christina had given her.

"Now, that's a caterer's dream." Mia smiled and stood next to Christina. "Where do I need to be?"

Christina pointed to the next item on the to-do sheet. Before Mia could move away to start her work, Christina grabbed Mia's hand. "You're sure everything's okay?"

Mia nodded. "We'll chat tomorrow."

Christina seemed to take the deferment well, but Mia saw Hailey watching the two of them whispering. It must be hard to be the third member of a team that had worked as closely together as she and Christina had. Mia hoped she'd be able to keep on her newest hire, but it was probably better not to mention the change up at the lodge until both of them knew each other a little bit better.

As she did the mental gymnastics to convince herself she wasn't really keeping secrets, Mia's phone rang. She checked the display; the call was from her grandmother. "Sorry, guys, I need to take this. I'll be right back."

She stepped out into the hallway by the kitchen and accepted the call. "Hey, what's going on? I've been meaning to call you anyway to see if you have plans for tomorrow."

"You shouldn't really ask a question, then not shut up long enough for someone to actually answer you."

Mia sighed. "You're right and I'm sorry. What's going on?" She hoped that would appease Grans, but she wasn't convinced. The woman in the much younger body appeared to be grumpier than her Grans and a lot less tactful.

"Well, you could have asked how I was rather than just jump into the discussion. Anyway, I think I might have found a removal spell. I tried to reach Mahogany, but there's some sort of crisis at the teahouse." Grans laughed and Mia didn't like the sound of her humor. "Like a teahouse could have a real crisis. Probably just ran out of Earl Grey."

"Grans, I'm getting ready for an event this evening. Can I call you tomorrow?"

"Did you not hear me? I think I've found a removal spell. What could be more important than that? At least for poor Mahogany and her desire to find out who killed her mom and why before someone kills her too."

Now Grans was overreacting to the issue at hand. Man, the woman liked to yo-yo her emotions. "I heard you, but like I said, I'm catering. I can't just jump up and head over to Mahogany's house. I'll talk to you tomorrow and we'll figure this out." Mia glanced at her watch. Time was slipping away. "Anyway, I've got to go. What time do you want me to call for you? I'll bring over muffins."

"Whatever time you can fit an old woman into your schedule. I'll be here, waiting." And with that dig, Grans hung up the phone.

Mia sighed and slipped the phone into her pants pocket. "What a freaking diva!"

Apparently, she must have said it a little too loud because the woman walking past her turned quickly and stared at Mia.

"Sorry, not you. I mean, I don't even know you. It was a phone call I took a few minutes ago."

The woman nodded, but the look in her eye said, *Stay away from me, you nut.*

Mia moved toward the door to the kitchen. She probably deserved that. Mia's work plans were interfering with the help she'd promised Mahogany. The problem was, Mia had too many responsibilities, with a ton of conflicting deadlines. She should start to learn to say no and build some boundaries for herself. Then she thought of the fact that James might be answering her problem. Something she didn't want. She wanted the control of saying yes or no to a new client. Not just losing everyone who was hiring her to do events at the Lodge. "I've got to get back to work," she said to the empty hallway. No matter what happened, she'd survive, even if her business didn't. And all she could do was continue to serve amazing food.

As she reached out to open the kitchen door, she saw Ginny Willis again, her arm around a guy who wasn't either of the two men Mia had been told Ginny was currently dating. She walked over and whispered in the woman's ear. "Wow, Ms. Willis, you realize there's a bit of a shortage around Magic

Springs of eligible witches in the area. Maybe you need to pick one boyfriend at a time."

Ginny looked up at her with fire in her eyes. "I don't know what you mean."

She tried to pull her date past Mia, but instead of following her lead, he held out his hand to Mia.

"Nolan Byrd. No need to introduce yourself. You've been cooking for me and my daughter for the last six months. She loves your macaroni and cheese." He stopped Ginny from leaving the area. "Ginny, have you tried this woman's food? It's high end."

"Thank you, Mr. Byrd. I'm sorry I didn't recognize you. I usually talk with an older woman at the house." Mia hoped she remembered exactly which house they were talking about.

"That's my mom, Donna. She moved in a few years ago, after my wife died, because she thought I was going to let Prudence starve. Luckily that didn't happen, but your meals are part of the reason. I think Mom's almost ready to move back out." He looked pointedly at Ginny. "Especially if she thinks I'm starting to get serious about someone."

That made both me and Ginny blink. Before I could do anything stupid, like ask Ginny how many men she was dating right now, I smiled and dropped his hand. "I'm glad your daughter is enjoying my meals. I'll drop off a free dessert next week as a thank-you for being such a great customer."

"Believe me, I should be paying you three times what you charge, just for the convenience. Especially because Mom has decided to go back to school and get her nursing degree. She wants to help more people than me and Pru." He stepped back and put his arm around Ginny. "I know you have to go. And I'm still talking."

Mia laughed and nodded. "Thanks again. It was nice to meet you."

Then she headed back to the kitchen, where she might be doing one of her last catering gigs for a while. Might as well enjoy it while she could.

CHAPTER 12

By the end of the night, Hailey had proven her worth as an addition to the team. Mia leaned against the wall, watching the three women plate up and serve Abigail's huckleberry crumble dessert with vanilla ice cream and a dark chocolate drizzle and a caramel twill to make it pretty. Hailey wasn't afraid to get her hands dirty and had been quick on her feet to notice when a plate didn't have the correct items or plating before she let it leave the kitchen. James had given them two servers to help in the dining room and they were currently refilling coffee and drink orders.

Watching them work brought her back to the one thing she'd filed away in her mind when she'd started cooking for the event. The new catering director position. She couldn't run Mia's Morsels and work full time at the Lodge. She blinked as the thought didn't leave. Or could she? She'd have to increase Christina's workload, but this was her last semester at school. Maybe Abigail could act as manager for a few months while Christina finished classes. She'd still work as much as she could in the business. Maybe increasing classes at night. She'd be ragged at the end of the year, but if she was on the inside, she could change the hotel manager's mind on being exclusive on events.

"You look like you're a million miles away." Abigail handed her a dessert plate. "I made too many servings. I think I'll be able to feed the entire kitchen staff dessert."

Mia took a bite of the crumble. "We're the lucky ones, then. This is amazing."

"Thanks. I never could master the art of making just enough. Even when the boys were at home, I'd have leftovers. Unless they brought one of their friends to dinner. I guess I'm always trying to feed the masses." Abigail nodded toward the chattering tables. "They enjoyed dinner. I've heard a lot of positive comments."

"I enjoy feeding the masses too." She took another bite of the dessert. "Abigail, can we have coffee on Sunday? I've got some things on my mind that I'd like to get your opinion on."

"Sure. I was planning on going to early service, so how about nine fifteen at Your Morning Brew? I've been meaning to try that place, but Thomas doesn't see the need to go out for coffee when we have a perfectly good machine in the house." She studied Mia. "Is everything okay? You look worried."

"I've got a lot on my mind right now," Mia admitted.

Abigail nodded. "Of course, you're worried about

your grandmother. I should have realized that. As long as Mary Alice doesn't try the spell again, it should wear off soon. Spells like that one need constant renewal."

Mia turned toward her. "So why hasn't the Medford house spell diminished? Someone must be keeping the spell active. For what purpose?"

"I don't know. If the plan was to kill Hetty, it worked, and there would be no need for the spell to continue." Abigail frowned, trying to work out the motivation behind the spell.

"The good news is, Mahogany is staying somewhere else. She was beginning to be affected. See, that's what I can't figure out. The person who set the spell has to know we've found out about it. Right?" Mia watched as people started leaving the banquet room. The woman who'd worked with her on the planning was walking her way. "Sorry, we'll have to continue this later. Duty calls."

"I'll start getting the dessert course packed up." Abigail moved toward the serving table, where Christina and Hailey were working.

Mia stepped away from the wall and went to meet the conference planner. She took a card out of her pocket to give to the woman. Maybe next year they'd consider holding the banquet off-site, at the school. As long as the wards hadn't fallen by then and it wasn't overrun with angry spirits. Pushing the thought aside, she put on a smile and went to schmooze the client.

With the final check for the event locked away in her office desk, Mia headed into the kitchen to see what else needed to be done.

"We're all unloaded," Christina called out when Mia came into the kitchen. "The linens are over by the washer and I'm starting on washing the serving pans."

Hailey held up her hand. "I just brought in the last tote. Where do you want me?"

Mia walked over to the washer and put the first load in. "I'll deal with the laundry. You help with the dishes. It's been a long day. Let's get out of here in the next thirty minutes, okay?"

Abigail had her own tote filled with her tools and put the lid on it as she spoke. "I'm heading home. Unless you need me, of course."

"No, we're good." Mia put the soap in the container and started the machine. "Let me carry that out to your car."

"No matter what my son and husband say, I'm not an invalid." Abigail put her purse over her shoulder and went to pick up the tote.

Mia beat her to it. "I know you're not, but I didn't carry anything in besides the first load from the van. Let me help."

Abigail said goodbye to the others and held the back door open for Mia. "I've learned not to argue, at least."

"I wanted some privacy to ask you about your thoughts on Hailey's performance tonight," Mia said as they approached the parking lot.

Abigail used her remote to open the back of the SUV. "I thought she was excellent. You can tell she's worked catering before. She was great with the servers, as well as the diners who approached her. And, best of all, she kept a positive attitude and a smile on her face all night. Actually, all day.

Even when we were in the weeds for the first course."

"She does handle pressure well." Mia closed the back of the SUV after putting the tote inside. "Thanks for the information. I saw the same things."

"I can't believe she just showed up on your doorstep," Abigail said as she got into her car.

"Wait, you didn't send her?" Mia had assumed Hailey had come from one of Abigail's contacts.

"I didn't even have a chance to let people know you were looking for help. I had a couple of people I was going to tell on Sunday at church because Thomas kept me busy this week with his travel plans." Abigail closed the door and rolled down the window. "Did she say I sent her?"

Mia shook her head. "I just assumed. Christina hadn't mentioned the job to her groups yet either. I wonder where she heard I was looking for help."

"It could be her gift." Abigail stared toward the lights of the kitchen. "She might just know where she's needed. I sensed a little magic in the girl. Not anything big, but some."

"I'll talk to her next week and see what she says. Tonight, I'm too tired to find out she's an evil changeling sent to ruin my life." Mia yawned as she looked at the house.

Abigail laughed as she started up the car. "Go get some sleep. You're being silly. There hasn't been a changeling sighting in years."

Mia was almost back to the kitchen when she realized what Abigail had said. She turned and watched the car drive away. She whispered in the dark, "So, changelings are real too?"

A wind came up and whistled through the trees at the back of the property. Mia was sure she could hear laughter. And it was aimed at her and her lack of knowledge of the magical world. She really needed to start working with Grans again on her witch training.

Maybe tomorrow.

Saturday morning, Mia was making a list for the day when Christina hurried into the kitchen. She was already dressed in jeans and a Magic Springs T-shirt. Her hair was up in a ponytail. Mia looked down at her footwear. "Hiking with Levi, I presume?"

"He found a waterfall, or at least someone told him there was a waterfall at the end of this trail. I told him I'd pack lunch, but he wants to be in and out. He took a shift this evening for someone. So much for Saturday night out on the town for me." She opened her backpack and put in several granola bars and took out her water bottles to fill. "Anyway, he's taking me to lunch after the hike, that new, casual Mexican place in Twin. I should be back around four if you want to grab some dinner with me."

"I'll cook something." Mia sipped her coffee. "Do you mind if it's soup? And maybe some corn bread? I've got some research to do in the library. I'm going to ask Grans to come over too."

"Oh, that will be nice." Christina's back was turned, but Mia could hear the tone from where she sat.

"If she's being a pill, we'll pack up her dinner and send her back to her house. Abigail said the spell should be wearing off, so maybe she'll be back to normal when she arrives." Mia pointed to an article in the paper. "Looks like the city council is sponsoring a summer picnic basket contest. And there's a professional category. We should enter something."

Christina stood behind her and read the notice. "That would be fun. We'd just need to be very creative in our basket items. You know the Lodge wins these things all the time."

"Then it will be our job to give them some competition." Mia wondered if she should ask Christina what she thought about the Lodge job. She decided not to bring it up. No need to stir the pot until Mia knew what she was going to do. She opened her planner, which she had set on the table. "Looks like the entry form is due by the end of the month. I'll do that today and we can brainstorm ideas tonight over some popcorn."

"Sounds like a perfect Saturday evening because both of our men aren't available to take us anywhere." Christina returned to packing her backpack. "Have you heard from Trent?"

"Not since dinner on Thursday. He's probably busy with his dad. And his dad's probably griping about how I'm running Abigail ragged. He's never going to like me." Mia ripped out the information about the contest and put the rest of the paper in the recycling.

"Don't think like that. Thomas is a nice guy. I think you'd like him if you got to know him." Christina zipped up her backpack and pointed to the security monitor. "And there's my ride. See you soon, Mia."

Mia called after the disappearing Christina, "Call me if you're going to be late."

"Yes, Mom," Christina called back.

Mia would have explained that it wasn't because she was worried about her taking off hiking, it was more the fact that people got lost in those woods all the time. The river that ran through the area was called the River of No Return for a reason. Mia had always felt there was something old in the woods, old and watching the humans. The one thing she knew about that feeling was it occurred before she knew magic was real and long before she knew of the existence of werewolves. The deeper she got into the local forest, the more uncomfortable she was. Almost itchy at the possibilities of danger, real or imagined. And now the real category seemed so much bigger.

Of course, Christina would have Levi hiking with her. Trent's brother wasn't only a trained EMT, he was also a witch. So if they needed help, he could reach out to his brother. The Majors family communication network was strong. Mia wouldn't put it past Abigail to be part of the telepathic group as their mother. She'd have to remember to ask her about it tomorrow, when they met for coffee.

Grans was supposed to be there soon. The monitor beeped and Mia watched as Grans's car squealed into the drive. She parked and Mia headed down to the front door to meet her.

When she opened the front door, Mia let out a gasp.

"Fine, I get it. I went a bit too far with the spell."
Mary Alice Carpenter stepped inside the school.
Mr. Darcy sat on the stairs watching, and he took
one look at Mary Alice and spit and ran. Grans
pursed her lips together. "Everyone's a critic."

"It's like I'm looking into a mirror. I mean, you
looked like Mom before, but I could still tell it was
you. Now, you look like me. Maybe even a younger
me, from five or ten years ago." Mia reached up to
touch Grans's cheek, but Grans slapped her hand
away.

"Stop. I get it. It's weird. You feel strange seeing
me your age. But I thought I might have had the
reversal spell, so I tried it and"—she ran her hands
over an imaginary outline of her face and body—
"this happened."

"Abigail said if you just stopped spelling, the effects would wear off. Do I need to lock you up in a
bedroom to keep you safe?" Mia shut the door and
started upstairs. "Anyway, I'm not going to give you
a hard time. Just don't do it anymore. You'll come
back to who you were in a few days."

"Unless I like the shape I'm in now," Grans muttered as she followed Mia up the stairs.

Mia stopped and turned on the second-floor
landing. "Now listen to me good. You are not
going to continue to spell. You need to go back to
who you were, I mean, are. If you don't stop, the
next time I see you I'll have to take you in and
raise you until you age out of the spell. High
school isn't as fun as it used to be. You wouldn't
survive a week."

"You don't have to threaten me. Besides, there

is such a thing as homeschooling now." Grans huffed as she followed Mia up to the third floor.

"Only good kids get homeschooled. I'm not doing something that will mess up my day. If you go back to being high school aged, you're going to class with the rest of the teenagers. Maybe having some structure to your day will keep you out of trouble." Mia opened the door to the apartment. "Tuck your purse in there and we'll go right to the library. I want to have plenty of time to bring out this ghost and make her comfortable enough to talk. Maybe she can tell us about the wards. And if there's anything we can do to shore them up. There has to be a book on it in the library."

"Or maybe they didn't want to write down their spells." Grans set her purse on the couch and came back out to the hallway. "I'm ready to go. You're wearing the protection spell I gave you, right?"

"I thought that was in case someone tried to attack me. We're dealing with spirits here." Mia turned to look at her grandmother. She could tell a lot from a look. Like if someone was lying to her. Grans didn't seem to be lying, but on the other hand, she wasn't quite herself these days. She didn't know if her grandmother would lie directly to her face, but it was possible.

"It's also a tracking and protection spell against the other side. You didn't think I'd let you live in this school without one, did you? Not with the ghosts on the north side trying to break down the walls." Grans shook her head. "Sometimes you surprise me with your naïveté."

"Good to know. And yes, I'm wearing it." She rubbed her neck where the pendant lay hidden under her shirt.

"Then let's go chat with some ghosties." Grans headed to the other room, and before Mia could stop her, she'd opened the door and stepped inside.

"In for a penny," Mia grumbled. She couldn't believe her grandmother had known. "Remember to tell me if you hear anything."

Mia walked into the library with a lantern in one hand and her amulet in another.

"It feels quiet. Peaceful, even."

The library was quiet. Sunlight streamed in through dirty glass in the windows. Dust mites danced in the light, tempted by the warmth of the sunshine. If Mia hadn't known that a young girl haunted the room and that the wards to the school were slowly breaking down, she would have spent hours in the room already. So far, she'd come in, grabbed books, and left, not wanting to be confronted with a ghostly visit.

The room felt warm, and by the time the sun came around to shine through the south windows, the room would be too hot to enjoy. Right now, the only part of the third floor with central air was her apartment. And, of course, the first floor. She might have to change that soon, if she was going to want to use this area as a home office.

But those were all thoughts for another day. She moved farther into the library and stood near the last place she'd seen the little girl. She'd thought she'd been looking into a painting, but then realized it had been a mirror. The girl had materialized onto the mirror to reveal herself.

"Hello? Are you there? Is anyone here that can speak for the girl who is locked in this room?" Mia turned in a circle and then paused, repeating her call. "We aren't here to hurt you. Only to help you fulfill your mission."

"If you talk to the girl, she will leave. And then we will be lonely once more. The girl has kept us sane while we waited for our deliverer." The voice seemed to come from all the places around them and from nowhere all at the same time.

Mia and Grans exchanged a look. Trent had been right; there was another entity besides the child ghost she'd seen before. Mia took a deep breath. "Okay, so we have a question. Do you know anything about the wards on the school? They are starting to fail and we need to reset them."

"If you reset the wards, we will be locked in here forever," the voice complained. "The school was in disrepair. We would have been freed soon."

Okay, so the voice wasn't going to be helpful in resetting the wards. Mia started to leave, but Grans caught her arm, silently telling her to stay.

"The ghosts from the cemetery—what do they want in the building?" Grans asked.

The voice didn't respond immediately. So they waited. Finally, a sigh came over the room. "Those souls are misguided. They think the path to freedom is in the school. I can tell you, it's not. We're tied here. They are the ones who are free."

Mia wondered if she talked to one of the other ghosts if they'd say the same thing. Maybe everyone was stuck because they assumed the answer was somewhere else. Just because the answer was coming from a ghost didn't mean they weren't subject to human fallibilities. Like the grass was always greener. And not knowing what they have. Mia wondered if she could give a ghost training in finding the answer within yourself to solve the problem. But that would assume the spirits were still able to learn and open to change.

Human or spirit, change was never easy.

CHAPTER 13

Mia made sandwiches in the kitchen while she and Grans talked about a game plan. "Obviously, the library ghosts don't want to help because they think the wards are keeping them in the house and this plane of existence. If we talked to the ghosts outside from the cemetery, I bet they'd say the wards are keeping them from escaping this world. I don't know, are either of the stories true?"

Grans was writing in her notebook. "I'm not sure. I never heard anything about the school being a portal to the next life. Even when I attended here. It was just the school. We played in the backyard, took classes in the second-floor classrooms, and learned about magic. You should text Abigail to see if she's heard anything."

"I'm talking with her tomorrow about some work stuff. I'll ask her then." Mia set down the plates on the table. She had a pasta salad she'd made a few days ago and added that to the plate with the turkey sandwiches. "I'm supposed to hear from Henry's relative today about the wards. Maybe that will answer our questions."

"Henry?" Grans asked, her fork paused in mid-air.

Mia pointed to the calendar. "In two weeks we're having a wedding here on the property. Either inside, if the weather is bad, or out on the lawn. The couple, May Hornbuckle and Henry Lasher, insisted. Their families attended the school."

"If they attended school here, it must have been when they were really young." Grans focused on her sandwich. "You should add avocado to this. It would make it creamier."

"I didn't have any on hand." Mia sighed as she took a bite of the sandwich. Her grandmother wasn't wrong. It was missing something, and a few slices of avocado would have been just the thing. "Henry and May's relatives attended school here. I don't think they did. Anyway, Henry said his great-uncle was part of the building team. Alphonso Lasher. He's supposed to call or come by this weekend."

"Al Lasher. I haven't heard that name in years." Grans set down her sandwich. "When is he coming?"

"I don't know. I haven't heard from him." Mia eyed her grandmother suspiciously. "Wait, did you know him? This Al?"

Grans nodded. "He was so handsome when he was younger. Strong jawline, dark, wavy hair. I didn't think he was old enough to be part of the school opening, though."

Mr. Darcy jumped down from the kitchen window seat, where he'd been sleeping. He meowed loudly and ran out of the room.

Mia shook her head. "Dorian hates it when you talk about other men."

"It's not like he's alive to date now, is he?" Grans picked up her sandwich. "Do me a favor and call me if Al shows up. I'd like to say hi."

"Which is impossible because you look younger than when you met him. Or at least I'm assuming you do." Mia focused on her food. "Another reason you shouldn't have reworked the spell again and tested it on yourself."

"I understand your concern, dear, and I won't perform the spell again. I promise. But Al knows I'm a witch, so he shouldn't be surprised at my appearance."

Grans had a point.

"Okay, I'll call you. Are you hanging around or going back home? I think we're at a dead end regarding the residents of the library." Mia finished her sandwich. She wished she had some cookies. She'd make some, but she needed to go downstairs to make more chicken soup. "Sarah Baldwin isn't feeling well. She's been down for about a week now. I need to make up a new batch of your soup. It's the only thing she can keep down."

"Sarah's sick? That's funny, I didn't sense anything when I drove past their house. In fact, the house felt happy." Grans tapped a finger against her lips.

Mia shrugged. "Maybe she's on the mend. But they all but depleted my stock of cure-all soup, so I have to make more today. Christina and I are making dinner in the kitchen after she gets back from her hike with Levi."

"Did Christina's mom contact her yet?"

The question came out of the blue. Mia narrowed her eyes at her grandmother. "What did you do?"

She held up her hands, "I promise, I have not contacted that horrible woman since you and Isaac had Thanksgiving dinner a few years ago. I can't even think about talking to her directly."

"Then why the question?" Now Mia was curious.

Grans shrugged. "Just a feeling I get. Maybe I'm way off, but I'd expect contact in the next few weeks."

"Great. That's one more thing on my to-be-worried-about list. Thanks for adding to my concerns." Mia finished her pasta salad and took her plate to the sink. "I'm heading down to make the soup. Do you want to help?"

"Heavens no. That's why there's a grocery store nearby and several eating establishments on the next block. So I don't have to cook. The only reason I have a pot is to make my potions." She finished her sandwich and put the plate into the sink. She took a lipstick out of her purse and reapplied the deep red color. "Thanks for lunch. It hit the spot. Remember to call me if Al shows up."

Mia followed her out of the apartment after picking up her cell, just in case "Al" called. She said her goodbyes at the door and went to the kitchen to work and to get one item off her rapidly growing list.

By the time the soup was done and cooling in the fridge before she packaged it up in the quart freezer containers, Christina was back. She popped her head into the kitchen and then came in when she saw Mia doing dishes. "Hey, I didn't know you were cooking today. I would have come back early."

"You need time off too." Mia set the soup pot on the rack to dry. "Besides, it was just what I needed. Some time alone with my thoughts."

"So, your grandmother is gone? I didn't see her car in the lot when Levi dropped me off." Christina came in the kitchen and opened the fridge. "I thought I smelled chicken soup."

"I had to restock after the Baldwins almost depleted our supply." Mia went over to the dryer and pulled out the last load of laundry from the catering on Friday. "So, how was your day? How's Levi?"

"He's good. He's up for some promotion at work, so he's taking as many shifts as possible. I probably won't see him for a few days now. But it's not like I'm not busy too." She came over and helped Mia fold napkins. "I'm thinking about asking Hailey if she wants to grab dinner sometime next week. Do you want to come along?"

"No, thank you. My to-do list is overwhelming me right now. Going out for dinner with someone I barely know seems like a lot of work. Especially in the conversation department." Mia folded a napkin and put it on top of the pile. "So you like her? Hailey? She did good work, right?"

"She was awesome to work with. She's like you. She sees the hole before it becomes a crater. And she had great suggestions on how to make service easier. Like setting up the plates a certain way so the waiters pick them up and serve them to the guests all the same way." Christina chattered away for a few more minutes.

As she listened, Mia saw a fog gathering on the other side of the doorway. She thought she saw a face in the fog, but when she turned back after grabbing another napkin, the face and the fog had disappeared.

"Mia?" Christina sounded concerned. "Everything all right?"

Mia turned her attention back to her friend. She hoped Henry's great-uncle would have a solution to her ghost problem. Otherwise, there might not be a Mia's Morsels to choose whether she decided not to take the catering director job. "Everything's fine. What did we decide on for dinner?"

After they ate dinner, Mia was watching a new romantic comedy with Christina, complete with popcorn and chocolate chip ice cream, when a beep sounded on her phone. She looked down and saw she had a message from an unknown caller.

She opened the message. It was Alphonso Lasher. The message was short and sweet. **I'll be at the school at one o'clock tomorrow afternoon**.

She texted **That will work** back as a response, then set down her phone, happy that the Goddess had directed her to make plans with Abigail early. Maybe her to-do list would actually decrease in the next few days. She set the phone aside and relaxed into watching the movie.

After it was over, she was in her room and reading, trying to unwind from the day, when she got a text from Trent, asking if she was still up.

She called him as his response and he picked up on the first ring. "Hey, you. How was your day?"

"You're wondering if I survived the trip to the library," Mia guessed from the tightness in his tone.

"I've been thinking about it all day. Are you okay?" Trent admitted.

She told him about the other entity and what he'd said. And she was pleasantly surprised when Trent's first words weren't *I told you so.*

"That's disturbing," he said instead.

She nodded. "Yes, it is. Although I'd rather know what they were thinking rather than just guess. And the other guy is supposed to be here tomorrow to look at the wards. Maybe Al will know more."

"Al?"

Mia laughed. "Apparently my grandmother and Alphonso Lasher had a little thing going on a few years ago. Or she just thought he was cute. I couldn't tell from what she told me. Anyway, she wants me to call her when he's here so she can stop by."

"In her new body?"

Mia nodded, even though Trent couldn't see her. "That's the problem. She's even younger now than she was when we went to Mahogany's house. Or appearing younger I guess is the correct terminology. But she says he's a witch too, so it shouldn't matter. Right now, I'm just hoping she doesn't do the spell again or I'm going to have to be raising a teenager until she stops messing with it. I'd hate for my first experience being a mom to be for my teenage grandmother."

Trent laughed. "Only in Magic Springs would anyone ever say something like that."

They talked for a while longer. She told him about making soup, and Christina and Levi's date, and the movie. He talked about spending time with his dad during the drive and watching him with his hunting clients. Mia could tell that Trent was proud of how his father had taken a hobby and turned it into a business he loved. Soon, she yawned.

"I heard that. I should let you go. I've got a busy day tomorrow. We've got breakfast with a local hunting group. I guess Dad's giving a talk on protecting our forests for future generations."

She set up in bed, hoping to stave off the sleep that was threatening to take her over at any time. "I'm having coffee with your mom tomorrow."

"Oh?"

"Yeah, we have some work stuff to talk about. Like the new employee."

He didn't say anything, but when she didn't volunteer more, he chuckled. "Fine, don't tell me what you're talking about. Just remember, the rumor mill is very active in Magic Springs."

"Are you saying you already know?" Mia should have figured that out. James couldn't keep a secret.

"I had coffee with James before I left. I'm supposed to sway you to his side. I'm not sure if that's the dark side or not, but I think you need to make your own decision. Mia's Morsels is your baby and my opinion is just that. My opinion." He yawned. "Now you have me doing that. I'll see you next week. Dinner Monday night? I'll take you out; you'll probably be tired of cooking by then."

"Sounds perfect. Good night, Trent." Mia hung up the phone and thought about what he had said. Mia's Morsels was her baby. But was it because she had carved out a struggling catering business that she was having a hard time giving it up? Or did she really not want to go back to being an employee? Yes, she'd have a lot of discretion in her job, but she'd still have to answer to the hotel manager. And if she didn't like the guy, she'd hate the job.

From what she'd heard already, the hotel manager didn't seem like an easy man to work for. This one thought was making the decision so much harder. Maybe she should talk to someone besides James to see if they liked working for the guy. She snuggled into the blankets, glad she had an action plan to work in the morning. Along with the rest of her many to-dos.

Abigail was already at the coffee shop when Mia arrived. A large cup with what looked and smelled like a café mocha with a pile of whipped cream sat in front of Mia's chair. "How did you know?"

"Dear, I've been a witch for more years than you've been alive. I sensed when you pulled into the parking lot. Trent texted me your favorite special-day coffee. And today is a special day, at least in my world. I love attending early service. The older group isn't there to be grumpy, so the music is much less traditional than the midday service. If you know what I mean." Abigail took a sip of her coffee.

Mia settled into the chair and pulled out a folder on the May/Henry wedding and gave it to Abigail. Then she took a sip of the coffee. It was perfect. She wiped the foam she knew lingered on her lips because it always did, and then leaned back. "I think that's all you'll need for the wedding in two weeks. I've given you a budget for the cake, which hopefully will be enough. I know the last budget was larger, but it was a bigger event too."

Abigail scanned the documents and then put the folder in her tote. "This will work perfectly.

But I'm pretty sure you didn't ask me to coffee for something that could have been emailed."

Mia winced. The woman saw right through her. She sipped her coffee again, then leaned back. "You're right. I have a few things I need to ask you. Like about the ghosts and the wards, and about my grandmother. But really, I wanted to ask you about taking over Mia's Morsels for a while for me."

"What? You're quitting?" Abigail leaned forward and took her hand. "You're all right, aren't you? I can't feel anything."

"I'm healthy." She pulled back her hand. "Look, the Lodge is bringing in a catering director. If they do, James won't be able to toss any jobs our way. So our catering will dwindle down to almost nothing. And I don't have the school set up to be an event center yet. Maybe after the wards are reset and maybe the gym going through a total remodel."

"Christina's been there longer," Abigail pointed out.

Mia nodded. "She'd do it in a heartbeat if I asked her. But she'd have to quit school and she's so close to finishing. My ideal would be if you'd take it over until Christina's done with school. Then she can take the CEO spot and I should have enough money to finish the changes and actually compete with the Lodge. And I should have enough contacts in the community that I could come back in seven to ten and take back over. All you two would need to do was keep it going until I could leave the Lodge and come home."

"You sound like you're being convicted of a crime you didn't commit." Abigail's voice was soft, comforting.

"I feel that way. All I want is to have a business that will support me and those who work with me. And if we have a little left over for fun, that would be the best. I'd like to visit Italy someday. And maybe Paris."

Mia didn't notice the tears that had started until Abigail handed her a napkin. Now, sobbing, she covered her face in her hands. How had everything gotten so out of hand?

CHAPTER 14

After Mia got home, she didn't want to talk to anyone. Abigail had agreed to run Mia's Morsels if Mia took the catering job. So that was one worry off her list. But Abigail had also strongly suggested Mia consider what she wanted. Abigail's words still echoed in Mia's head and now, as she sipped her cup of tea with the job description in front of her, she repeated them. "'Our lives are given to us to enjoy, not do the things we think we must. If you don't love your work, you're doing it wrong.'"

Mr. Darcy looked up from the window seat and meowed.

"Apparently you agree with Abigail's advice?" Mia smiled at the gray-striped cat. Some days he looked more gray, sometimes this striped version, and other days, Mia could swear Mr. Darcy was pure black.

She got an answering meow, then he jumped off the cushion and headed to the apartment door. As she watched, the locks disengaged and the door opened a few inches, just enough for a cat to escape. Then it slammed shut and the locks reengaged. Mr. Darcy's resident spirit, Dorian, had taken over the cat's care. He used his magic to open doors, refill the food and water dishes, and Mia swore he brightened the sunshine coming in the kitchen when the cat was sleeping.

And witches thought their magic died with them. Or was transferred to someone else. Not in this situation. Mia wondered if Dorian's power was still around because his daughter hadn't taken possession of his grimoire yet. Or she should say "again." The girl had gotten it after the funeral but had misused the spells when she was on her own. Once she had started training with the new power, she'd decided to leave the book in Magic Springs until she could take the time to finish her training.

Mia called Grans.

"What?"

"Good morning to you too." Mia knew the pleasantry would only aggravate her grandmother more, so she hurried to ask her question. "Do you think Dorian's stronger because his grimoire is nearby?"

Grans didn't respond quickly. Then she said, "Maybe. It's a possibility. Even though Cindy has taken legal possession, she doesn't have the grimoire. The book could be looking for its new master and, when it found Dorian, it gave him back some of his powers."

Mia whistled. "We really need to get Dorian out of Mr. Darcy and off to his next life."

"Don't you think I know that? I've been a little busy trying to figure out why this spell won't reverse and keeps making me lose years. Do you realize the pizza delivery guy thought I was you last night?"

Mia could hear the anger seething from her grandmother's words. "I know you've been busy. This idea just popped into my head and I needed to figure out if it was possible."

The sigh from her grandmother was so deep, Mia almost felt bad for calling today. "I know you're doing your best. It's my fault we haven't finished your training. If we had, you'd know these things and not have to rely on an old woman being silly."

"You're not old and you're definitely not being silly. Not to poke at the wound, but have you found anything in your library that could help?" Mia pulled a notebook closer and started making out a list of her worry items. Including Mr. Darcy and Mahogany's mother and now Grans. Mia's Morsels and the job offer. And the wards on the school. It seemed like the more she wrote down, the more she remembered things she needed to fix.

She glanced at the clock. Al was supposed to be here at one. She had ten minutes to get out of this funk. And she realized her grandmother was talking.

"I found a letter from the coven I thought was interesting. It asked about my estate plans and contact numbers for my next of kin. Some kind of investment guy was coming into town, and he'd love to buy me dinner and talk." Grans chuckled. "Like I'd just give someone access to my investments."

"I wonder if Hetty Medford got the same letter." Mia wrote down Hetty's name on her worry list.

"I thought you'd be more interested in who sent it. It was Ginny Willis. It says here that she's in charge of coven foundation gifts." Grans must have been looking at the letter because Mia could hear the paper crackling. "Call Mahogany and see if Hetty got the same letter. I don't know if we can get into Theresa's house legally, but I know someone who might have a key."

The security system beeped and a car pulled into the parking lot. Alphonso Lasher had arrived, five minutes early. "Hey, Grans, I've got to go. Your 'Al' is here to talk about the wards."

"I'll be right over."

The line went dead and Mia put her phone in her pocket and went downstairs to meet her guest. Before she left the apartment, she called out to see if Christina was home. When there was no answer, she assumed she was out with Levi. Not a bad idea. Mia wasn't sure what would happen when Mr. Lasher messed with the wards. But the library ghost or ghosts didn't want them rebooted. And the cemetery ghosts were actively trying to break them. The school might not be the safest place for a mortal to be right now.

She shut the door and hurried downstairs to meet Alphonso Lasher.

When she opened the door, she was taken aback at his appearance. For a man who must be in his late nineties, he looked at least thirty years younger. A touch of gray at his temples was the only thing that hinted at his age.

He smiled and held out a hand. "I'm Alphonso Lasher. Silas Miller told me you were beautiful, but he downplayed your power. I'm surprised you need help with this problem at all."

Mia shook his hand. "I think you're overestimating my abilities. I'm still in training. And besides, I'm a kitchen witch. I'm more into the domestic arts and spelling for world peace."

"Argue your limitations and they're yours. A little bit of wisdom from *Illusions* by Richard Bach. You should read it, if you haven't yet. I'll send you a copy." He squeezed her hand and then let it drop. "Just remember, words have power. Whatever you are, you're not *just* a kitchen witch."

"I don't understand," Mia said as he walked past her and into the foyer.

He nodded as he studied the area around them. "You will. Soon, I believe, but you will. Now, tell me about what's going on with the house. Henry said you were worried about some ghost activity during the wedding."

Mia let the power comment drop. Lasher wasn't here to train or assess her or her power. She'd mention it to Grans, but she knew her grandmother would laugh it off. Maybe it was the residuals of their family history passing down from one witch to another. She did have witch royalty in her ancestral line. "For the last few months, we've been having issues with ghost sightings near the side of the house. A negative spirit is hanging around where the trash bin is located. Recently, he moved to the side porch. I don't know if it's just one or if there are more. I've done some research, and there was a cemetery next to the school before it was built."

He shook his head. "All those graves were moved and reconsecrated at the new town cemetery. The coven paid the fees to have it done correctly. If you have a ghost, it's probably a residual who didn't want to leave when their bodies did."

Relief filled Mia. She hadn't realized how much of a worry having that cemetery being filled with unmarked graves had made her anxious. "That's such a relief to hear. I also have at least two ghosts in the library upstairs. They believe they're stuck in the house and can't move on until the wards come down. They believe the outside ghosts think the way onward is somewhere in this house."

"So, the grass is away greener, even after you die." He pointed toward the kitchen. "Show me that room."

Alphonso was big into mottos and quotes, she thought as they moved to the kitchen door. She pulled out her keys and unlocked the door. "Here you go."

"You have a lock to a room inside the house?" He studied her face for what Mia could only think was emotion or tells.

"There were some issues with people breaking in. I wanted my kitchen to be secure. It's where all my tools of the trade are located." She stepped inside the kitchen. "I'm a caterer and own Mia's Morsels. Which is, basically, this kitchen. We do classes and food delivery for local families as well as big catering events."

"That's nice." He pointed to the side door. "That's where you're having your unwelcome visitors?"

"That's the place. At first, it was just a feeling of being watched when we took out the trash. I saw an apparition one day. Then the feeling became more. Stronger." Mia walked over and started to open the door.

Alphonso grabbed her hand and stopped her from opening the door. "Let me feel out the health of the wards. Anything else I should know? Do you have any enemies?"

"No, not that I know of. Well, except John Lewis. He wanted to buy the property, but then I won the board's approval. But he's in jail. The school is on the list for historic preservation. Not there yet, thank goodness, but it might wind up there soon."

"When it makes the list, you'll be limited to what you can do. Basically, it means you can't change the property from its historic state. No new appliances or plumbing. You need to get your renovations done soon." He nodded to a table. "Mind if I set up here? You can go about your business. In fact, it's probably better that you do."

"I'll be in my office. Go out the same door we came in and turn left. I'll make a pot of coffee if you're interested." She handed him a key to the kitchen doors. She didn't point out that she actually knew what getting on the historical register meant to her and her plans for the school. Why pick a fight when you're asking a favor from the other guy?

"Just stay out until I come to get you. Researching wards can be a bit tricky." He chuckled and made a back-and-forth motion with his hands.

Mia had been excused. And, at the same time, she wondered if he'd "heard" her last thought. She went into her office and started working on the weekly menus for next month's delivery service. She liked to rotate the dishes through the menu, keeping a few standards for customers' favorites, but adding new dishes as the ideas came. She had two brand-new dishes she still needed to field-test. She printed off the recipes and then added a taste test dinner to her personal calendar. She could invite both Levi and Trent. That was so it seemed special and not just the fact she wanted some guinea pigs for her dishes. She added the ingredients to her shopping list and then went back to working on the menus, leaving two slots open for the new dishes if they turned out well. If not, she'd rotate in another tried-and-true recipe into the mix.

Happy with her schedule, she turned to accounting. One of the tasks she hated the most. Okay, to be honest, it was the *one* task she hated the worst. She would put it off for months, but with changes happening in her life, she needed to know where the business was at financially.

Mia had keyed everything into her software when the security system alerted her to a car entering the parking lot. Grans. She left the office and hurried over to the front door. Al wouldn't be happy if she let someone barge into the kitchen, especially not a woman living out some childhood crush.

She stood in the doorway while Grans got out of her car, wearing what looked like three-inch heels and a miniskirt. Oh, my word. When she'd hobbled to the door, Mia shook her head. "Seriously?"

"I'd forgotten how hard these shoes were to walk in." Grans swerved and almost fell.

Mia caught her arm. "You're going to break an ankle, or maybe a hip. You know the spell is mostly glamour, right? You're not really in your twenties. If you fall, your bones are going to be the ones in your real body. And they'll snap like a twig."

"Mia, sometimes you're a real buzzkill." Grans

leaned down, holding on to the wall, and took off the shoes. She replaced them with a pair of flats she had in her tote. Tucking the dangerous heels into the tote, she met Mia's gaze. "Happy?"

"I'm freaking joyful." Mia held the door open. "He's in the kitchen, but he doesn't want to be disturbed. He's working."

"What does he look like?" Grans settled on the couch where she could see the kitchen door. "Is he still hot?"

"I would say yes. Especially for his age. He looks handsome. Not old at all, even though I know he has to be older than you." Mia sat on the arm of the couch, watching the kitchen door. "It's like the power is keeping him young."

"It probably is. Strong power can protect the body from such things as wrinkles or a beer gut." Grans glanced down at her much younger body. "I wish this wasn't just a glamour. I'd love to be able to stay young."

"Are you sure we don't?"

Grans turned and looked at Mia. "Sure we don't what, dear?"

"He said I'm powerful. Much more than a kitchen witch. Did you know?" Mia watched her grandmother. "Or was that some sort of witch pickup line?"

Grans didn't say anything for a while. Then she curled a leg up underneath her. "I haven't been able to do that for years."

"Grans, answer my question."

She looked up at Mia. "I am answering your question. I was taught magic by my mother, who was taught by her mother. We were told that our gifts were there to support the others. To heal, to calm, to save the world. We were told our powers were less than the other witches in the coven. That we should honor our heritage by taking care of the world. Sure, we were less powerful, but we had more. We could make people well again. We could ease people's pains, both mental and physical, and I did. But I knew my limitations. Her mother had taught her and her mother and so on. We had a strong lineage. But when I started researching our background, I found much more about our family. We've been limiting ourselves."

The words Lasher had said came back to me. She turned to Grans. "Argue your limitations and they're yours."

"Where did you hear that?" Grans studied her.

"Your boyfriend in there."

"Well, I'm beginning to think he might be right. That I was taught to be less." She held up her hand. "Let me finish. I don't think they did it to hurt us. I think something happened, and we voluntarily toned down our abilities. Maybe the coven didn't like our power. Maybe it was the Salem hearings. Something convinced our ancestors that living undercover was the smart way to go."

Grans looked down at herself. "I think that's why I can't 'fix' this, or Mr. Darcy. I think there's something in our witch DNA that keeps making the spell bigger rather than reducing it."

"Who would know that? Who would be able to help?" Mia took her grandmother's hand.

Someone cleared his throat. They looked up, and Alphonso Lasher was watching them.

"I think that answer is me. Or at least, I'm a start. Nice to see you, Mary Alice. You're looking lovely, as always."

Grans stood and stepped toward him. "Thank you."

At the same time, Mia said, "You should have seen her last week."

Grans turned and glared at her. "Sorry about my granddaughter's rudeness. I'm surprised you recognized me."

"I see people by the soul, not the body they currently inhabit." Alphonso looked at Mia. "Because I live longer, I see people in several lifetimes. The body may change, but the soul? It's always the same. Good or bad. The soul can't hide."

CHAPTER 15

They'd moved the discussion upstairs and Mia was cooking dinner. Christina was still out with Levi, so it was just the three of them. Well, four if you counted Dorian. Lasher recognized Dorian immediately, and the two talked for at least thirty minutes while Mia started dinner. Grans came into the kitchen and opened a bottle of wine. "Is Dorian still giving Lasher his list of grievances?"

"Dear, it's nothing like that. He's just telling him what he knows about the house. He's been trying to figure out a way to fix the wards since he died."

Mia stopped chopping mushrooms and turned to look at her grandmother. "He has?"

"That's why he's going out at night. He's been working on the wards." Grans blushed. "He always was a good man."

"Cat, Grans. Dorian's a cat now," Mia reminded her.

"He might be in a cat's body, but he's a good man. You heard Al, the soul can't hide."

Mia was starting to question Al's sanity because he was in full, face-on, conversation with Mr. Darcy, but then she shook her head. "I guess there are more things on earth than I know."

"Isn't that Shakespeare?" Grans poured wine into two glasses. She held the bottle toward Mia. "Do you want some?"

"Definitely. I need to be a little less skeptical for this conversation." Mia put the mushrooms into the pan to cook and took the glass of wine. "Dinner will be ready in about thirty minutes. I need to cook off these mushrooms; then I'll be able to sit with you all for a while. Please don't talk about how he's going to fix the wards until I'm there."

"We won't leave you out." Grans took the wine and left the room.

Mia wasn't sure that was true, so she hurried with the prep and left her glass untouched. She slid the chicken into the oven and turned on the timer. Then she took off her apron and grabbed her notebook and a pen. She wanted to get this process down in case she needed something tweaked in a few years.

Mr. Darcy jumped down from the chair where Mia was about to sit and then left the room. She watched him leave. "Apparently he's done talking?"

"Mr. Darcy thinks there's a mouse in the kitchen. Dorian keeps telling him it's the pipes rattling, but I guess they haven't solved the mystery yet." Al leaned back on the sofa with Grans next to him. Right next to him.

Mia wondered how Dorian had taken the attraction, but then pushed the idea away. Could a ghost be jealous of two living creatures? She settled onto the chair and set down her glass. "Okay, so tell me what we need to do. Your nephew Henry and his future bride are insistent on getting married here. Is it going to be safe?"

"Of course it is. I'll come back tomorrow to work on fortifying the wards. After talking to Dorian, I'm concerned that not all the graves were moved. He's reporting that he's seen several ghosts where the cemetery was located." Al leaned forward. "You have to understand, I wasn't part of the committee to move the cemetery. All I can do is report what they told us. That all of the graves were moved. Maybe these were unauthorized burials or interred before the records were kept. I need you to go to the cemetery board to see if you can get a list of who was moved and, if possible, any listing of who was buried here in the first place. I don't think it will solve our immediate problem, but after we deal with any clerical mix-ups, we can bring someone in to sanctify the land. Those bodies will still be there, but the process will send the souls to the afterlife." Al sipped his wine.

"Wait, why don't we just ask the spirits where they are buried and move those bodies now?" Mia set down her pen.

"Sometimes spirits are too far gone to communicate with the living." Al spoke like Mia was a small child having trouble with a history lesson.

"And it's a longer process that way. If we want to totally clear the area before the wedding, this is the most efficient."

"I understand efficiency, but the coven didn't do their due diligence when they moved the cemetery. Now, they should come back and fix the problem."

Al started to say something, but Grans put her hand on his leg, stopping him.

"You're right, of course, Mia, but the coven hierarchy may not see this as their issue."

"Not their issue? They bought the land. They built the school. It was their responsibility to make sure the cemetery was cleared before they built. I'm not here to place blame unless I have to; I just want the land cleared." Al started to say something, and Mia waved him down and kept going. "Without just whitewashing the problem. Who knows if the souls would even leave if the graves were still there? It's a matter of principle. We want to do this right."

Al nodded slowly. "I have to agree, you're right. Honestly, I would have just cleared the souls, but I understand where you're coming from. You care about people."

"Yes, and if those souls are too far gone to know where they are, we need to search the ground for any bones. Maybe if we move all the graves, the souls will just move on." Mia saw the look that passed between Al and her grandmother. So she sighed and added, "And if we can't find their graves, we'll have to use the other process. I don't want anyone stuck here who doesn't want to be on this plane. And this can't affect Dorothy."

Grans nodded. "I understand."

The timer went off in the kitchen. Mia stood. "Dinner will be on the table in five minutes."

She heard Al's whisper when she left the room: "Who's Dorothy?"

Over dinner, Al explained the process through the coven. "I'll try to expedite it for the wedding, but there may be some hiccups."

"As long as they don't goop on my wedding cake, I don't mind the ghosts hanging around for a few weeks." Mia cut into the chicken. It was just right. Anytime she put something in the oven to finish, she always worried she'd leave it in too long. The mushroom sauce had not only seeped into the chicken but kept it from overcooking. "Can I ask you another question?"

"This is the best meal I've had in a while, so you can keep asking me questions." Al smiled at her and she saw kindness in his eyes.

"You're welcome any time you're in town. Anyway, we have a spell on a house that has been aging the resident at least in the eyes of the town. She's not really aging, or wasn't before she was killed, but everyone thought this fifty-something-year-old woman was in her seventies by the end. Have you ever seen a spell like that? Grans has been having trouble finding a reversal spell."

Al glanced over at Grans, who was sitting next to him. Her cheeks flared red. "So, that explains your appearance. I thought maybe you were just vain. Anyway, there is a spell that does that. It's been banned almost everywhere. Have you told the coven?"

"No. Should I have?" Mia wondered where this was going.

"Of course you should tell the coven. They can use their best to find out who set the spell. And then maybe you'll find out why. Although that's not always the case. The motivation is left on the side when humans are looking into people who could have murdered someone." He pulled out a card and wrote a name on the back. "Go talk to Malcolm McBride. He'll get someone over to the house to look at the spell. You should have an answer in a few days. He's really quick when he thinks the council may be sued."

"Sued?" Mia took the card and tucked it into her planner, which sat next to her on the counter.

"Only the council is supposed to have the directions to this type of curse. It's supposed to be kept under lock and key, which, of course, means no one was watching the store. I swear, our current board is totally useless."

As she said goodbye to Al and Grans that night, she was pleased with what she'd accomplished that day. She'd located a possible manager for Mia's Morsels, just in case. She'd gotten someone over to work on the wards. And she'd found another clue in Hetty Medford's case. One that Baldwin wouldn't love hearing about, unless she could point a mortal finger at the guy.

She locked up, leaving off the dead bolts because Christina may come in later, and as she turned off the lights, she saw Mr. Darcy watching her in the darkness. She went and picked him up, hearing his purr against her chest. There was nothing more calming than a purring cat. They went into her room and she lay him on her bed. She lay down too and checked her emails and voice mail on her phone. There was a text from Trent, saying he'd just gotten in and was beat. He also reminded her of their dinner plans tomorrow night. She texted back a see-you-then and then set down her phone. Curling up on the bed, she pulled a blanket over the top of her and promptly fell asleep.

The pounding on her door awakened her. She turned on a light and looked at the clock. It was two in the morning. "Christina?"

The door flew opened. Christina flipped on the overhead lights. "Oh, my goodness. You won't believe what just happened."

"Calm down and tell me." Mia wrapped a blanket around her and sat on the side of the bed.

"Levi dropped me off at the front door and so I went inside, and then I saw lights on in the kitchen. I thought maybe you were working on something. You know, like you do when you can't sleep. But the lights just kept flashing. I walked over and knocked on the door and called out your name, and then the lights went out. I was so scared, I ran up the stairs and dropped my keys several times before I could get inside. What do you think's happening?" Christina sat next to Mia on her bed. Her hands were still shaking, but her voice had started to calm as she told the story.

"I think the ghosts didn't like whatever modifications Lasher did on the wards last night. Because the light show stopped, maybe we should just go to sleep now. I'll call him in the morning. I wish he'd warned us about possible aftereffects." Mia saw Mr. Darcy was now on Christina's lap, rubbing his head against her hands. "I think Mr. Darcy and Dorian agree. You can take him to your room if you want some company."

"I'm thinking about dragging a blanket and pillow in here and sleeping on your floor," Christina said, but Mia could see she wasn't serious. Christina took a breath. "Okay, so we're good. No more light show. Just tell me you'll wake me up if something weird happens."

"Weirder than flashing lights?" Mia teased as Christina stood with Mr. Darcy in her arms.

"Okay, so it was just flashing lights, but that's not supposed to be happening, right?" She paused in the doorway. "Sorry I woke you up."

"No worries." Mia crawled back into bed. "Sweet dreams. We'll get more information on this tomorrow, I promise."

After Christina had gone to bed, Mia lay in her bed and worried. She hoped she hadn't opened up some spiritual can of worms like the voice in the library had warned her about. She hadn't mentioned the spirits in the library to Lasher. She'd tell him tomorrow. She rolled over and turned off the light.

The next morning, she was surprised to see not only Christina in the apartment kitchen making breakfast but Levi and Trent were there as well.

"Good morning, sleepyhead. I would have thought you'd be the one up and baking this

morning after the night Christina told us about."
Trent stood and gave her a kiss. "I'll get you some
coffee."

"You called them over for breakfast?" Mia sat
down, watching as Christina put a plate of eggs
and bacon in front of Levi.

"You were asleep when I got up. Then Mr. Darcy
went out. And I was alone," Christina said. She
didn't meet Mia's gaze. "So I called Levi, and he
offered to come over and keep me company."

"And Levi called me," Trent added as he put a
cup of coffee in front of Mia. "Now that we're
caught up, tell me about this Lasher person. What
exactly did he do yesterday?"

"I'm not sure. I left him alone in the kitchen."
Mia sipped her coffee.

Trent stared at her.

"What?" She put a hand up to her hair. "Do I
have something in my hair? A cat toy?"

"No, you're fine. But you left him alone? He
could have done anything, like left the door open
to come in and do the light show later. Or even set
up a machine down there." Trent leaned back in
his chair. "Look, I don't mean to tell you your business, but what if he's a scammer?"

"You mean there are people who go around pretending to 'fix' wards?" She leaned over and grabbed
a book from the counter. "It's one of the guys in
the picture in this old book. The ones that protected the school. Besides, Grans knows him. Not
to mention he's Henry's great-uncle. And he talked
to Dorian."

"The cat?" Trent took the book and stared at
the picture.

"Grans said he was talking to Dorian, the man."
She took another gulp of coffee. "Look, I know
this sounds weird—at least it would to normal people—but three of the four of us aren't normal."

"Thanks, I think," Christina said as she put a
plate in front of Mia. "I tried to make your eggs
sunny-side up, but I think they're hard."

Mia smiled at her assistant. "They're fine. Thank
you for breakfast. And I didn't mean normal in a
bad way. I just assumed my witchy friends here
would be more open to working with a probably
one-hundred-plus-year-old man who looks like he's
in his late sixties."

Trent blinked at that and looked back at the picture. "Brody's in the picture too. And he looks the
same. Is this guy a werewolf?"

"Not that I know, but you know my witchy limitations." *Argue your limitations.* The thought came
back full force again. She looked over at Gloria,
the kitchen witch doll that served as her familiar
along with Mr. Darcy. The doll giggled. Mia rolled
her eyes. "Anyway, I didn't even think to check any
were-vibes from him. Grans might know."

"I'd wait to call her," Levi said, then blushed.

Mia narrowed her eyes at him. "What don't I
know?"

He turned even more red and glanced at Christina, who turned her back and focused on the stove,
even though Mia knew there wasn't anything else
cooking since she'd seen Christina plate up her
own breakfast and Trent already had his plate.
"Well, when I drove by last night, there was a car in
the drive that wasn't your grandmother's."

"Maybe Lasher stayed around to have a drink or something." Mia could see where this was going and she didn't like it one bit. She looked under the table to make sure Mr. Darcy hadn't come back inside.

A look from Christina made Levi continue. "And it was still there when I drove past this morning."

Mia felt her eyes widen. "Grans let him stay over?"

Trent laughed. "You sound like you just found out your grandmother was with a man. Ever."

"I was just getting used to her dating. Well, the *idea* of her dating. Dorian died just before I moved here, and then there was some guy last year, but I don't think it went far. Anyway, I don't want to talk about this now or ever." Mia focused on her breakfast. Then she looked up and met everyone's gaze. "And don't talk about this in front of Dorian."

Christina's hand flew to her mouth. "Oh, that would be awkward."

"Exactly." Mia rolled her shoulders. "Anyway, Mr. Charming seems to think he might have an idea of who cast the spell on Hetty Medford's house. He says only the coven council has power like that. Or someone who used to be on the council. So we're looking at an inside job. We need to be careful and not leak that we're looking into this."

"Sounds good to me." Trent cleared his plate and took it to the sink to rinse. "Can I have your keys? I want to check out the kitchen before I have to go open the store."

"What do you think you'll find?" Mia grabbed the keys from the counter and singled out the one for the kitchen. "Maybe some mini disco balls?"

"That would be nice. But now that we know Lasher was busy last night, I'm concerned that instead of strengthening the wards, he loosened them. I want to make sure nothing got in." He took the keys from Mia. "I'll run these back up when I'm done."

Levi stood and rinsed his plate. "I'll come too. I've got a shift in a few minutes."

Christina sat down at the table with her plate. After the men had left, she looked at Mia. "I'm sorry I called them. I was just freaked out a little bit. And you were asleep."

"It's not a problem. I was bothered by the whole thing too. I'm hoping the ghosts were just woken up from what Lasher did to the wards and he didn't weaken them, like Trent thinks." She pushed away the half-eaten plate. "I should have just told May and Henry no when they asked to have the ceremony here. Then all we would have to deal with is the Hetty Medford issue."

"Do you really think it was one of the coven board?" Christina sat up. "Maybe it was Bethanie's dad. He was a coven big shot."

"If it was him, the spell would have disappeared when he went to prison. They strip you of all magical abilities when you get arrested. That way, they can't use the coven as a bargaining chip based on something bad they chose to do." Mia scratched her head. "This isn't adding up at all."

"Don't you need to call Ginny Willis and remind her about her outstanding debt? I wouldn't put it past her to spend all the money and then decide she wasn't responsible because you didn't give her the bill." Christina brightened. "You could ask her about it, then."

"What if she put up the spell? She'd know if anyone tried to bring it down, right?" Mia thought it was a good idea, unless Ginny was part of the plan. Then she'd turn on them, and everyone Mia cared about and loved might be harmed. But Christina was right. It wouldn't hurt to make a follow-up call on the outstanding bill. She would do it first thing after her day started. Right now, it was time for breakfast.

CHAPTER 16

Levi left right after checking out the kitchen and the state of the wards. But Trent paused at Mia's office door, gently knocking before coming in. He nodded to the coffeepot. "Any chance I can get one to go?"

"Of course. You ran over here this morning to make sure we were safe, how could I deny you a cup of coffee?" Mia stood and poured coffee into one of her travel mugs. "Just bring back the mug, and the other ones you haven't brought back yet."

"I have them clean and lined up on my counter. I keep forgetting to put them in my truck. Maybe I should make you dinner one night so you can pick them up?" He took the coffee and sat in one of the chairs.

"Sounds like a plan, but you're sitting down. Something wrong with the wards?" Mia refilled her own cup before joining him. It was going to be a long day.

"I don't think so. They seem stronger. Mr. Darcy

followed us all along the kitchen, then the first floor, meowing all the time. Do you really think Dorian has been trying to repair the wards?"

"As weird as it sounds, yes, it's logical. He's always going out at night lately. But how strange is it that a cat—okay, a spirit in a cat—is the first one to see cracks in the wards?" Mia rolled her shoulders. "This has been an odd week. I'm glad you're back in town. Are we still on for dinner?"

"Unless you don't want to. I know you have a lot on your plate. I don't want to be another to-do item." He stood and paused by the door.

"Honestly, you'll be doing me a favor. I'm going to need a break by the time we're done cooking today. I want to hear all about how the trip with your dad went." She heard the security alarm. "And Hailey's here. Do you mind letting her in?"

"I can do that. Is she working out?"

Mia nodded as she booted up the computer. "She's fitting in perfectly. I couldn't have asked for a better team member. Tell her to go on into the kitchen with Christina."

"Six thirty too late for dinner?" he asked. "I'm pretty sure I'm going to be swamped at the store after being away for a weekend."

"It's perfect. See you then."

Mia opened her weekly order list and printed it out for them to work through in the kitchen. She'd let Christina and Hailey get started on prep as she finished some administrative tasks, like calling Ginny. Mia probably should call Grans and tell her about the light show last night so she could tell Lasher. After the printer stopped, she looked through the orders. One caught her eye.

The Baldwins were ordering more soup. So,

Sarah's flu bug hadn't gone away. She picked up the phone and dialed Mark's number.

"Good morning, and no, I haven't determined that Hetty Medford was actually murdered. I'm talking to the coroner in person today," Mark grumbled through the phone.

"Good morning to you. And thanks for the update, but I was calling to see how Sarah was doing. I saw your online order."

"She's doing a lot better, but for some reason, the only thing she can keep down is your soup. And dill pickles. I insisted that she go to the doctor this week. I'd take her to the emergency room, but she doesn't want to be a bother for anyone. Sarah can be a bit stubborn." He chuckled after saying the words.

"I hope you're in your car, because if you're somewhere your wife can hear you, you might be the one who needs a doctor." She ended the call, then dialed Mahogany. No answer. She left a quick message about getting together. She wanted to go through Hetty's desk to see if there was anything from one of the coven's board talking about estate planning. If she could match Hetty with a council member, maybe then she could talk to someone about the spell. It was risky, but she needed more information. And she wasn't going to solve Hetty's murder sitting here waiting on Baldwin to follow up with the coroner. Especially since he had the autopsy report. He just didn't believe in what it was telling him.

She called her grandmother but didn't get an answer. There she left a message as well. Finally, she called Ginny. This time someone answered, just not Ginny.

"I'm sorry, she just stepped out. Can I take a message?" a crisp female voice asked, low and slow with her word choice.

"Please have her call Mia's Morsels and let me know when she'll be paying the final installment of the Holly wake catering charges. They were due last week." Mia threw in the last bunch because she hadn't pulled the actual invoice.

"Of course, so sorry. Can I get an amount?"

Mia pulled up the invoicing software and quoted her the final payment. "I'll have to charge late fees and interest if this isn't paid this week."

"I'm sure we can meet that deadline," the woman assured her. "I'll bring a check down Friday myself if I have to."

Mia looked at the short to-do list she'd made when she first came downstairs. The only thing left on it was to call Malcolm McBride regarding the spell on the Medford house. Technically, the call probably should be coming from Mahogany as next of kin, but she'd asked Mia for help, so she was helping.

Malcolm answered on the first ring. "This is Malcolm. How may I help you this fine Magic Springs morning?"

Mia introduced herself, then got right to the issue at hand. "I need some help."

"With the school? I thought Lasher was coming in to help with the wards."

So, he was on the pulse of what was going on in the community. "Actually, we're working on that, but I need help with Hetty Medford's house. Apparently there's an aging spell on the property and it's affecting her daughter. Mahogany asked me if I could help get it removed, but it's way above my skills. Maybe someone at the coven could help?"

"I've heard you're quite the witch in your own right, but with an aging spell, that's tricky." He paused for a minute, and Mia heard paper turning. "I could come by the house tomorrow at eleven if you or Ms. Medford could meet me there."

"Sure. I'm not sure I can, but someone will be there to let you in." Mia glanced at the list of deliveries she had to do for tomorrow. Then, in her mind's eye, she saw the gray in Mahogany's hair. "Scratch that. I'll be there at eleven. I hope you can reverse the spell. I understand that only a board member could have set it. Do you have any clues on who could have done such a thing?"

He coughed, and Mia wondered if she was supposed to know that about the spell. Too late now; she'd let the cat out of the bag. "Truly, anyone who has ever been a board member has the ability to cast long-term appearance curses. They really are nothing more than a glamour; the person who is affected by the spell doesn't actually become younger. It's just an appearance of being at peak conditioning."

Grans knows that but she still is acting differently, Mia thought as Malcolm continued to explain how almost everyone knew someone who used to be on the board, so anyone could have cast the spell. Mia wasn't really listening until he'd mentioned Ginny's skill in illusion.

"Ginny Willis used to be on the board?"

He paused a second time. Mia wondered if he realized what he was saying or if he always just said whatever popped into his head. "It's a small coven. Most of the members have served on the board, including your grandmother when she was an active member. Ginny's too busy with the coven bequeaths now to be on the board. You must have worked with her on Ms. Holly's wake, correct?"

"Yes, I did." Mia didn't mention the fact that Ginny still owed money on that event. "Ginny must have an official office for the fundraising?"

"An office and funding for a full-time clerical assistant, although I believe she has two part-time people, for some reason. I'd love to have one full-time assistant. As a board member, I work out of my home and get two hours of office help a week. It's not nearly enough. But you're not concerned about the petty disagreements inside the coven. You probably just want your friend back in her house." He tapped what sounded like his pen on his desk. "I'll be there tomorrow to solve your problems. And maybe I can take you to lunch to talk about joining the coven this year? I'm in charge of membership and losing your family from the rolls has always been a black mark on our coven's history."

"I'm not sure I have time to commit," Mia said, but then she decided waving the carrot wasn't a bad idea. She was asking for a favor. "However, I'd love to go to lunch to discuss what would be expected of me if I did join."

"Splendid. I'll see you at the Medfords' at eleven."

Mia hung up the phone and had just written the appointment down in her paper planner when the phone rang. She jumped, then scolded herself as she reached for the phone to answer. "Mia's Morsels, may I help you?"

"It's Levi."

She reached for the Hold button. "Hold on a second, I'm in my office. I'll go get Christina."

"Wait," he called out, and she sat back down to listen. "I called to talk to you. There's a bunch of dead birds out here at the Holly farm."

"Theresa's farm?" Mia asked to clarify.

He dropped his voice. "Yeah. We were called out because the cleaning lady thought she fell and broke her hip. She's banged up from falling down the basement stairs, but I think it's all just bumps and bruises. She says she's twenty-eight, but Mia, she looks like she's in her late fifties. Maybe older. She's been in the house for a week now, cleaning it up so Ginny can sell it. She even got permission to sleep in one of the bedrooms because she lives in Twin. Hey, hold on a second."

Levi paused and said something to someone on-site. Then he uncovered the phone.

"As we were closing up the house to take her to the hospital just to make sure, I walked out back to check the back door lock and there were a ton of dead blackbirds all over the backyard. I think we have another aging spell. Only this one didn't just affect the person in the house, it affected the birds that fly over the house." Levi whistled. "I didn't know any spell could do that."

"Give me the address. I'm having lunch with a board member tomorrow. Maybe he knows something about this. Either way, I need to go out there today to see if it's the same spell." Mia wrote down the information. "Don't say anything about this. Well, except to Trent and Christina. We need to keep this under wraps. Especially if it's the same spell. Maybe Hetty isn't the only one who was targeted."

"This is getting creepy, right?" Levi's voice trembled a little.

Mia nodded, "It is definitely creepy. Just stay safe today."

After Levi had hung up, Mia picked up tomorrow's orders and went into the kitchen to help the others cook for tomorrow's deliveries. And to tell them she wouldn't be in the delivery van. Hailey was strong enough to help Christina. And besides, she thought, as the idea swirled around in her head, this way, she could really make sure the two of them could work together.

When Trent came to pick her up for dinner, she met him downstairs. She saw the truck pull in and hurried outside to greet him rather than waiting for him coming inside. She climbed in and leaned over to give him a quick kiss. "Do you mind if we make a quick stop first?"

"Sure." He waited for her to put on her seat belt. "Don't tell me you want to go out to the Holly farm."

"I take it Levi called." She shut her door and nodded. "That's exactly where I want to go. Let's go make sure this is the same spell. I'm meeting with Malcolm McBride. I want to have all my ducks in a line."

"In a row," he said, but when she gave him a quizzical look, he shook his head. "Never mind. Just so we don't disappear with no one knowing where we are, did you tell anyone your plan?"

Mia bit her lip. She hadn't. She'd told Christina not to expect her tomorrow for the delivery day. If something happened and they disappeared, no one would start looking until late tomorrow at the earliest. "Maybe we should call your mother. Grans hasn't called me back. I think Lasher is still in town."

"You call Mom. I'm driving, and she gets mad when I call from the truck." He backed up the truck and headed out of the parking lot.

"Don't you use your Bluetooth?" She pointed to his phone, which was hooked up to the dashboard.

"Yes, I do. Mom still yells at me." He shook his head as Mia laughed.

After she'd let Abigail know what they were doing and listened to a few minutes of directions on what they should be looking for and promised a few times to call as soon as they left the farm, Mia hung up her phone. "That's done."

"I thought Lasher was coming back today to finish the wards," Trent said.

Mia nodded. "I did too. But about four this afternoon, I got a text that said three tomorrow. Nothing else, just three tomorrow. No explanation or even asking if that was a good time for me."

"He's used to people working around his schedule. My dad said he was always that way, even back in the day." Trent pulled onto the highway away from town. "The farm's about five miles this way. Just on the edge of the fire district. That girl's lucky Levi got to her first. If anyone else had, they would have thought she was actually elderly and treated her differently. Levi says she's dehydrated but fine. No broken bones but a lot of bruising.

She'll probably go home tomorrow and Ginny will need a new housekeeper."

"Does this let Ginny off the hook for the spell? Would she send someone in a house that had an aging spell on it deliberately?"

"According to Levi, the woman said she didn't ask Ginny; she asked her clerk, who hired her. So maybe Ginny doesn't know she was there," Trent countered Mia's theory. "Anyway, we need to verify it was the same spell first."

Mia glanced over at him in the cab of the truck. "Seriously? You think there might be two witches putting aging illusion spells on single women in the coven who just happen to have a sizable estate?"

"You can't think the coven has anything to do with this," Trent said.

That was exactly what Mia was thinking. Now she just had to prove it. Instead of answering Trent, she pointed to the creek running by the road. "The water's high for June, don't you think?"

"It's been a late spring. Snow stayed on the mountain longer this year." He continued talking about snowmelt and water levels until they got to the farm. The sun was just starting to set behind the mountain when they arrived. He handed her a flashlight. "We've got about thirty minutes before it gets too dark and we'll have to come back."

"I don't think it will take thirty minutes." Mia stepped out of the truck and walked the dirt path to the small farmhouse where Theresa Holly lived. "I started feeling the spell as soon as we got out of the truck. It's the same spell; I'd bet money on it. I can't tell if it's the same caster, but it feels like it might be. I'm not sure what I'm looking for."

Trent came up next to her and lifted her hand. "Feel the edges. If it's the same person, the edges are going to feel the same. It's like how I can feel your spells when you make them. I'm in tune with your vibrations. You might have to go back to the Medford house to verify, but if you 'think' it's the same, it probably is."

"You're a good teacher." Mia leaned into him as she studied the house. "It feels wrong that someone took a life. The house isn't happy."

"Would you be?" Trent asked, then a light shone in their eyes.

"Who are you and why are you here?" a man asked, holding a flashlight on them.

Mia held up her hand, blocking the light. "I'm Mia Malone and this is Trent Majors. I did the catering for Theresa's wake?"

"There's no one here to pay you, if that's what you're looking for. You need to call that witch that wants to sell the farm." The flashlight dropped and a man stepped out of the shadows. "I'm Jack Farnell. I ran the farm for Teri. And according to her will, I'm the new owner. But that witch, Ginny Willis, is fighting me on the estate."

"Hi, Jack, nice to meet you." Mia exchanged a glance with Trent. She thought Jack was using the label "witch" as an unpleasant woman, not a noun. But she didn't know for sure. "How long did you know Theresa?"

He smiled as he walked closer. "About five years now. Or it would have been five years. We met at a farming convention in Iowa and because we were both from Idaho, we had a lot in common. Last year, I sold my farm in Rigby and moved up here to help Teri out. We were . . ." he choked on the word, "going to be married next year."

After that bombshell, there wasn't much else to say. They said goodbye to the bereaved boyfriend and drove back into town. They were almost to the Lodge when Mia remembered she was supposed to call Abigail. She dialed and met Trent's gaze. "Sorry, we're on our way back now. No problems at all, but I'm sure it's the same spell and probably the same caster. I'm meeting Malcolm McBride tomorrow at eleven. I'm going to break the news that he has a serial spell caster, if not a murderer in his coven. Do you want to join me?"

"Of course. I love seeing McBride squirm. He's a true politician and a typical weasel. Are you sure you can tell the caster from the spell?" Abigail asked.

"Maybe not the caster, but Trent showed me how to find out if it's the same person." Mia reached over and squeezed Trent's hand. "I just want Malcolm to take off the spells. We'll deal with the question of who did this later."

After Mia hung up the phone, she stared out the window at the darkening night. "It's not fair that this person has run both Mahogany and now Jack out of their homes. We need to get the spells lifted."

"Jack's not in the house because Ginny's fighting his inheritance, not because of the spell," Trent reminded her.

"Yeah, but if the spell wasn't there, at least it would be safe for us to tell him to physically claim the house. Isn't possession nine tenths of the law?" Mia studied the way the dash lights lit Trent's face. Even in the darkening light, she could see he was thinking.

Trent pulled into the restaurant's parking lot. "I don't think that's going to be enough in this situation."

Chapter 17

Trent dropped Mia off at the school after dinner. She curled up on the couch with Mr. Darcy on her feet. She was reading when the phone rang. "Hello?"

"Mia, you won't believe what I found," Mahogany chattered excitedly.

Mia closed the book and sat up, getting a dirty look from Mr. Darcy, who jumped down and stalked off. "What did you find?"

"My mother was dating someone."

Mia's eyes widened. First, they'd found out that Theresa had a boyfriend, now Hetty? It was a romance-gone-wild kind of day. "Seriously? How did you find out?"

"In the house, Mom had several journals. I gave you the planner, but her journals I kept to see what she was thinking these last years. I don't know, it comforted me, knowing she had a good life here before she died." Mahogany let her voice trickle off. "I wasn't living here to be part of it. And you just get busy, you know? I never thought she'd go this early."

"It must be hard." Mia felt for the tea shop owner and made a note to call her own mother as soon as this phone call ended.

"Yeah."

Mia heard the swallow from the other side of the line. "Did you know him?"

"No. And I'm not quite sure who he is from the writings either. The name Jerimiah is in her journals. And it was, at least on Mom's side, a pretty steamy relationship."

The name rang a bell. Not someone she'd met or worked with. It was something else. Jerimiah. Oh, that was the guy who Ginny had dinner with. She didn't out him to Mahogany on the off chance he wasn't the guy. It was a slim chance, but Mahogany needed to know the truth. Just like Mia did.

"Well, that's news. I've got some too." Mia went ahead and told Mahogany about the possibility that Malcolm could remove the spell. "At least you'd be in the house and not renting a hotel room or sleeping at the restaurant."

"That's the best news I've had in days or weeks." Mahogany laughed. "Maybe in months or this entire year."

"Well, I'm glad you're happy. Abigail's going with me just in case this guy is full of hot air, but I'll call as soon as we're back to the house." Mia twisted two fingers together in a cross, just to make sure she wasn't telling a lie. She had barely remembered to call Abigail and that wasn't over a day between the promise and the action. It was time to cut her losses and go to sleep. "Talk to you tomorrow? I'm beat."

"Not a problem. Thanks for checking out the house and finding this guy. You're the best."

Mahogany hung up before Mia could explain that this wasn't her finding things and keeping the lights on at the house. Maybe if she practiced harder, she might just be able to snap her fingers and keep the cat from starving. Mia had always been told that she didn't dream big enough. How funny would it be to go back to one of her elementary school teachers and write them a letter about how screwed up this situation was and ask for advice?

Maybe that was her destiny in life: to help others who found life scary and full of questions. She could be Magic Springs's version of a psychic hotline. Of course the answer most people got when they called was to "find the solution within." Most problems could be solved with just a little brainstorming.

Unless your problem consisted of someone spelling your house with an aging spell. Or murdering your mother. One of those Mia could help solve, and she was going to do that tomorrow for Mahogany. The other needed to be left in the hands of Magic Springs's police chief, Mark Baldwin. If he could focus long enough to really think about the task. And as long as the actual murder didn't have anything to do with magic.

She set down the book and decided to let the decisions and her thoughts muddle through until tomorrow.

* * *

Tuesday morning, Mia woke to the smell of cinnamon rolls baking in the oven. For the second day in a row, Christina had been the early riser. She'd taken on Mia's habit of baking when she was stressed. Mia threw a robe over her pj's and pulled her hair into a ponytail, just in case they had visitors again.

Instead, when she reached the kitchen, all she found was Christina reading a book and drinking coffee. She nodded when Mia came in and put the book down on the table. "Good morning."

"Hi, Mia. I've got a to-do list for today that I'd like you to look at before Hailey and I start packing for the deliveries. I think I remembered everything, but you said there was a new customer you wanted to send something special to? And I've forgotten their name." Christina handed Mia the clipboard with a page full of tasks.

"Thanks. Let me get coffee and I'll look at this." Mia set down the clipboard and poured herself a cup. "Nolan Byrd—that's the newish customer. Although he's not really new; I just met him. You'll probably talk to his mother, Donna. I told them I'd add a free dessert to their order this week. Something kid friendly; he has a daughter, Prudence. She loves our mac and cheese."

Christina pulled back the clipboard. "Ooh, that's a good catch. Maybe we should add a descriptor of the most-ordered items for each client and their family makeup. Like the Byrds, you'd have 'mac and cheese' and 'kid friendly' on the list. We could even ask for birth dates, and then we could give them a free dessert then."

Mia listened to Christina brainstorming as she sipped her coffee. "This might be a horrible idea because it's so early, but what if we do something like a kid's club? That way, the kids sign up, give us their favorite food choices, and then we give out a free cookie each month and a dessert for their birthday."

"I like it. That way, they want to give us the information because they're getting something back for it. We'd have to put in some disclaimer like we don't sell their information." Christina took her notebook, which was sitting next to her, and started writing down ideas as they came. "We could add the questionnaire to the website. And maybe even reach out to the kids at school. Offer to do a free cooking class?"

Mia thought about the ideas Christina was listing off and then about the application for catering director still in Mia's purse. If she took the job, extras like this would drop to the wayside.

"What are you thinking about? You look a million miles away." Christina's question brought her back to the current.

Mia smiled, hoping her sadness didn't show. She still needed to run numbers, taking out all the catering that had come from the Lodge to see if what was left would at least pay the business bills and Christina's and Abigail's salaries. It would be a step back, but if they kept having great ideas like this, maybe the business could grow in spite of the new catering director trying to take all their contracts. "It's just early. Let's go over this list to see if you forgot anything. From the size of it, I don't think it's possible."

"You're just saying that. I want this delivery to go like clockwork, as if you were there in the van with us." Christina stood to refill her coffee. "Levi says you're meeting one of the coven board members today?"

"Yeah, that's one of the reasons I put the delivery on your shoulders. You'll be fine." Mia read the next task on the list. Christina was being very thorough. "He needed to meet at eleven. Then I'm taking him to lunch to talk about the house and the wards. And now, Theresa Holly's house too."

"What about the Holly house? What did I miss?" Christina asked right as the oven buzzer went off.

"Check your rolls and I'll tell you what Trent and I found out last night." Mia's stomach growled at the smell of the cinnamon rolls. She was hungry, probably because she'd only picked at her dinner after meeting Theresa's boyfriend, Jack Farnell. Christina dished out two hot rolls and drizzled glaze over the top as Mia told her about last night's adventure with Trent.

After she'd filled Christina in, she whistled. "I can't believe the coven would try to take the farm from him. That's sad."

"If he's who he says he is. He could have just been a drifter who was selling me a line." Mia broke off a piece of the roll and dipped it in some of the excess glaze on her plate.

"One way to find out, if they were on social media. Maybe they put each other in a relationship with." Christina opened her laptop and went to Facebook to search for a page under Theresa or Jack. "Great, nothing. Why don't people use Facebook more? It's a great way to see what other people are doing."

"So you can stalk them more effectively?" Mia smiled at Christina's motivation.

She nodded. "Exactly. Oh, I know who else we should check on: Hetty Medford."

Mia held up a finger. "You do that. I need to grab something."

She went into her bedroom and got Hetty's planner from her purse. If she could finish reviewing the planner for clues, she could give it back to Mahogany today when she saw her. No, she reminded herself, she told Mark she'd drop it off. This week was getting more and more filled with to-dos, and Mia needed to make her own list to keep on track of things. Especially when she needed to make a decision on the job soon. But not today.

She set the planner down and grabbed a notebook from her kitchen desk. "Mahogany asked if I'd seen anything about Hetty having a boyfriend. Apparently she wrote about him in her journal."

"And on Facebook," Christina added, excitement in her voice. "Maybe he's the guy who put the spell on the house."

"Maybe. What does he look like? Any pictures?" Mia asked as she opened the planner. It was last year's because Hetty had died early this year. Mia wondered if there was a second one. She always started the next year's planner as soon as she got her first catering job of the coming year. Then she'd go through the empty planner and add in things she'd done the last year and move it up a few months to check in to see if she could get the contract for the following year.

"Not yet. Apparently he didn't want them announcing their relationship until they were sure." Christina bit her lip. "Does that mean the boyfriend was probably a total jerk and most likely married?"

"Maybe, or maybe he was just cautious. Magic Springs is a small town. If you break up with someone, you'll probably see them the next day. Maybe he was just being careful." Mia scanned through January with only one appointment. pausing her finger over the date. "This is interesting. She had an appointment on January eighteenth with Ginny Willis."

"Maybe they were friends and were having lunch," Christina suggested.

Mia turned to the detail page for that week. "Not unless it was brunch. The appointment was at 120 Main Street, Suite A. I wonder what's at that address."

"Hold on a second—let me open the maps browser," Christina said.

While she waited for an answer, Mia saw that there were a lot of pages after December's calendar pages. She turned back to look at them. Hetty had listed out a set of goals. Goals for the tea shop, financial goals, personal goals, which, of course, had one about losing weight. Women were predictable. She found the financial goals. They seemed normal. Pay off debt. Increase the emergency fund. And then she saw it. "Set up an estate plan." Under that one was a memo to talk to Ginny Willis about a gift to the coven.

Mia swore under her breath. "The address is Ginny's office for the coven. She went to talk to Ginny about leaving the coven money in her will."

"You're right. It's listed as the Economic Development Office of the Magic Springs Society for Magical Realism." Christina leaned back. "I guess they don't like using the word 'coven.'"

Mia had already known that when the coven interacted with the nonmagical world around them, they used a cover name, so this didn't surprise her. Had Ginny set the aging spell on Hetty because she thought the coven needed the money? Or was this a coincidence? Either way, Ginny Willis was at the middle of both women's financial life. She wondered if Baldwin had made the connection yet. She needed to call him again today. With Sarah being sick, at least she had a non-investigation reason to start a conversation.

"Maybe I can see if Malcolm has more information about Ginny's department. Or about the status of the coven's financial health. If this is about money, Ginny's got to be in the middle of it."

Christina closed her laptop. "And you need to find out from Mahogany just what she got from the will. Maybe Hetty didn't have much money to give. Why else would Mahogany uproot her life to take over her mom's tea shop if she didn't need the money? I can't think that most local businesses are rolling in dough around here."

"Solid questions. I think the merchants in Sun Valley are doing okay, but Magic Springs is just far enough away to be out of range for most of the high-end buyers." Mia glanced at the clock. "Hailey should be here in about thirty minutes. You may want to get dressed for the day."

Christina looked down at her shift nightgown and grinned. "Maybe this is my delivery outfit."

"We might get more orders from the male clientele, but I think our family orders would drop like a stone if you wore that to deliver." Mia stood and cut another cinnamon roll. "These are amazing, by the way. I love the orange-flavored drizzle."

"Thanks. Our chef used to make them every

Sunday morning. I loved them so much that as soon as I was old enough, I begged her to teach me how to make them. I had to promise never to tell my mother. She wouldn't have approved of me doing servant's work." Christina stood and put her plate in the sink. "Make sure you review the rest of my checklist. I'd hate to forget anything."

Mia picked up the checklist and made notes here and there, mostly to let Christina know that she'd looked at the whole thing. It was good and thorough. Someday Christina would be running her own business, and it would probably be sooner rather than later.

Her phone buzzed and she checked a text from Trent that she read aloud. **"Mom and I will meet you at the Medford house at eleven."**

She keyed in a quick thanks and went back to Hetty's calendar. When she hit July, she started to see dinners scheduled with "J." Was this the Jerimiah that she'd written about in her journal? Mia listed the dates and places as she went through the planner. She'd ask Mahogany if the dates matched the journal entries.

When Christina came back into the kitchen, she'd finished going through the planner and had crossed one thing off Christina's to-do list. "I'll handle the Baldwin delivery."

"Seriously, Mia, I can do it. Besides, he's probably going to be at work. Sarah doesn't hate me." Christina picked up her clipboard and reviewed her notes. "These are good additions. Thanks."

"Actually, I'm not handling the Baldwin delivery because of your relationship with Mark. I need to drop off this planner and my notes to him. I think I have a possible suspect, or at least someone he needs to interview about Hetty's death. And if I can get the name of the spell caster from Malcolm, we might just have solved this murder."

"I'm glad. Mahogany seems really sad about her mom's death still. I don't think she has closure because no one believed her that she was murdered." The security alarm went off and she looked up at the monitor. "And Hailey's here, ten minutes early. She's really fun to work with. I'm so glad you found her."

Mia watched as Christina headed downstairs to start her day. She wanted to remind her to knock hard at Mrs. Packer's house and to schedule extra time with Mr. Terns because he loved to talk. Mia knew she was probably one of the few people he saw during the week because he was homebound. The delivery service was more than just dropping off food. It was a way to check on and be part of the community. But these were things Christina needed to learn on her own or, Mia hoped, she'd already learned by watching Mia complete the deliveries.

She had to let her baby bird fly sometime. Today was that day.

Chapter 18

Trent and Abigail were already at the Medford house when Mia arrived. She'd packed a cooler with the Baldwin order into the back of the side-by-side Trent had given her for Christmas. The small utility vehicle was great for trips to the store and around town because it was licensed. However, it didn't go very fast, so she didn't take it on the highways or for long distances. It wasn't enclosed, so it wasn't warm enough for long trips anyway. She needed a second car, but she also needed a better van. She had a savings fund for the new van and, when she bought that, the old van would be her second car until it finally died.

Before she went to meet them on the front porch, she reset her ponytail. Riding in the open vehicle made her hair go crazy, even when she tried to contain it in a scarf or pony. And hats had a tendency to fly off at the worst time, so she just put up her hair and reset it when she arrived at her stopping place.

The planner was in her tote, along with her phone and a notebook. She'd drop off the copy of her notes with the planner to Baldwin with the food. And maybe she could have Trent follow her to the house and give her a ride to the restaurant. The windblown style wasn't her best look. Especially when she wanted to be taken seriously.

Trent stepped off the porch to greet her. He pointed toward the side-by-side. "I could have picked you up on the way."

"I forgot I didn't have the van until I walked outside with the cooler. I need to stop at the Baldwins' before lunch, but if you could take me to the Lodge after that, I'd appreciate it. I can walk home if I need to." Mia stepped up on the porch to greet Abigail and felt the spell surround her. She paused for a minute and, following Trent's instructions yesterday, felt the outside of the spell. The edges matched the spell on Theresa's house. "It's the same person."

"Hello to you as well, dear. What are the two of you talking about?" Abigail came over and gave her a hug. "Oh, do you mean the spell? You can feel the caster's energy?"

"Yeah, Trent taught me a trick yesterday. The edges are the same. I practiced last night on a spell I did to bless today's delivery and found the edges and felt the difference between that and the Holly farm spell. This one matches the one we found last night. My edges are wavy and sunny, if that makes any sense. This spell has hard edges. Almost like glass." Mia turned to Trent. "You were right."

"I didn't do this. I just told you how to find it. When I do it, I see the edges, not feel them. I guess we're all a little different." He nodded to the car coming up the drive. "That must be Malcolm."

Abigail watched as the Lincoln pulled into the driveway. "One thing to mention: Malcolm feeds on praise. If you want him to do something he doesn't want to do, feed his ego. It might work. He has a vested interest in protecting the coven, so he'll want this spell gone, but he's not going to give up the maker easily."

"Got it. Praise him for his work, thank him for coming here, and lay it on thick. Maybe he'll slip." Mia smiled and waved at the car and its inhabitant. When he got out, Mia was surprised. Instead of a powerful, magical wizard, Malcolm portrayed more of a high-tech geek, right down to the comic book hero T-shirt and jeans. "Okay, I thought he'd be older."

"Malcolm is older than he looks. He's been off and on the board for over thirty years now." Abigail waved at the new arrival. "He's got a lot of clout with the other members."

"He thinks we're talking about me joining the coven at lunch, by the way." Mia glanced at Trent. "For some reason, he's been told I have more power than a kitchen witch should have."

Trent snuck a glance at her and she knew he thought the same thing. But his response was a generic, "Oh?"

"We're going to talk about this later," Mia said before she stepped off the porch to greet Malcolm. She held out a hand to shake, but he opened his arms for a hug instead. She followed his lead, stepped in for a short hug, and tapped him on the back several times before stepping back. "Oh, well,

I'm so glad you could make it. Mahogany's been beside herself with the house and the spell."

He smiled at her discomfort, and in that instant, Mia knew she didn't like him very much, or at all. The hug had been a test. One she'd apparently failed, and he thought he knew something about her boundaries.

"Well, you brought friends; isn't that nice." He stepped toward Abigail, but Trent blocked him with an outstretched hand. "Trent Majors. I'm surprised to find you here meddling in the affairs of witches. I thought you passed your power to your brother."

Trent nodded as he shook Malcolm's hand. "I'm here to support Mia. We've been dating."

And with that one sentence, Trent had laid claim to Mia in front of Malcolm. Mia felt the energy of his protection spell cover her as the men poked at each other. This was getting out of hand. She stepped toward Trent to break the testosterone battle, but Abigail was two steps ahead of her.

"Malcolm McBride, I haven't seen you since your wedding. How is Barbara? I haven't seen her in years." Abigail's statement pierced the battle between the two men. If Mia was right, she'd just canceled out Malcolm's possible claim on Mia by bringing up his current status. If this mental battle was a coven tradition, what had instigated it here? The spell on the house? Or Malcolm's desire to win her over as a coven member?

Trent stepped back, looking a little dazed. He met her gaze and shrugged, indicating he wasn't sure why he'd responded in the full-on, defend-your-woman, caveman mentality. Maybe Abigail could explain what just happened later. Right now, they needed Malcolm's help to get the spell removed here and on the Holly farm.

Feeling the de-escalation of tension, Mia stepped closer to Trent. "Malcolm, what do you think about the spell? Can you reverse or close it?"

He took Abigail's hand and helped her off the porch. "Let me see what I can do. You're right, it's very powerful. The spell itself had to have been made by someone with board-level magic. No one else could have sustained this level of power for this long. Hetty died, what, six months ago?"

"Yes. At the beginning of the year." Mia felt the pull of the spell. Malcolm must be trying to close it because it wasn't happy.

Malcolm closed his eyes, whispered a few words, and just like that, Mia felt the spell dissipating. Like a cloud of smoke from a fire, it waved through the air until there wasn't anything left. Malcolm took a step toward the house and almost stumbled. He lurched over to one of the porch chairs and fell into it.

"Malcolm, are you all right?" Abigail stepped back on the porch and hurried over to where the man was on the chair. He looked pale and he was breathing very quickly. Worse, his eyes were still closed.

"Mom, be careful," Trent said in a low tone. Mia could hear the worry.

Abigail glanced back at him. "It's fine. I know you can't feel it, but the spell is gone. Do either of you have something with some sugar?"

Mia ran back to the side-by-side and opened the cooler. She'd brought a bag of cookies just in case

Malcolm was late. She had almost said something stupid back there to Abigail about how Trent could definitely feel the spell, but she realized Abigail was trying to keep Trent's secret. When he gave up his power to his brother, the result should have been a complete transfer. Instead, both brothers now shared the power, and they were both as powerful as Trent had been when he gave up his power. At least in the coven's records.

She grabbed two peanut butter cookies from the bag and wrapped them with a napkin. Then she also grabbed a bottle of water. Malcolm looked like the reversal had taken a lot out of him. She ran back and gave the items to Abigail.

On the porch, she couldn't feel anything. The spell was finally gone. Now, Mahogany could return to the house and making a life here in Magic Springs. Mia just needed to find out who had placed the spell and why, so she could find a way to give that information to Baldwin so he could put whoever killed Hetty in jail.

After a few minutes, Malcolm's color returned. He smiled weakly at the three who were watching him. "Who's up for some lunch? I definitely need some fuel intake."

"I've got to stop at Baldwin's to drop off his order." Mia looked at Trent. "I can meet you at the Lodge."

"Why don't you drive Malcolm to the Lodge in his car?" Abigail looked at Trent. "I can pick up Mia at the school, then we only have two cars to deal with."

Trent held out his hand to Malcolm. "Sounds like a plan. Can I get your keys? That Lincoln's really sweet."

"It drives like a dream. You can't get it up to speed on these mountain roads, but get it on a highway and it purrs." Malcolm handed over the keys and the men left the porch and walked to his car.

Abigail and Mia stood, watching them. "That was smart, getting Malcolm to accept help. He looked like he couldn't even walk after he lifted the spell."

"The spell fights back if it's not the original maker trying to cancel it." Abigail took Mia's arm as they walked toward Trent's truck. "I'm not sure he'll be able to remove a second spell today."

"I'm hoping he can tell us who put the spell on the house in the first place. If we get that person talking, maybe they'll take off the spell." Mia watched as Abigail climbed into Trent's truck. "I'll see you at the school in about fifteen minutes. Thanks for the ride to the Lodge."

"No problem. I knew Trent wouldn't allow me to drive Malcolm to the Lodge. Sometimes those boys of mine are a little overprotective." She started the truck. "I'm going to call Mary Alice to see what she's found out from Lasher. I'm planning an elaborate cake for this wedding and I don't want any slime monster to ruin it."

"Are there really slime monster ghosts?" Mia's eyes widened. She'd seen the movie but thought it was all make-believe. Well, she had until she'd met Dorothy, Magic Springs's resident ghost who hung out at the hospital where she'd passed. Now, after meeting real live werewolves, she didn't know what was real from the ghost stories and fairy tales she'd read as a child and what wasn't.

"Of course not. But some of the older ones, like those on your property, have lost connection to what it means to be human. That makes them harder to deal with." Abigail paused. "And angrier."

Mia thought about angry spirits during the drive to the Baldwins'. When she got there, Sarah Baldwin answered the door. She looked like she'd been rode hard and put away wet, as the saying went. "Sarah, I didn't mean to get you out of bed."

"I've been resting for weeks now. If I watch another daytime talk show, I'll be throwing shoes at the television. I can't believe how stupid some people can be. If they'd just follow the golden rule, none of that stuff would be happening." Sarah turned back toward her living room and the offensive television. "Oh well, so much about my life. I take it you're dropping off food. Where's the van? Isn't this your normal delivery day?"

"I wanted to bring this personally." Mia smiled and held out the bag. "I've got soup and a few dinners in here, along with some cookies. Can I put it away in your kitchen for you?"

Sarah looked at the bag like it weighed fifty or more pounds. She reached for it, then dropped her hand. "I guess I'd better accept help. If I take the bag and drop it, soup will be all over this new Oriental rug I just talked Mark into getting. And I don't want a bunch of men in here cleaning carpets while I lounge on the couch. I'd better start feeling better soon or I'm going to go crazy."

Mia stepped inside and closed the door. "Mark said you have a doctor's appointment this week. Maybe they can find out what's going on and give you something."

"Better health through modern medicine. Take a pill and everything will be all right." Sarah pointed the way to the kitchen and slowly walked with Mia. "Sorry, I'm grumpy. I guess I'm not a good patient. But I feel like we take too many pills for things that just need to run their course."

"You've been sick a while," Mia reminded her.

Sarah met her gaze and then dropped it. "You're right. I'm scaring Mark, so I'll go to the doctor and let him poke and prod. I'm sure it's just a stomach bug that went crazy. I ate mall food a month ago and started feeling bad right after that. I should know better."

"Let's hope it's just food poisoning." Mia set the bag down and took out the three quarts of soup. "I'm going to put one of these in the fridge and two in the freezer, if that's all right. Or should I warm some up for you? It's almost lunchtime."

Sarah sank into a chair at the small table near the window. "I'd love it if you did. That way I can tell Mark I ate today. He makes me oatmeal before he leaves for work, but I worry he's doing too much. Have you heard that Hetty Medford was murdered? I met her at a spring pie festival a few years ago. She won the apple pie division every year. I tried to compete one year but switched to cherry pie the next. She was unbeatable."

"I didn't know she or you baked pies." Mia took a pan from the hanging rack and put half of the soup from the container into it. She put the rest into the fridge and saw a fruit salad in Tupperware and pulled that out to go with the soup.

"I love baking. I'm not as good with cakes as I am pies. Cakes want to be decorated. I can do layered cakes with just regular frosting and maybe some toppings, but for sheet cakes you need to have some decorating skills. Like Abigail Majors. She's amazing." Sarah watched as Mia dished out a bowl of the fruit. "I'll take that now. I guess I was hungry."

"Fruit is always a good appetizer." Mia set the bowl on the table and went back to stir the soup. "Abigail's doing the cakes for my catering company now. She's so creative. I'm good with a basic cake sponge and maybe filling and frosting, but don't ask me to make it pretty."

"Cake decorating is an art. I like feeding people." Sarah took a bite of the salad and grinned. "You're actually very nice. I can't believe I felt threatened by you."

Mia set cookies on a plate on the counter so Sarah could get to them easily. The woman needed calories. "Wait, you were threatened by me? Why?"

"Everyone talks about your meals and how amazing they are. I didn't let Mark order food from your company because I felt like that was my strength. Then, when your soup was the only thing I could keep down, I thought God was teaching me a lesson in pride." She sipped her water, not meeting Mia's gaze.

"Well, that's just silly. My delivery service is for the families who don't have amazing cooks in the household. You didn't need me until you got sick. And once you're better, you won't need me again." She looked around the kitchen. A bowl sat near the stove, waiting for the soup to warm up. "Can I get you anything else to go with the soup? I left the cookies out for a midafternoon treat."

"The soup will be fine. You don't have to stay and serve me. I can get it to the table once it's warm."

"It's almost done. Let me put these meals in the

freezer and your soup will be ready. Then I'll get out of your hair." Mia wanted to unload the dishwasher, but Sarah had already disclosed her uncomfortable feelings about Mia's kitchen skills. She didn't want to push it. Besides, she might feel like unloading it this afternoon after she took a nap. "It's too bad about what happened to Hetty. I didn't know her, but her daughter, Mahogany, is really nice. Have you been to the teahouse?"

"Not yet." Sarah watched as Mia bustled around the kitchen. "I didn't know she had a daughter until Mahogany moved back. It's too bad they didn't have more time to spend together."

"It is." Mia stirred the soup, measuring the steam coming out. It was ready. She poured it into the bowl and walked it and a spoon over to the table. "There you go. Anything else I can do for you?"

"I'm good. Thank you so much. I'm glad we got to spend some time together." Sarah started to stand.

"It was very nice to meet you as well. I can let myself out. Should I lock the door on the way out?"

Sarah nodded as she picked up a spoon. "Please. Mark worries about me being alone in the house. I always ask him who he thinks is big enough to break into the Magic Springs police chief's home."

"He worries. That's cute."

Sarah beamed. "He's a keeper."

Mia picked up the bag and realized it wasn't empty. She held up the journal. "I told Mark I'd bring this over. It's Hetty's day planner."

"Just set it on the table by the front door. That way I won't be tempted to search it for Hetty's recipes." Sarah took another bite of the fruit salad. "I'm feeling better already."

"It's the sugar rush. Remember the cookies

later if you run out of energy. It's not a long-term solution, but cookies work in a pinch." Mia waved and headed out to the front and to her side-by-side.

When Mia got home, Abigail was sitting in Trent's truck, waiting. She was on the phone, and Mia remembered she was going to call her grandmother. She wondered if they'd been talking since she left the Medford house.

She opened the passenger door when Abigail waved her inside.

"Hey, Thomas, I've got to go. Mia just got here." She paused, listening. "Yes, we're going to lunch, and then I think we'll have to make a plan for the Holly house. Don't worry, I'll be back home to make dinner."

She listened again and added, "I love you too."

Mia busied herself with the seat belt and looking out the window as Abigail and her husband said goodbye. Obviously they were still in love after all these years. And he worried about her. Which was the same comment she'd gotten from Sarah about Mark. She wondered what made a relationship work like that. Was it the fact they genuinely cared for each other? At the end of her last relationship, Isaac would disappear for days without even telling her where he was going sometimes. And she hadn't pushed. She hadn't even worried. She thought they were strong when, in reality, they were falling apart, even then.

Abigail started the car. "Sorry about that. He's being a little clingy lately. I think it's the job. I've always depended on him to bring in the money. Now I have my own and he's not sure how to deal with that."

"Some people would just spend it." Mia smiled as they drove out of the parking lot.

Abigail nodded. "He's not just anyone. And he's right, we don't 'need' the money. I just like the job."

"I could not pay you, if that would make him feel better," Mia offered.

Abigail laughed. "It might make him feel better, but I'd be upset. No, I can handle my husband's tender feelings. You just keep paying me. I like having some money I can call my own. It makes me feel powerful."

"Okay, if you're sure." Mia pointed out a parking spot near the front of the Lodge. "Front-row parking; you're the best."

CHAPTER 19

As they finished lunch, Malcolm promised to meet up with her and Abigail same time, next day, at the Holly farm. "We need to get this settled," he admitted.

It looked bad for the coven to have unauthorized magic being started on his watch. Mia knew Malcolm would work with them to get the spells neutralized, but he wasn't going to give up the caster. Even though he knew they'd probably killed two coven members.

"Tom is waiting for me in the parking lot. He wants to go shopping for a new couch for his office." Abigail gave Mia a hug. "I'll see you around noon tomorrow, then? I'll drive."

Trent opened the door to his truck for Mia after his mom and Malcolm had left. He paused before he shut the door. "You okay?"

"Fine. Worried about Sarah Baldwin. She looks horrible. She's going to the doctor and I really don't want to guess what he's going to say." Mia put on her seat belt and leaned back against the seat as Trent closed the door and walked around to the driver's side to get in.

Trent started the engine and followed up on the comment as they pulled out of the parking lot. "You think something's wrong."

Mia sat up straight and looked out the window. "I couldn't get a handle on it. It doesn't feel like a disease. Maybe she's right and it's a horrible case of food poisoning, but I don't think so."

"Did you find out anything about Hetty's case?"

She shook her head. "Strike two on that. All Sarah said was Hetty was the queen of the apple pie contest."

Her phone rang as she opened the front door. Trent had dropped her off and gone back to work to deal with an issue. This call was probably Christina with a question about the delivery schedule. Work never stopped. "Hello?"

"You need to be careful and stay out of other people's magic. People die when they go messing with traps," the man said.

Mia clutched the cell tighter to her ear, trying to recognize the voice. He obviously knew she was behind killing his spell at Hetty's. If Malcolm was up to it tomorrow, they'd drive him over to the Holly farm and end that spell as well. "Who is this?"

"I would have thought you'd have figured that part out already." The man chuckled. "Now I feel like I've overestimated you. Just stop messing around with my spells. I'd hate for you or your grandmother to be in harm's way."

The line went dead.

Mia tucked her phone in her pocket and locked

the door. Christina and Hailey were still out on deliveries, so it was just her in the school. She went into the kitchen to finish cleanup from yesterday, as well as check inventory. Besides, she hadn't worked in the area since Lasher had shorn up the wards. She wanted to see if they were holding.

Mia finished the few things Christina had left from yesterday and ran the last load in the dishwasher. There would be more work when they came back, like cleaning the travel tubs, but for now, the kitchen was almost back to normal. She started a load of laundry and looked out the side-door window. No mysterious fog hanging around the dumpster. She didn't feel like she was being watched. Maybe Lasher had helped. Looking around the kitchen, the only thing she had left to do was inventory. Then she'd go into the office and start making calls for May and Henry's wedding. It looked like the school was going to be a safe place to hold the event after all.

She'd finished inventorying the frozen meals and making sure the oldest stock was still good and in the front to use. Now she was in the office, keying everything into her online inventory system. She needed to run a special on the vegetarian lasagna next week because that hadn't been selling as well as their other options. Mia thought about her drop-in clients and wondered how to increase that foot traffic. Of course, she didn't have someone at the school every day to sell meals, so that might be hurting that side of the business.

A noise from the kitchen startled her. and she grabbed her clipboard and went out to greet Christina and Hailey, back from deliveries.

But they weren't who stood in her kitchen. It was Grans and Alphonso Lasher. "Oh, I didn't expect you today."

"I thought I left a message that I would be here at three." He frowned at her and reached for his phone.

"My bad. I guess. I thought it was tomorrow." She glanced around the kitchen. "The school feels better. I don't have that impending-doom feeling that was seeping into the kitchen."

"Short-term result. I need another day or two to make sure the patches are going to hold. It's delicate work." He put his bag on one of the prep tables and started taking things out of it. A cauldron, his grimoire, and tiny bottles with different-colored liquids and dried concoctions lined up on the table.

As he was finishing, Christina unlocked the back door and came inside with a stack of empty tubs. "Oh, I didn't realize anyone was in here."

"No worries. Is there any food in the van?" Mia hurried over to take the tubs from Christina when she saw the look on Lasher's face. Apparently he did think it was an issue.

"Nope, we sold out of everything, even the extra desserts I packed. Hailey mentioned them every time we delivered and we were sold out about half way through the delivery cycle." She handed a bag with the credit card reader and the cash box to Mia. She nodded toward Lasher and asked in a quiet voice, "Do you want to just clean out the van later? I can send Hailey home. When do you want her to come back?"

"Tell her I'll have a check for her on Friday for the work she's done so far." Mia walked with

Christina toward the back door. Thank the Goddess Christina knew about the special parts of Mia's life. This could be hard to explain. Which was why she was trying to keep Hailey in the dark as long as possible. "Thanks for handling this. And make sure you come in the front door when you return to the apartment today."

"Sounds great. Nice to see you, Mary Alice and, um, Mr. Lasher." Christina hurried out the door and Mia relocked it. She waved to Hailey, who had been walking toward the kitchen with bins before Christina caught up with her. Then Mia closed the blinds on the door.

She turned to Lasher and her grandmother. "Sorry about the interruption. Like I said, I thought you were coming tomorrow."

"I need this area cleared of all life." He looked pointedly at the two women still in the kitchen.

"I was just leaving. Grans, I need to talk to you anyway. Mr. Lasher, we'll be in the third-floor apartment when you're done. Or you can just call one of us." Mia took her grandmother's arm in her own and they left the kitchen. As they walked up to the stairs, she asked, "Do you want to tell me what's going on with the two of you?"

"I don't know what you mean." Grans pulled her arm away from Mia's grasp. "Al is just here to help with the wards."

"Al spent the night at your house," Mia pointed out.

Grans paused on the stairs. "Are you checking up on me? You know, despite my appearance, I've been taking care of myself longer than you've been alive."

"I know. And I'm sorry to be intrusive. Levi said

he saw Lasher's car at your house. I'm just concerned about you."

Grans turned and headed up the stairs again. "Dear, I know what I'm doing. Al was trying to help me reverse this spell. It got late, so I put him up in the guest bedroom rather than him having to find a hotel. No scandal there."

Mia's face heated. She'd come to the wrong conclusion. She hurried to catch up with her grandmother. "Sorry I jumped to conclusions. You've been different since the transformation and I was just concerned."

"Dear, I don't sleep with every man who visits my house." Grans glanced down at her younger body. "Although I feel like I'm wasting my time in this thing. I haven't felt this strong in years. I actually ran on my treadmill yesterday morning rather than taking the walk I do every morning."

"It must feel weird." Mia opened the apartment door to let them inside.

Grans grinned at her. "It feels glorious. I'm tempted to keep this body."

That afternoon, after Lasher and Grans had left, Mia got a call from May. "Hey, I was just working on your plans. We said blue and silver, but I don't think we settled on a specific blue, did we?"

"Light blue, almost lavender? I think the color is periwinkle. As long as it looks more blue than green, I'm good. I'm not too picky about things like colors. I just want to be Mrs. Henry Lasher by the end of the event." May laughed, then continued, "Anyway, I'm calling because his great-uncle said the school was going to be available. Did he tell you?"

"It feels better, but no, he didn't say it was fixed yet. I'm just going on faith with the Goddess that we're going to be able to pull it off, now we've set a budget and the location and the color scheme. Are you sure you don't want more input into the details? There are a ton more steps to this. Do you want a rehearsal dinner? Here or somewhere else?"

"Let's do the rehearsal there, but we'll handle the dinner. Henry already set it up at the Lodge with a guy named James. That way we're not in your hair all weekend. I've already done the invites and have confirmed most of the two hundred guest spots. You handled the reception at the school, and as long as you stay in your budget, go wild with whatever you want to serve. I'm not much of a food person. As long as it's yummy."

Mia was scribbling notes as they talked. "One more thing: I'm going to have Abigail send you pictures of the finalized proposed cake. Let me know if there are any changes you want. I'm assuming you're handling the dress? Do you need any referrals for that, or the bridesmaid dresses or the tuxes?"

"Suits. The guys are wearing black suits. We've already verified they have some. My friends and I are going to Boise to get dresses and pick up my wedding dress this weekend. And we'll stay over for a kind of bachelorette party. Mostly food and some theater, but we'll have fun." May paused, "Oh, I don't have a photographer. I had one lined up out of Boise, but he dropped out when we gave him the date. I guess he's got a previous commitment."

"Okay, I'll find someone." Mia wrote that down. "I think I have everything I needed. I'll give you a call if we need something else. You're making this wedding planning way too easy."

May laughed. "Too many years as a corporate event planner. I know what needs to be done and what's just the toppings. And neither one of us are very picky. We just want to get married. It took a long time for us to find the one. Now we want to live our lives together."

Mia kept working after the call ended. It felt good to be back in the planning stages. Her first wedding planning experience, she'd stepped into the wedding two weeks before the event. This one might be a lot smaller than the first, but it would give Mia's Morsels a different type of event under their belt, and one she could feel comfortable bragging about because it would be her design. She broke the to-do list up into days and people responsible.

Christina came out of her bedroom as Mia was finishing up the schedule. "What are you working on now?"

"The wedding for next weekend. We've got a lot of stuff to get set up in not a lot of time. I guess Lasher called and told his nephew the wards would hold up for the wedding. So that's good news." Mia moved a list over to Christina's side of the table. "This is your list. Let me know if we're missing anything as I go through the plan."

Then she went step-by-step through the checklist to make sure they'd covered everything. When she was done, Christina had made some notes on her sheet. "I'll match this up to the checklist we made after Amethyst and Tok's wedding, but I think we've got everything covered. Nothing in the plans for this weekend, right?"

Mia shook her head. "All we have on the books is next week's delivery, and then the wedding that weekend. We don't even have to do the rehearsal dinner."

"So that should take some stress off you." Christina set the paper aside. "How did the spell busting go today? Any thoughts about who killed Mahogany's mom?"

Mia stood and grabbed a soda out of the fridge. "The spell is gone. I'm glad I asked Abigail to come with us and verify the reversal worked. I felt it leave, but I don't trust my 'skills' in that area."

Gloria, Mia's kitchen witch, giggled.

Mia ignored her.

Christina frowned and looked around the kitchen. Then she shook her head and asked another question: "What about the Holly house?"

"We're going there tomorrow. I guess the reversal spell took a lot out of Malcolm. But there's something else I need to tell someone. I got a call after we took down the spell from a man who said I should stop messing with his spells." Mia wished she'd recorded the conversation now. Or just let the guy leave it on voice mail. But would he have made the same threat? "I don't remember now exactly what he said, but it was clear he didn't like us taking the spell off the house."

"Do you think he's going to try to stop you from removing the spell off the Holly house?" Christina asked.

Mia sat back in her chair. "I hadn't thought of

that. Let's just hope he doesn't know that we know about that one."

The next morning, Mia worked on the wedding until it was time for her to meet Abigail at the Holly farm. She had the additional information for her for the cake and she needed to verify what design she wanted to use so she could let May and Henry know. Although they'd been given so few guidelines, she was sure Abigail could do almost anything she wanted with the cake as long as it was pretty.

The farm seemed deserted, but the air was warm, so Mia went to sit on one of the chairs that surrounded a stone firepit in the front yard. She checked her watch. Abigail was five minutes late. She must have gotten hung up at home with Thomas. Mia wasn't sure he would ever be happy about Abigail working, whether it was for Mia or anyone else. He'd grown accustomed to her being around when he needed her. Mia shut her eyes and let the sun warm her face as she got lost in her thoughts.

Her cell phone ringing woke her. She blinked and checked the time as she answered Abigail's call. She'd been out for almost ten minutes. She must have been tired. "Hey, Abigail, are you hung up? No worries. Malcolm isn't here yet either."

"Oh my Goddess, Mia, that's why I'm calling. He's not at his house. He asked me to pick him up this morning for some reason; I really didn't listen to the specifics. Anyway, I got here a few minutes before eleven because his house is on the way to the farm. I called, but no answer. I went to the door to knock and it was open. The house looks like there was a struggle."

"You need to call Baldwin." Mia sat up straight and looked at the house. Now, it felt like the house was watching her. Or at least the spell that hovered over the actual house.

"I did. And he told me to stay here until he had time to talk to me. Then I forgot you were waiting until now. I'm so sorry," Abigail ranted on.

"It's fine. We just need to find Malcolm and hope he's all right." Mia needed to let Baldwin know about the call she'd gotten yesterday. She hadn't recognized the voice, but maybe Baldwin could track the phone number. She went to stand, then saw a piece of paper in the firepit. The pit had been used recently, but this page was stuck on the side, out of view unless you were sitting down. She pulled it out. The edges were scorched, but the words were still clear. It was a list of women's names. Mia recognized a few of them, including Hetty Medford, Theresa Holly, May Hornbuckle, and, near the bottom, her grandmother, Mary Alice Carpenter.

CHAPTER 20

Baldwin met her at the edge of the police tape at Malcolm's house. Mia had made a stop before she'd gone to the crime scene. She'd gotten two quarts of the soup and made a copy of the list. That copy was in her tote in a plastic sleeve, as was this one. She wanted an excuse besides copying the list to run to her house. And bringing Sarah more soup would hopefully cover up her deception.

"Thanks for bringing this by. I was going to stop by Friday and get more. Sarah's going to the doctor today and I hope they find something. I'm getting worried." He took the soup and handed it to a deputy. "Would you run this over to Sarah and tell her I won't be home for lunch?"

"Yes, Chief." The young officer carefully took the bag from his boss and ran toward a cruiser sitting on the edge of the crowded street parking.

Baldwin turned back to her. "Now, what did you find?"

Mia told him the story of meeting Abigail and Malcolm at the Holly ranch this morning. Then she lied. "The magical society has a ritual they do on all houses where a member has passed on. It's very sweet, and Abigail thought I should see one. They're trying to get me to join the group, but I'm so busy. But Abigail is Trent's mom, so I didn't want to argue with her."

He nodded. "Sarah's mother can be a bit of a control freak too. She's all about how I should join the Elks to meet people who can introduce me to people who can build up my career. What's wrong with being a police chief? I know it's a small town, but we're happy here."

"I think it's a great job for you," Mia said, supporting him.

He groaned. "Sorry for dropping that on you. Anyway, you were waiting for Abigail and Malcolm to show up and you found this. A list of women in Magic Springs?"

"Yes. Well, two of them, at least, are dead. And Grans's on the list. What do you think it means?" Mia pointed out the three names she recognized on the list.

"Maybe it's the women's group for this sorority Abigail wants you to join. Or maybe the older women's group, no offense to Mary Alice. Aren't most of these women elderly?" He scanned the list.

"I don't know. But Hetty was only fifty-five, right? We verified that. So she and Grans shouldn't be in the same women's group if they divide it up by age." Mia was trying to feed him the conclusion she'd already come to. That this was a hit list. For some reason she didn't understand. Yet.

"I'll look into this. And thanks for the soup." He

turned away and headed back into the middle of the chaos.

Abigail came over from where she'd been standing on the other side of the crime scene. "Baldwin said I can go, but my car is blocked. Do you want to give me a ride?"

"Sure, come over to the house. I'll text him that you're there and ask him to let us know when your car is clear and you can come back to get it." Mia pointed to her work van. "I'm over there."

Neither of them said anything else until they got in the van and were driving away. Then Mia spoke first. "I got a threat last night after we took down the Medford spell. He said to stay out of his spells."

"Did you tell Baldwin?" Abigail asked.

"No. I couldn't think of a way to say what he said without messing with Mark's vision of reality. Or sounding so crazy that he threw me into a jail cell until he could get my sanity tested." Mia sighed as she turned off the private road and back onto the highway. "So I told him a version of the truth. That you were pressuring me to join the 'society' and we were supposed to be doing a ritual to cleanse the house."

"Wow, so I look like the heavy-handed mother-in-law to be." Abigail smiled.

"Yep, that's what came to me." Mia shot her a look. "Of course I didn't mean it."

Abigail waved her hand. "No worries. Besides, sometimes you have to lie, especially to nonmagical folk. They just don't get it. Do you think Malcolm was kidnapped to keep him from taking off the spell?"

"That's the only reason I know he'd be kidnapped. Tell me about the house. Was it destroyed like someone was looking for something?"

Abigail nodded. "Totally trashed. Do you think he was looking for the list?"

"Maybe that's what he thought we were using to find these spells of his." Abigail added, "Too bad you gave it to Baldwin before letting me look at it. Maybe there's some similarity with the names on the list."

Mia reached over to her tote and handed a copy of the list to Abigail. "Home copy machines are amazing."

Abigail took the list and scanned it. "You think ahead."

"I just want this to be over before whoever's killing these women reaches my grandmother's name." Mia pulled into the school's parking lot. "Let's go figure out who everyone is and why they're on this list."

"Don't you have any Mia's Morsels business to get done?" Abigail got out of the van and shut the door.

"It's called multitasking." Mia pulled out the sheet she'd made for the wedding cake for Abigail's use. "I was planning on giving you this at the Holly house. And I need to call Hailey to tell her we won't need her until Monday and then to expect to work all week, including Saturday for the wedding. I'm not sure our hours are going to work for her, but I hope so. She's been amazing so far."

"I'm glad." Abigail walked next to Mia to the house. "Besides adding bits of the color to the cake, I have full artistic control?"

"Within budget and with a sketch for the couple

to approve before you start decorating. So just let me know when you have it and I'll email it to May. She's very organized, so we should get approval or comments back within twenty-four hours. She knows we're on a tight deadline here." Mia unlocked the door.

Mr. Darcy sat on the stairs and started yowling as soon as he saw her. The lobby area was filled with a ghostly fog and Christina waved from the second floor.

"What on earth is going on?" Mia called up to her.

"I'm not quite sure. I was leaving for a lunch date with Levi, but Mr. Darcy wouldn't let me past this landing. Then he ran down the stairs and has been talking to the fog ever since. I tried to call you, but my phone seems to have lost service." Christina leaned against the railing. "Is it the ghosts?"

Abigail nodded and pointed up to the apartment. "Go upstairs and use the house phone to call Levi. Tell him to get over here, with his brother. And call Mary Alice to see if Lasher is still in town. We're going to need as many hands as possible to get this under control."

"Okay. I'll be right back." Christina turned, but Mia called after her.

"No, stay inside until we come get you. They can't possess us, but you're human, so you're an easy target. We don't need to have to do an exorcism as well today." Mia glanced at Abigail, who nodded. She was feeling the same pull from the ghostly fog. "Are these ghosts from the outside? Did the wards fall?"

Abigail concentrated for a minute, then shook

her head. "No, I think these are ones that were stuck inside. I guess there was more than just the two in the library. These were dormant until Lasher started working on the wards. He woke them."

"Awesome." Mia turned to Abigail. "Teach me what to do."

They didn't get the house ghosts under control until close to six that night. Trent and Levi moved the last of them into a second-floor classroom Abigail had turned into a storage closet, so to speak. They came down to the living room and collapsed on the couch. Levi closed his eyes. "Someone should tell Christina it's safe."

"I already called her," Abigail said from her place at a table. "She's bringing down cookies she's been baking all afternoon. She's going to fit right into this family. She cooks when she's anxious."

Mia laughed and held up a hand. "That's my bad. She's been around me too long."

"Either way, it's not a bad stress reliever." Mary Alice turned to Al Lasher. "I thought you said the wards were strong."

"That's the problem," Lasher said. "The wards are a lot stronger than they've been. These ghosts floated between the inside and outside. Then they got stuck inside after today's warding and didn't know what to do. I told you this wasn't an exact science."

"I told May we could have the wedding here. Having an out-of-bounds room filled with ghosts seems like a security issue for the wedding." Mia stretched her neck and shoulders. This had been a crazy week. "If I can even get the supplies ordered. The wedding is next weekend. And she's already invited guests."

"You'll be fine," Abigail assured her. "I've worked on weddings with a much tighter deadline. As long as the ghosts are dealt with."

Lasher nodded. "I get it. I need to get these guys on their way to the next road before the wedding rehearsal next Friday. I guess I'm just going to have to stay in town this week until it's done."

Mary Alice turned away, not meeting his gaze. Then she said, "Sounds like you need a hotel room."

By Friday, Mia was starting to believe Abigail's claim that she really could pull off a wedding next week. She looked at her clipboard. She had made a list of must-dos for each day running up to the day of the ceremony. She was caught up and actually on Friday's list after a few items were finished from yesterday's list this morning.

She closed her eyes for a minute, making sure she wasn't missing anything, and realized she hadn't heard from either Mahogany or Mark Baldwin for a couple of days. She texted Mark to see how Sarah was doing. She'd call him later to see if he had gotten any more information on Hetty's death. Those types of calls were tricky because he didn't really want to share information with her at all.

Then she called Mahogany.

A chipper, "Good morning, Mia," greeted her call.

"Hi. Sounds like you're doing well." Mia put the phone on Speaker and flipped through the notes she'd taken about Hetty's new boyfriend.

"The house is wonderful. So much lighter. I feel like I can breathe in there. I don't know what you did to get the spell off, but it worked." Mahogany paused for a second, and Mia realized she was at the tea shop. "What have you found out about Mom's death? The coroner called and asked me to sign some papers as they were going to reopen the autopsy. He said it would only be reviewing the results."

"I did have a question for you. Do you know if your mom talked to the coven about her estate plan?" Mia was certain Hetty's death had something to do with Ginny Willis. And, as she was thinking about the woman, realized she still hadn't received the last payment for the Holly funeral. She made a note on her calendar to call the office again on Monday.

"I know she was talking to someone. She called me in Portland and asked about some of the house furnishings. There are pieces there that came down from several generations. I guess she wanted to make sure I wasn't going to just sell off the house and furnishings without realizing what was there. As far as family history, I mean."

Mia had Hetty's planner on the desk. She pulled it closer. "Do you remember what month she called? Maybe there's something in the planner."

Mahogany laughed. "You realize I can't remember where I left my keys one day to the next, right? But I'll try. I was still working at the Portland shop. And it was good weather, rainy but warm. I stepped outside to take the call, so I'm pretty sure it was spring? Portland doesn't get warm until May or June. April we have some pretty days, but around that time? I'm not much help, am I?"

"It wasn't snowing, so it cuts off some of the months I need to look through." Mia smiled, even though Mahogany couldn't see her. "I'll look through her planner. Thanks for this."

"No, you deserve the thanks. I'm moving back into the house this weekend. And the first thing I'm going to do is bake a frittata for breakfast. I'm missing cooking, and the kitchen staff here isn't happy with me trying to use their toys."

"Enjoy the house. And let me know if you find anything. We still need to find your mother's killer." Mia decided not to tell Mahogany about the threatening phone call. Especially since the spell had been lifted from the house. He'd probably be watching the Holly house now because they weren't able to get that spell off.

And, she reminded herself, Malcolm McBride was still missing. She needed to see if he'd just taken off because he didn't want to take off the spell, or if he was taken because he could. If there were others who could clear the spell, taking Malcolm didn't make sense unless there was some other reason he was kidnapped.

Her phone beeped, and she saw that James was trying to call. He probably wanted an answer about the job. Was she even applying? She hadn't made up her mind yet. She looked at the list of things she was supposed to do today and wondered what it might be like to assign some of this work to someone else. She'd had an assistant when she'd worked at the Owyhee Plaza, but she'd done most of the planning and scheduling herself. This time, if she took the job, she'd hand over as much as possible, so she'd still have time to help Abigail with Mia's Morsels. Especially because Thomas was going to kill her for dragging Abigail into working more hours.

She let the call go to voice mail and tuned back into Mahogany's story about the rabbits in the backyard of the house. That she hadn't seen them since she was a kid. She broke into the story. "Wait, so when you came back for the funeral, when the spell was on the house, the rabbits weren't in the backyard?"

"No." Mahogany paused. "You think it was because of the spell?"

Mia didn't know what to think, but she was reasonably sure it was important. She thanked Mahogany for her time, then listened to James's message.

She wrote herself a note on the calendar to make a decision by next Friday, which would give her the weekend before the application was due on that following Monday. She still needed to review finances without the catering part of the job to see if it was even doable without her taking the position.

Her phone rang again. James just wasn't giving up. She sighed and picked it up. "Hello."

"Well, you sound depressed. What's going on? I can tell you, it's not as bad as what's happening in my mirror." Grans was on the line, not James.

"Sorry. I thought you were someone else." She leaned back in her chair. "What's going on that has you depressed?"

"I look like your mother."

It took a minute for Mia to realize what her grandmother was saying. "Oh, good, the spell's wearing off?"

"Not so good when you have a man in town who's used to seeing you a certain way." She sniffed. "Anyway, it wouldn't have lasted. Al's too tied up in his work to be fun. How are your ghosts today?"

"I haven't even been up there to check. I'm working on the wedding planning." Mia glanced at the ceiling, like it could tell her what the confined ghosts were doing.

"You should check the wards at least every couple of hours. You don't want angry ghosts floating around your business," Grans suggested.

Mia swore under her breath. "No one told me that. I don't want any ghosts floating around here. What time did Lasher say he was coming over?"

"I'm supposed to pick him up at the Lodge after noon. He's doing some research this morning on the school and talking to the others who helped put up the wards years ago."

Mia nodded like her grandmother could see her. Who knows, with Grans's powers, she might be able to. "Like Brody McMann. He was one of the original spell casters. I saw him in the picture."

"Yes, that's the problem with photography; it tends to show when someone isn't aging normally. It used to be weres would just move and begin a new life when they should have been showing some signs of age. Now, they're on social media, so it's harder to start all over."

"Wait, I thought Lasher was a witch, not a were." Mia stared at the doorway like she expected someone to burst into her office and attack anytime.

"Al is a hybrid. He has were blood in his family, but his skills are more on the witch side. It was hard back when he was growing up. If you were a hybrid like Al back in the day, you had to pick what you were and then ignore the other part. So he's a witch in all intentions. But he doesn't age due to his genealogy."

"Oh," Mia wasn't sure what else to say. It didn't matter to her if Lasher was werewolf, witch, or human. She just wanted him to fix her wards, and the side effects fixing her wards had caused. Magic always came with a price, even when it was to do good.

Chapter 21

Mia had all the wedding planning done she could do. Abigail had sent her a cake design and she'd sent it over to May. Not expecting a quick answer, she decided to look at her financials for the last year. Grans and Lasher were due at the house in an hour and she didn't want anyone seeing her reviewing the books.

Trent came in with a tray about noon. The smell of tomato soup and grilled cheese made her stomach growl. She moved papers off her desk and motioned for him to set down the tray in the middle. "What are you doing here?"

"I figured I could help with finding Malcolm. I don't think modern human methodology is going to work in this case." He moved to the fridge and pulled out two sodas. "Christina said you hadn't been upstairs to eat and from the lack of dishes, she thought you probably didn't eat any breakfast."

"She's beginning to see and decipher details of my life. She was right, I haven't eaten. I was working on the business numbers. I need to see what areas of the business are bringing in the money." She picked up a half wedge of the sandwich and took a bite. "I love it when she fuses the cheese. I would have just done cheddar, but is this a provolone and cheddar mix?"

"I think that's what she said. I wasn't really listening. Especially when she started talking about food. That girl can talk about ingredients like she was reading out of a novel." He picked up one of the piles and looked at it. "Trying to figure out where the money for your business is coming from? I can tell you right now, it's catering."

"I was afraid you were going to say that. But even I have to admit, it's not even close." She set down the sandwich, her appetite gone. "And looking at the venues? It's probably over seventy-five percent being held at the Lodge. If they bring in an on-site catering director, I'm going to go under in less than a year. I can't survive without the catering."

"But if you take the job, you won't have time to build up new venues and client referrals." He picked up his soup bowl. "Eat; Christina is worried. She cooked."

Mia laughed and tried to finish her food. Now that she knew the facts, she was going to have to bite the bullet and take the Lodge job. "Well, I have a solution for this problem. I'll take the Lodge job, and your mom and Christina will run Mia's Morsels. Mostly your mom until Christina gets out of college. By then, either she can take it over or I'll have enough saved from this job to come back."

"That's not what you want to do," he reminded her.

She looked around the office. "Sometimes you have to make sacrifices to save the ones you love."

He blinked at that analogy, but he let it go. "Maybe the Lodge will get a new manager and he won't want a catering director."

"One can only hope. And pray. And maybe send anonymous letters to corporate, telling them how much work the current hotel manager was taking from the local economy." She tapped her computer screen. "I have my first one already drafted."

"So you're going to sabotage your own job?" Trent whistled. "That's cold."

"I don't want to ruin the guy. I just want my life back."

"You know that never happens. Anyway, let's get off this topic. So, the wards feel good. I stopped in to visit your ghost guest room and they seem to be holding steady." He returned to focusing on his sandwich. "When is Lasher coming back?"

"Around two. Grans's bringing him." Mia went on to tell him about Grans's spell wearing off. "At least I don't have to look at myself all the time when she's around. That was a little freaky. And Mom would have had a cow, so let's just hope the rest wears off before she comes to visit."

"You've got a lot on your plate." He nodded to the sandwich. "And I mean more than just what you still need to eat."

She laughed. That was one of the reasons she

loved hanging out with Trent. He got her, and he could make her laugh even when she was in the dumps. "Well, this problem I can take care of right now. Thanks again for bringing down lunch."

"No problem. I like having lunch with you. It's like sneaking off to have a date."

"You always do like being the bad boy," Mia teased.

He shook his head. "Maybe before, but not now. Now, I let that role fall to my baby brother. Levi's good at playing the bad boy. Or he was until Christina came to town."

"The Major boys, all domesticated and grown-up. I'd say my work is done, but I think you girls ran the last leg of the race." Abigail stood in the doorway. "Sorry I disturbed your lunch, but I was coming in to talk to you about the cake and some-one had dropped this envelope on your doorstep."

Mia stood and took the envelope. "It's probably the last payment for the Holly wake. The woman I talked to at Ginny Willis's office said she was going to drop it off. I bet I didn't hear her arrive."

"I would have thought the security monitor would have seen her car." Trent looked over at the television that was tied to the security system. "Is that off?"

Mia swore and reached over to grab the remote. She turned it back on. "Yes. I turned it off last night when I was working on the wedding. There was a hawk that kept flying by the camera and set-ting off the alarm. I forgot to turn it back on."

"The security company still has the recording, just in case something happened that you didn't see." Trent finished his soup and stacked his dishes on the tray. Mia was done as well, and she put her dishes on the tray.

"I'll take this upstairs so the two of you can talk. I've got to get back to the store, but it's afternoons like this that make me happy to be a small business, where I can cut out when I want to during the day." He nodded to Mia and kissed his mom on the cheek. "I'll pop in before I leave to say goodbye. You don't have an event this weekend, so what do you think about dinner out either tonight or tomorrow? We could drive into Twin for something special."

"I don't really want to be that far away, just in case." Mia watched as Trent stood and his mother switched places with him. "There's just a lot going on."

"No trouble. So, dinner in town. I'll set up reservations at the Lodge." He paused in the doorway. "If they're too busy tonight, I'll sign us up for a seating on the first available day. Then I'll call you."

"Sounds good. Thanks, Trent."

Abigail glanced at the piles and picked up an invoice. "You're checking financials. I told Thomas I was going to do this for you if you asked."

"I bet that made him love me even more." Mia opened the envelope. She could run by the bank when Grans showed up with Lasher and deposit the check. She examined the amount, then realized the paper with the check wasn't blank. She opened the folded paper and gasped. It was a list of women. It appeared to be the same list as they'd found before, but this one had the title, *Single women with no family and at least half a million in as-sets.* And it wasn't half torched. She scanned the names: Hetty, Theresa, her grandmother, and one more she knew on the burned sheet, May Horn-buckle.

"What's wrong?" Abigail reached out her hand and took the paper. She handed it back with a frown. "So, Ginny was targeting coven members who didn't have families for her fundraising efforts. That's not unusual."

"Is that what this list is? A list of possibilities for fundraising? Or is it a hit list, one where the estate funds would go to the coven? The unusual part is the spell on Theresa's and Hetty's places." Mia tapped on the paper. "And someone else thinks this is unusual too. The woman who works at Ginny's office. She must have put this into the envelope with my check because she wanted me to see it."

"Or she put the page on a pile of paper and didn't realize it had something on the back." Abigail shook her head. "You don't have anything to prove that Ginny's a killer. And that spell was made by a man. We both felt that."

"Okay, maybe Ginny isn't doing the deed, but she's selling the women's information to someone else. Like the guy who called and harassed me after we took down the spell at Hetty's." Mia picked up her phone. When someone on the other end answered, she said, "This is Mia Malone. I'm trying to identify who just dropped off a packet for me, but I had my monitor shut off. Can you send me a copy of the last two hours to my email?"

She listened to the security technician asking

for more information as well as verify her identity. Then she said, "Thank you," and hung up. "The file will be in my email this afternoon. Then we can go talk to this person and see what she meant by sending it."

"I really don't think Ginny is a murderer. A little crass, self-absorbed, and unfeeling, but not a killer." Abigail nodded to the piles on Mia's desk. "So, did you make a decision on the catering director job yet?"

They talked about the pros and cons and what Abigail would be expected to do, including telling her to step back if she got too controlling. Mia started putting away the files. "I know it's my business, but if this is going to work, I need to trust you to run it while I save money from the job at the Lodge. Once I hit a certain, preset number, I'll quit, and you can go back to being the cake lady."

"I like the title 'pastry chef' better." Abigail stood with her tote in hand. "Are you sure you want to take this job? You could probably scale back and fight your way through the next couple of growth years."

"I just hired Hailey. And you. And scaling back might even mean cutting Christina's hours. People are counting on me and Mia's Morsels." Mia put another file away in her desk. "It's not a perfect solution, but it's not horrible either. I just need to make sure you know to tell me when I'm overstepping and trying to do too much."

"I think that will be a daily task." Abigail pulled her into a hug. "We'll get through this. I promise."

As Abigail left the office, Mia wondered if even her assurances were going to keep Mia's Morsels going without the catering at the Lodge.

Gloria's voice echoed in her head. *Tomorrow's worry is for tomorrow. Today has its own concerns.*

She took a deep breath, sent her worries up to the Goddess, and cleared her desk of anything except what dealt with the wedding. She had a business to run today. And who knew if Lasher was going to kick her out of her office when he and Grans arrived.

Hanging up the phone after making the floral order, she saw Baldwin's truck pull into the drive. There was no way he needed more soup, not after her second delivery this week. She tucked the floral notes into the file and highlighted the "order tables and linen" to-do on the list before closing the file to go meet Baldwin.

He looked up at her with a grin when she opened the front door. "Good day, Mia."

"What's got you all chipper? Oh, I know, Sarah's feeling better. I'm so glad." Mia leaned in the doorway as they spoke. "Do you want to come in for some coffee?"

"Actually, no, I'm on my way back to work. And no, Sarah's still feeling horrible. At least just in the mornings now. I wanted to tell you the coroner has a cause of death for Ms. Medford." He took off his baseball cap and rubbed his head. "I'm reopening the case today."

"That's good, but what's wrong with Sarah? Did she go to the doctor? I'm worried about her." Mia felt confused. Baldwin was so happy about just reopening the case.

He grinned again. Speaking slowly, he repeated, "Sarah went to the doctor this morning. And she's only feeling bad in the mornings."

Mia knew there was a message in there somewhere; then she got it. "Sarah's pregnant again? That's why she couldn't keep anything down?"

"Doc said it was the worst case of morning sickness he's seen in a while. He gave her some pills, but knowing Sarah, she's probably just going to be making do. Keep making that soup. It's the only thing she can eat right now." He took a breath. "The last time she wasn't sick at all. Maybe this is a good sign."

"Oh, my goodness. I'm so excited for you and Sarah." Mia hadn't even thought about the chance Sarah could be pregnant. "Let me know if you want to do a gender reveal party, or even just a baby shower. You'll get a friends and family discount."

He grinned and put on his hat. "We're a long way from where we began. I'm even beginning to like Ms. Adams since she's kept her nose clean here in town and stopped looking like she was trying out for a horror movie in her all-black garb."

"Be careful, you may just have a daughter who decides Goth is the bomb," Mia teased.

He put a hand over his heart. "I can just hear Sarah now. I'm not sure I'm going to live through the teenage years."

"You'll be fine. Besides, you've got a lot of time to practice." She giggled. "I'm so glad Sarah's okay and that there's a baby coming. You've made my day. Grans will be excited too."

"I need to get back to the station. I'm behind now that I've reopened the case and took this morning off to drive Sarah to the appointment. Thanks for being so kind, Mia." He sniffed. "We appreciate you and your grandmother."

After Baldwin left, Mia saw her grandmother's car coming down the road. She looked at her watch. The day had gotten away from her. She'd go back and get the file from her office and take it upstairs to work while Lasher was doing his spell work on the wards. She needed him to release the ghosts in the second-floor classroom as well. She didn't need any non-witches checking out the place during the wedding reception and being scared and hurting themselves running down the stairs.

She had an off-limits chain she had installed on the stairwell she could put up, but some people saw a limitation as a challenge. The school already had a lot of rumors going on around it. She didn't need it becoming the "haunted" event site. That might just kill Mia's Morsels even with her current plan of taking a second job.

Mia waited in the foyer for Grans and Lasher. Grans had aged in the last few days. The spell must be wearing off. One part of her felt bad for her grandmother; being young again would have its advantages, but then again, life happened to us all. Well, all of us except the werewolves and whatever hybrid status Lasher had. Mia embraced her wrinkles and scars. They gave her character and she'd never been one to worry about her appearance. In fact, the last time she'd put on the full makeup look was the night Trent had taken her to dinner.

Grans came and gave her a short embrace. "I'm so happy for Mark and Sarah. A baby in the Baldwin house. That will be such a blessing."

"How did you know?" Mia frowned as Grans and Lasher came into the school and shut the door.

Grans looked over at Lasher, who laughed. He nodded to the stairs. "I'm heading upstairs before this conversation starts. I told you to stay out of her thoughts, Mary Alice."

Mia turned to her grandmother. "You've been reading my mind?"

"Only when you get excited or have a strong emotion. How else can I protect you?" She walked toward the kitchen. "Do you have any food? I'm starving. I was working on some spells and didn't get lunch."

Mia took a deep breath, a practice she'd been doing a lot with her grandmother recently. Then she followed her into the kitchen. "Actually, I haven't eaten yet either. Let's grab something out of the freezer. How do you feel about vegetarian lasagna?"

They were eating in the living room when a car pulled into the driveway. Mia went to the door and Hailey came inside. "Hey, I have your check for last week in my office. Come on in." She pointed to her grandmother and made introductions. "I'll be right back. Do you want something to eat? I can heat up another lunch."

"I only have a few minutes," Hailey said as she slowly walked into the living room. She nodded toward Grans. "Hello."

"I'll just be a second, then." Mia hurried to the office and grabbed Hailey's envelope. She had already paid Christina and Abigail through direct deposit. She hurried back to the living room and handed Hailey the check. "Next week, bring in a voided check from your account and we'll get you set up on direct deposit. That way you don't have to stop in if we're not doing a weekend event. I emailed you the schedule for next week, but basically, plan on working all week if you can. With the wedding coming up, we're going to be swamped."

Hailey took the envelope and nodded. "I'll make arrangements. I'll see you Monday at nine, right?"

"That will be perfect. Thanks for such great work this week," Mia called after her as Hailey had already turned and headed to the door.

After she'd gone, Grans stared after her for a long minute.

Mia went back in the kitchen and grabbed some sodas. When she came back, she nodded to the doorway where Hailey had left. "I really like her. She's a good addition to the team."

"Oh, really?" Grans picked up a fork and took a bite, then set down her fork again.

"Okay, what's wrong? You're quiet and recently, that's not like you at all." Mia opened her soda and took a drink. "You don't like Hailey?"

Grans followed her actions. "I don't not like her. I have this feeling that we've met before. I can't quite place it."

"She's new to the area. I'm not sure when you would have met. Besides, she didn't seem to recognize you." Mia took a bite of the lasagna. It was perfect. She always worried about the quality of the meal after it froze. You never knew what could happen when you heated it.

Grans set down her fork. "You realize I look different than I did a couple of weeks ago."

"True." Mia paused. "You think you've seen her before, then? I could have sworn she said she'd just moved here."

"Maybe she looks like someone I know." Grans

picked up her fork again. "But there's something there. I can't remember what, though. It will come to me."

"The ghosts have all been released and sent on to their next stop," Lasher announced as he came down the stairs. He sniffed the air. "Hey, that smells amazing. Do you have more?"

CHAPTER 22

The doorbell rang at the kitchen door at about nine the next night. Mia was alone in the apartment. Christina and Levi were on a date. Trent had just left. Mia glanced at the security monitor, but the back camera didn't show the door; it looked like it had been adjusted to just show the parking lot. She'd have to fix it tomorrow. It was always being moved; by the wind or the spirits outside, she didn't know.

Mr. Darcy followed her downstairs. She smiled at him as they went down, "Are you my bodyguard?"

The cat stopped on the second-floor landing, looked toward the room that had held the ghosts from Lasher's ward work, and then looked back at her. The meow that came out of his mouth seemed to be as close to a "duh" as she'd ever heard one. Especially from a cat.

"Okay, then, I've got my phone on me, so if something happens, dial 9–1–1. Baldwin shouldn't think it weird that my cat knows how to use a cell. Or maybe you could just reach out to Grans if you still have a connection there." As Mia got closer to the kitchen, she wondered if going to answer the door was a good idea or not.

The knocking got louder as she unlocked the door from the kitchen to the rest of the house. She flipped on the lights and saw a man standing outside her back door. He was looking over his shoulder. Then he turned, and Mia realized it was Malcolm McBride standing there. She hurried over and unlocked the door.

"Thank goodness. I was beginning to wonder if you were home." He hurried into the kitchen, turning to lock the door behind him.

"Where have you been? You're considered a missing person. The police are looking for you."

He scratched his head. "The police? Why?"

"Abigail went to pick you up on Wednesday and you weren't there. It looked like there had been a struggle." Mia nodded to the coffeepot. "Do you want some coffee or cocoa?"

"Coffee would be great. I'm not sleeping anyway, so bring on more caffeine." He sat down at one of the tables. "I left my house because I got a threatening message about releasing the spell on the Holly house. I'm not sure how the guy knew we were going there, but he did. And he wasn't happy. I went out to my lake house for a few days. Then I felt like I was being watched there. So I decided to come here."

"I got an angry message about the spell as well. But no one's been hanging around here. I hate to tell you that it looks like someone trashed your place after you left." Mia poured water into the coffeepot

He shrugged. "I'm not very neat. And the night before, I'd been looking for something in the old board meetings. It could have been me who made the mess."

"Well, I'm glad nothing happened to you. I thought you'd been kidnapped or something worse." Mia wondered why Baldwin hadn't checked Malcolm's lake house, or maybe he had and hadn't told her. He had been a little distracted. "Maybe you saw the police at your lake house, looking for you."

"Impossible. It's in a shell corporation name to avoid taxes." He took one of the cookies Mia had set out on the table after starting the coffee. "I love peanut butter cookies. A lot of people shy away from peanut butter due to so many people having allergies. I'm not sure if it's the peanut butter or all the toxins in the world today. Fifty years ago, you didn't have all the air pollution or pesticides. I guess they were using them, but not the way they are today. I went to a store the other day and nothing was fresh. Frozen, canned, or prepackaged. That why people are getting sick, at least in my opinion. No one does fresh anymore."

Mia appreciated the diatribe on the state of the food delivery industry, but she tried to refocus Malcolm. She poured him a cup of coffee. "Cream or sugar?"

"Sugar, please." He picked up a spoon and waited for Mia to give him the sugar container she kept on the counter. "Thank you for opening the door. You wouldn't have an extra bedroom for me to hide out in for a few days, would you?"

Mia paused just long enough for him to look up from stirring the sugar into the coffee.

"You did talk me into removing those spells, so in a way, it's your fault this guy is after me." He sipped his coffee, confident in his argument.

"Of course." Mia would call Trent over as soon as she could. "So, did you recognize the caller?"

Malcolm frowned, "You mean the guy who threatened me?"

"Yes, that guy. You said that to set this level of spell, the caster would have had to have been on the board at one time or another. Maybe you know him." Mia poured herself a cup. She'd call Abigail too.

"You're right, I should have recognized his voice. And now, thinking back, it was familiar, but not too familiar. If you know what I mean."

Mia had no clue, but keeping him talking was probably best. And at least the man was alive. "Okay, let's go back to the board meeting notes. What were you looking for?"

"When I released the spell on the Medford house, I got an impression of the caster. And a name."

"His name?" Mia took a cookie.

Malcolm shook his head. "No, not the caster of the spell I released. Another name. Richards. It's not anyone I know, but I thought maybe there was a witch with the coven by that name. It can be a first or last name, which makes it harder."

"You said 'the spell I released.' That's odd phrasing." Mia set down her cookie.

Malcolm leaned forward. "I can't be sure so I didn't say anything earlier, but I think there were two spells. The one I released—it couldn't have been more than three to six months old. I think that's why it wasn't as hard to release."

Mia thought the man had looked like heck when he'd finished. She'd hate to see him when the spell was hard to release.

Malcolm yawned. "I'm sorry, I need to sleep. Can you show me to the bedroom I'll be using? I have a feeling I'll be home in a few days, but I appreciate your hospitality."

Mia left the lights on in the kitchen and they went upstairs to the apartment. She put him in the spare bedroom and told him she needed to go back downstairs and she'd be there if he needed her.

Mr. Darcy jumped on the couch as she went to go downstairs.

"You'll watch him?"

The cat nodded, then lay down on the couch, his face toward the bedroom hallway and his ears up, listening.

"Thank you," Mia said as she stepped out of the apartment. She called Trent first. "Hey, any chance you can pack an overnight bag and come spend the night?"

He paused, and for a minute, Mia thought she might have gotten the wrong number. "Trent?"

"Sorry. I was just processing what you said versus our evening. I would have stayed if you'd asked." He dropped his tone into this sexy growl.

"Slow down, big guy." Mia laughed at his misunderstanding. "I have another man in my apartment and I'd feel better if I wasn't alone. I'm not sure if Christina is coming home or staying the night with Levi."

"And who's the other man in your apartment?"

Trent asked. Mia could hear doors opening and closing and assumed he was getting an overnight bag ready.

"Malcolm McBride."

"The missing person, Malcolm McBride?" Mia heard Trent start up his truck.

"Yeah. He showed up just after you left. He's been hiding from the guy with the threats." Mia tried to remember if she'd told Trent about her call. "Anyway, I'll explain more when you get here. I'll leave the front door unlocked. I need to call your mother."

"My mother . . ."

Mia heard the question, but she'd already started to hang up. She'd explain that too when he got there. For now, she needed to finish making calls. She dialed Abigail's cell.

When Abigail answered, she asked, "What's wrong? Are you safe? Is it your grandmother? Trent?"

"Everyone's fine. Can you come over for a few minutes? I need to tell you something that's probably better in person." Mia tried to sound calm, hoping Abigail wouldn't freak out.

"You're sure you're okay?" Abigail asked again.

"I'm fine, and Trent's on his way over too. We just need to talk about the Medford place." Mia added some information to calm Abigail's emotions.

"At nine at night?" Abigail sighed, "Okay, I'll be there in a few minutes, but be warned, Thomas is probably coming with me. He's feeling a little overprotective right now."

Mia hung up and went into her office. She grabbed a notebook and a few pens, then went back into the kitchen to wait. While she did, she wrote

down everything she could remember from what
Malcolm had said. And the questions that his
words had caused. Especially when he said he
thought there was a second spell. What had the
caller said about his spell? He'd called it a warning; no, not a warning, a trick. An ambush; no,
he'd called it a trap. The spell had been a trap.
And if it had been the second spell, like Malcolm
thought, it wasn't the caller who'd killed Hetty. He
was trying to find out who had killed her too.

She sipped her coffee. Maybe she was tired, but
she felt like she was going in circles. She needed
Abigail and Trent to help her think this out.

Abigail had been right, Thomas also showed
up, and for the next two hours, the four of them
tried to figure out who had put the trap spell on
the Medford house and why. And why he thought
the original caster would come back to try to remove it.

Trent held up the empty coffeepot. "Should I
make another?"

Mia shook her head. "I think we're done for the
night. Unless one of you guys think we're on to
something?"

"I remember something about a Richards a few
years back. Maybe it was someone on the board?"
Thomas picked up the last cookie and offered it to
the other three. Everyone shook their head, so he
took a bite. "Nothing bad. Not like they were ban-
ished or anything, but the weird part is, the memory is fuzzy. Like what I feel when I think about
Hetty Medford. Even after knowing she wasn't in
her early nineties now, she's a bit fuzzy, and I think
about her as older."

"Okay, newbie here. Could someone have put

this type of spell on the Richards person? A forgetting spell?" Mia took her coffee cup and put it in the dishwasher. She wouldn't run dishes for several days, but at least the kitchen would look clean. Impressions counted, even if they were false images. Like dirty cups hidden away. Or people who weren't who they showed themselves to be. "I'm beat. I've got to get some sleep. Trent, you're in Grans's room."

"I could sleep on the couch," he offered.

"Your feet would hang over and Mr. Darcy would be annoyed because that's where he likes to sleep if Christina's not home." Mia turned to Thomas and Abigail. "Thanks for coming over. I know we could have done this tomorrow, but I just had too much in my head to sleep."

"Not a problem, dear." Abigail gave Mia a big hug. "And anytime you need us, we'll be here."

When Mia and Trent went inside the apartment, Mr. Darcy was still on the couch and on guard. When he saw them, he meowed and jumped off, heading off into the kitchen. Mia locked the door. "I'm going to make sure Christina isn't coming home, then I'm going to crash."

"I'll check on your guest first, then I'm following. We've got deliveries at the store tomorrow. I'm going in to help unload because summer folk are starting to arrive." He kissed her on the cheek. "Sleep well and lock your door. If you need me, text me. I'll have my phone next to the bed."

"I don't think he's dangerous." Mia texted Christina as they talked. She stood in the living room and waited for an answer. When it came, she threw the dead bolt. "They're in the middle of some game, so she's going to crash over there."

"Knowing my brother, it's probably a fantasy role-playing game. You know, like Dungeons and Dragons? He's always trying to get me to play, but I can't see being in a game for hours on end." He walked with her to the bedroom door. "I'll see you in the morning."

Mr. Darcy ran into her bedroom just before she shut the door. She smiled as he jumped up on the bed and made a sleeping spot near the end. "I take it you're my bodyguard still?"

The cat blinked at her and then lay down to sleep. She turned off the lights and joined him.

The next morning, Mia was in the kitchen cooking breakfast when Levi dropped off Christina. She had her own key, so Mia didn't go down to the front door to let her in, but she did undo the dead bolt and leave the apartment door open. Last night had been unremarkable, at least after she'd fallen asleep. She'd tossed and turned and written down every idea that came to her until she'd fallen asleep. Looking at the notebook now, it looked more like a list of people than any tangible idea. She ran her finger down the page, pausing on Hailey's name and then Jerimiah. Ginny was on the list, of course; she'd been on Mia's mind for months now. And now the new name Malcolm had given her, Richards.

She needed to call Baldwin to tell him that Malcolm wasn't lost. That he was in her spare bedroom and they could end the manhunt. But she'd wait until he was awake to make the call. That way, he could talk to Baldwin and explain his actions.

Christina came in the kitchen and poured a cup

of coffee. "I'm going to grab a shower and change clothes; then I'll be out for some of that coffee cake. It smells amazing."

"Thanks. I tried a new recipe. Oh, and we have a guest. Malcolm McBride is here. I'm not sure for how long, but I didn't want him to scare you."

Christina blinked. "Wow, I'm gone one night and when I come back, we have another room-mate?"

"I'm hoping he's going to be more of a short-term guest. Oh, and Trent's here too. He's in Grans's room." Mia looked up at the beeping monitor. "And now Grans is here. It's a busy morning."

"I hope there's still coffee," Trent said from behind Christina. "Good morning, I take it my brother didn't bore you to death with that game."

"He's really into it." Christina shook her head. "I think it's going to be one of those things we agree to disagree on. I was bored out of my mind most of the time."

Trent held up his hand for a high five. "I'm right there with you."

Christina left the kitchen and Trent came inside to pour his coffee. "Was that your grandmother pulling into the parking lot?"

"Yes, and could you go open the door for her?" Mia poured milk into the powdered sugar she had sitting in a bowl. "I need to glaze this coffee cake."

"You had me at coffee cake." He set down his cup and headed out of the apartment. "Be right back."

Mia focused on the coffee cake and wondered if she needed to make a frittata to go along with the sweet. Especially since the number of people just kept rising. She took eggs and peppers out of the fridge, then grabbed an onion from the basket hanging near her window.

Mr. Darcy meowed and jumped on the window seat to watch birds outside.

The apartment door opened and Grans came inside with Trent behind her, carrying Muffy, her terrier, and an overnight bag. Mia met Trent's eyes, but he just shrugged. The story would have to be Grans's to tell. Mia stepped closer to give her a hug, then realized she had aged even more. She still looked like Mia's mother, but now she had a touch of gray in her hair and a few more wrinkles on her face. Like Mom before she hit the salon and her plastic surgeon for an injection. "I didn't expect to see you. Are you staying?"

Grans sat in one of the chairs. "Be a dear and get me some coffee. I left the house without my first cup. And, yes, if you couldn't tell from the overnight bag and Muffy, I thought it better if we stayed together. I got a call telling me I needed to watch your back because you were messing with things you didn't understand. I recognized the voice. It was Jerimiah."

CHAPTER 23

Mia set a cup of coffee in front of her grandmother. "I don't understand. Jerimiah from the Twin coven? Why would he be threatening people?"

Muffy ran to the window seat and lay next to Mr. Darcy. He licked the top of the cat's head and Mr. Darcy swatted at him.

Trent came back into the room. He had his tote in his hand and he set it on the counter behind them. "I'll change those sheets before I go to work if you tell me where I can find fresh linens."

Her grandmother set down her cup and frowned at him. "Why were you sleeping in my room?"

"I put him there because Malcolm McBride is in the other bedroom," Mia explained as her grandmother glared at Trent.

Now Grans's glare turned to Mia. "Malcolm is here? Why? I thought he'd been kidnapped."

"Well, so did I until he showed up at the kitchen

door last night. He came through the trail system so no one would see his car parked in the lot." Mia put the chopped onion and peppers into a pan and started to sweat them a bit before mixing them in with the frittata. She didn't have anything else to put inside except for cheese, so this would have to do. She'd pull out food from the freezer downstairs if she needed to feed this crew lunch. Then she'd have to do a grocery run. "Anyway, he showed up and needed a place to stay. I'll call Baldwin when he wakes up and let him know to call off the manhunt."

Grans shook her head. "You gather strays like cats. Anyway, one of your strays isn't who she says she is."

She set down the bamboo spatula she'd been stirring the vegetables with and turned to face her grandmother. "Who are you talking about?"

"Hailey Berger. Or she might be Hailey Berger now, but when I met her, she was Hailey Richards." Grans let that set for a second. "I met her at Ginny's office a few years ago, when Ginny was trying to get me to put the coven in my estate plan. I thought I recognized her the other day. But I was going through some old paperwork to shred last night. It gives me something to do when I can't sleep. And I found the workup Ginny had proposed. I'd get a life estate in the house and then, at my death, all of my assets would transfer from the trust into the coven's coffers. I told her then that I'd be willing to leave the coven a gift, but that I was going to leave most of my estate to my family."

Mia frowned as she turned back to stir the vegetables. "Why didn't she know about the family? Isn't that where most people start with wills— giving to the next generation?"

"That's the thing. I heard Ginny yelling at the girl when I left that she hadn't vetted my situation enough. I'd felt sorry for her. She was so young, and Ginny was just ripping her a new one." Grans sipped her coffee.

"Hailey Richards." Mia looked at Trent. "Your dad said she was discussed during one of the board meetings. I wonder if the board hires and fires Ginny's staff?"

"I'll give Mom a call and ask. She should know." Trent pulled out his cell phone and went into the living room.

"Of course that doesn't connect Hailey to the killings. Just puts her in Ginny's office." Mia poured the vegetables in a casserole dish to cool while she mixed the eggs. "And gives me a reason to talk to her again about her history here in Magic Springs."

"Are you talking about Hailey?" Christina came into the kitchen with a towel, still drying her hair. "So, she called you last night?"

Mia shook her head. "I didn't get a call from Hailey last night. Why?"

"She called and told me she'd been called back to Walla Walla for family stuff and she'd have to quit. I told her that you were the boss, but she said she felt more comfortable talking to me. Anyway, I repeated that she needed to call you too because you handled all the employment stuff. She said she understood and that she'd enjoyed working with us." Christina leaned against the counter, watching everyone. "But you didn't know that."

"No. We just found out that Hailey had worked for Ginny Willis at the coven foundation." Mia sprinkled the cheese over the now-cooled veggies and poured the egg mixture over the top. She tucked the dish into the oven and set a timer. "We need to know more about the Richards family and how they fit into the coven. Maybe Hailey's connected to the killings somehow."

Christina shook her head. "I don't see how."

"Well, we just need to look into her history. Especially now that she's disappeared." Mia could see the hurt in Christina's eyes. She'd started to see Hailey as a friend.

"Mom says Ginny has full control over her staff. It's not a board decision," Trent said as he came back into the room.

"I'll dig into the coven records, at least the ones Adele had." Grans tapped Trent on the arm. "Can you go out to my car and bring up those two boxes I have in the trunk? I had a feeling I might be needing them. Adele had every coven member and their genealogy for the last twenty years. She was working on a project. If Hailey or her family was part of our coven, we'd have the information in there."

"You may want to transfer all that to digital records," Christina said as Trent took Grans's keys to go get the boxes. "I can scan it for you if you want to leave them here. That way, we just have to do a keyword search. It takes a lot less time."

"If you want to waste your time, go ahead. I like paper. It never disappears or gets corrupted unless someone spills something on it. So, no coffee while you're searching for the Richards family." Grans nodded to the coffee cake. "Mia, cut me a slice of that so I'm not starving while we wait for your frittata."

"Sure." Mia pulled out small plates and sliced off several pieces.

"I'll take mine to go, if you don't mind." Malcolm McBride stood in the kitchen doorway. He'd showered and changed clothes.

"Malcolm, I don't think you should be hiding anymore. Why don't we call the police and let them know you're not missing? They can put an officer with you to make sure no one hurts you." Mia handed Grans her coffee cake.

"No need, my dear. I'm sure I'll be fine now. I have a feeling. Next week we'll meet at the Holly farm and get rid of that last spell. I'm sure it's a cover spell like this one was. I've already called Abigail and she says she can do it on Wednesday, if that works for you?" He tore off a paper towel and held it out for a slice of coffee cake. "I've also called Mark Baldwin and explained the confusion. He was quite gracious about it."

"The confusion?" Mia put a slice of cake on the paper towel.

Malcolm nodded. "I told him I took off for my lake house and forgot that Abigail was going to meet me. He gave me a lecture about leaving my door open, but that's that."

He took a bite of the cake.

"You're not afraid to go home?" Mia asked.

"Heavens no. I'm sure Jerimiah was just ruffling feathers with the call. I told him that I would remove the spell on Wednesday if it was still there. He said he'd remove it before that, but that he'd appreciate a visit from you. He thinks you have some things to talk about."

"You're not going alone." Trent came back into the room. "The boxes are in the living room. I don't care if he's being all reasonable now. Two people are dead and he put a spell on their houses. I want to know why before we welcome him back with open arms."

"That's outside my role as the membership committee chair." He stared at Trent for a full minute. Then he turned back to Mia. "I would still like to take you to lunch and talk about you joining us."

"Maybe sometime later," Mia said, dodging the invite. "I'm down an employee as of this morning and I've got a full day of deliveries and a wedding this week."

"I'll be looking for your call." He tipped his head. "Thank you for the hospitality yesterday. It was very kind."

They all watched as he left the apartment, then watched on the security monitor as he left by the front door. He walked down the hill to the road and got into a taxi he'd apparently called before leaving his room.

"That was weird, right?" Christina looked around the table at the others.

Mia was the first to respond. "That was really weird. I guess we," Mia looked at Trent, as he nodded, "will head over to Twin to talk to Jerimiah to see what he knows. Christina, call Levi to see if he has time to help scan these records for anything with Ginny or Hailey or the name Richards."

"Levi's working a shift, but Mom will be here in a few minutes. Dad would come, but he's got a fishing tour booked today." Trent sat down at the table. "So, we have time to eat, right?"

"The frittata needs a few minutes, but there's coffee cake." Mia handed out the plates she'd just filled. "Grans, do you want another slice?"

"Please. I need to take advantage of this metabolism before it disappears like this tight skin." She patted her cheeks.

They sat down to eat while they waited for the frittata and Abigail. When she arrived, she ate too, while the group filled her in on the happenings that morning. When they were through, Abigail whistled. "You all know a lot of the players. I'm sorry to hear Hailey left. She was a joy to work with."

"I'm sure we'll find someone else soon." Mia met Abigail's gaze. "But for right now, let's just slow down a beat on hiring. So don't tell your friend I need help. I might need to back up a few steps with Mia's Morsels."

"You're not shutting it down, are you?" Christina set down her fork. "I need the part-time job. I've built my class schedule around cooking and delivery days. Besides, this is what I want to do with my life. I know it."

"Nice speech, but not necessary." Mia sipped her coffee. She explained the catering job and then went into the specifics. "Abigail and I have a plan for the next few years while you're still in college. She's going to run the business while I work at the Lodge as their catering director. Maybe they'll change their mind about outsourcing their catering. Then I'll quit and come back and we'll pick up where we left off. Or if we get too busy, I'll come back. Right now, we need the income to stay afloat."

"I can help if you need me," Grans offered. "Maybe we can have the office open for drop-ins on Monday, Friday, and Saturday for a few hours. That way you have someone here at specific times to pick up food. I think that would help."

"I think that would be amazing." Mia smiled at the group. "I'm so happy you all are in this with me. I can't do it without you."

Grans nodded to the stove. "Your buzzer's about to go off. Let's eat and then we'll finish figuring out what Hailey has to do with the murders. I do hope that girl isn't responsible. She's got a kind soul."

Mia got the frittata out of the oven and cut it into triangles. For the next few minutes, the group ate and enjoyed one another's company. She'd made true friends here in Magic Springs, not just acquaintances. And she knew the business would work itself out. She'd be open to whatever opportunities arrived due to her new catering job and Mia's Morsels would grow without the Lodge's business.

This time Gloria's giggle was one of comfort, not something scary. Mia had found her tribe.

Now, to find the murderer.

Mia sat in Trent's passenger seat, looking at the small ice cream shop in Twin, where Jerimiah worked. Or, more accurately, he owned the pink building with a happy, black-and-white cow grazing on the roof. She looked over at Trent. "He doesn't look busy. Shall we go inside and ask him what he's doing with the spells?"

"Sure, and probably have him produce a small ball of sparkles while we grill him on his magic." Trent shook his head. "Coven leaders don't talk about coven business when they can be overheard by mortals."

"Well, we're just going to have to hope no one else is in the shop. I need to help Mahogany figure out who killed her mom. It's not enough that we got the aging spell off the house. What if the person keeps killing? Grans is on that list." Mia turned from watching the white building with its sunny personality. It felt wrong to be talking about murder here. This was a place where happy families got a midday treat. Or milkshakes after the baseball game.

"Okay, we drove all this way, we might as well try. But don't say I didn't warn you." He turned off the engine and climbed out of the truck.

Mia followed and met him in the doorway. She looked through the window. No one, not even a clerk, seemed to be in the store. She opened the door and bells rang through the empty dining area. "Hello? Is anyone here?"

A man in an old-fashioned soda jerk outfit including a paper hat came out with a box. He set it down behind the ice cream display and turned to them. "Sorry, I was in the back. Oh, it's you. Lock the door and put up the 'Closed' sign, please. We can talk in my office. I'm not expecting customers for thirty or so minutes."

Trent followed his instructions and Mia stepped forward. "You're Jerimiah, right? I saw you having dinner with Ginny a few weeks ago."

"That's me." His narrow face looked more menacing without the smile he'd had when they first walked in. "Look, I know you're here about the calls. I'm sorry, but I was trying to fix this before it got any further out of hand. I was helping, really."

"Helping? At least two women were killed by a spell that looked a lot like the one you put on the property after they died." Mia followed him into the back, where he stood by a white door, holding it open for her. Was it a trap? She pushed out her senses but didn't feel anything but the residuals of happy ice cream customers. Glancing back at Trent, she nodded and went into Jerimiah's office.

"I'm not going to hurt you." He stepped around her and sat at the wooden desk, which held a computer and a line of toy trolls. Their hair blew in the gentle breeze of a fan in the back of the office. "Look, I noticed the spell when I came to town to talk to Hetty Medford about her tea shop selling my ice cream. I figured it was a long shot, but we'd chatted online for a few months and she seemed open to some specialty items. We started to talk a lot. One day, after I hadn't heard from her in a few weeks, I went to the shop and her daughter told me she was dead. When I found out she'd died of old age, I knew something was wrong. We graduated the same year from Twin Falls High."

"So you knew it was an aging spell. Why didn't you talk to the Magic Springs's coven leaders?" Mia couldn't believe someone had known Hetty had been murdered all this time and hadn't told anyone. And this was the "boyfriend" Hetty thought she had?

"I did, but they blew me off. Said that Hetty was old and it was a natural death. That they'd talked to the police chief there to make sure." He picked up one of the trolls that had fallen over, brushed its hair up and in place, and returned it back to its place in line. "I didn't know who to trust. So I put the spell on Hetty's house. I hoped the actual killer would return and think their removal spell hadn't worked. But then Theresa died, and I knew someone was targeting single witches in Magic Springs. So, I set the second trap. But when they weren't triggered, I went to talk to Ginny about what was going on. I thought she was killing people to get their estates for the coven. Ginny always has been a big spender. She told me I was imagining things. But I saw the worry in her eyes."

"So, Ginny knew that people she's been soliciting to leave their estate to the coven are dying. But she didn't do anything either." Mia swore under her breath. What did it take for the coven to step up and protect its members?

"I don't know what she did. The next thing I knew, you and Malcolm were bringing down my traps. I should have come by to talk to you, but it's been crazy around here. I lost my best server a few weeks ago. Hailey just up and quit with no warning." He pulled out a pile of applications. "I've been calling job applicants ever since, but no one wants a part-time job with no benefits with what I can pay them."

"Yeah, I had the same problem." Mia froze as her mind caught up with what he'd said. "Your employee was named Hailey?"

"She was only here a short time, but she was amazing with the customers. Especially the little kids." He nodded to the last troll, who was dressed as an ice cream cone. "She gave me that."

"Long blond hair, blue eyes, pretty?"

Jerimiah nodded. "Yes. About five eight, I think. I'm six foot and she was almost as tall as me. Why?"

"Because I think she's the same Hailey who worked for me for a week and quit this weekend." Mia stood and thanked Jerimiah for his time. She let him know that Malcolm was taking the spell off the Holly house on Wednesday.

"No need. I've already removed it. After I talked with Malcolm, I realized my efforts to find the killer weren't working. I was just making it worse." He followed them out to the front, where he opened the door and turned over the sign. "If I can help in any way, please let me know. I feel bad that this guy is still out there."

Back in the car, Mia sat back, thinking about what she'd learned. Jerimiah wasn't the killer she'd been looking for. In fact, he'd been the one trying to stop the killings. At least if she believed his story, and she did. "So, Jerimiah didn't kill Hetty and Theresa. And if he thinks Ginny didn't, I'm not sure who to look at."

Trent leaned forward. "There seems to be a common denominator here. Hailey. And didn't you say that someone sent you a list of the women Ginny was targeting for the fundraising? Maybe it's someone in Ginny's office."

"Well, I can't stop by today to see if my ex-employee is actually working at the fundraising office. I guess I'm going to have to put this aside and work on the wedding coming up. According to Lasher, the wards are as good as new. I'm not sure I totally believe that. I sent an email to Silas Miller and he said he'd come by on Monday, just to make sure."

"You're having someone check Lasher's work?" Trent snuck a look at her as they drove through town and back to Magic Springs. "I should have thought of that. Especially after the ghost thing."

"There's just something about him I don't like. It may be that he was dating my grandmother and they apparently had a falling out, but there's something I can't put my finger on. Yet." Mia looked around the road they were on. "It looks like we missed all the fast food and I'm starving."

"I can turn around, or we can do an early dinner at the Lodge. Your choice." He stopped at a red light and looked at her.

"Better make it the Lodge; I've been avoiding James's calls. I need to tell him I'm applying before he thinks I'm not interested in the job." She faked a smile. "'Yes, I'd love to be your catering director.'"

"You'd probably better practice that in the mirror because it looks like you're signing up for having a root canal with no nerve-deadening meds." He turned onto the highway that would take them home.

"I'll try. Besides, James isn't the one I have to convince; it's his boss. I just need to get the application and fill it out. I need to do this for the business." She stared out the window.

"We do a lot of things for the business. I just hope you don't wear yourself out while you're trying to be superwoman." He turned on the music and they spent the rest of the drive avoiding talking about the murders, or the new job, or anything about business.

* * *

At the Lodge, they'd ordered and been served their drinks and, as their waiter put a basket of bread on their table, Mia asked, "Is James in today?"

The waiter nodded. He was one of the regulars James loaned her when Mia's Morsels did events at the Lodge. "He's in the banquet area, setting up for the dinner tonight. It's for the Magic Valley Golf Association's annual event. I'm working there as soon as I get off shift in the dining room. I need the overtime to pay my car insurance this month. Do you want me to ask him to come over?"

The dining room was busy and Mia knew the waiter had several tables. "No, I know where the meeting rooms are. I'll just pop over and find him."

Trent held up his phone. "I'll call Mom to tell her about the Jerimiah trip."

"Sounds good. I'll be right back. Don't eat all the bread."

He reached for a slice as she walked away from the table. She left the dining room and headed to the main ballroom, but although it was set for dinner and there were several servers putting the final touches on the tables, James wasn't there.

She'd turned and gone down a hallway that would take her to the kitchen the back way when she heard angry voices.

The door to a small meeting room was cracked open. She glanced inside and saw Hailey talking— no, yelling—at a man. When he turned toward Hailey, Mia recognized him. It was Alphonso Lasher. Mia pulled away from the doorway and called her office number. When it went to the voice recording, she punched Speaker and held it closer to the entry.

"I'm not doing this anymore. These people are nice. They aren't the monsters you told me they were." From the tone in her voice, Hailey was on the verge of crying. "Just because they're witches doesn't mean they're evil. I know that now."

"You'll do what I say. You're the one who gave me the names. Once we kill a third woman, the authorities won't have any choice but to close down the coven and Ginny Willis will go to jail." Lasher laughed at the idea.

"I didn't kill anyone. You set the spell and then strangled those women," Hailey said. "And I'm not helping you anymore. I'm quitting my job with Ginny and leaving town."

"That's not going to stop me. And if I get caught, you're going down with me. Just remember that if you try to get a conscience. You wanted to be a witch hunter. You were the one who believed they were evil. You can't just walk away scot-free now. Besides, I've already chosen the next target. Mary Alice will regret the day she turned me away. And she's already been messing with her time line. She's perfect."

Mia's hand started shaking and she almost dropped the phone. She had to get out of there and tell Baldwin. Or Malcolm. She hurried away from the room, back the way she'd come, and turned off her phone.

Trent pointed to her plate. "Just in time. The food just arrived."

She looked up at him and whispered, "Alphonso Lasher is the killer. I have a recording that proves it, but I don't know who to give it to. Trent, he's going after Grans next."

*   *   *

Mia had never been at the coven's headquarters. Now, she sat outside the board office on a leather couch. Grans, Abigail, Thomas, Trent, Levi, and even Christina were in the room as well. There had been some grumbling from the board about Christina being let into the building because she wasn't a witch, but there was no way Mia was going to leave her alone at the school. Not when Lasher was still at large.

After she'd told Trent at the Lodge, he'd paid the check without eating and they'd headed to the Majors house. He'd called Levi and asked him to pick up Christina and Grans. When they got there, Malcolm was waiting. Mia told her story, and while they waited for Malcolm to make arrangements with the board, Abigail had fed them.

When they'd arrived at the coven headquarters, Mia had told her story again. Then she played the recording. Now they all waited outside the board room. Mia turned to Abigail. "Are you sure we shouldn't call Baldwin?"

"He'll be called as soon as the board figures out a way to remove the magic part of the crime. Lasher has made it pretty easy for them. He got Hailey to give him the list of names Ginny had curated. Then he just picked one. If Baldwin had gotten suspicious, all the evidence pointed at Ginny and her need for money to keep up her lifestyle. They would have assumed she'd hired someone and killed them too." Abigail looked over at Grans. "You're lucky he didn't kill you."

Grans, who now looked like herself after the last of the reversal spell had dissipated, shook her head. "He didn't have a chance. He thought he was being so charming when he was with me. I knew something was off, but I couldn't put my finger on it. I thought it was the aging spell. Then that girl showed up at the school and I recognized her. I just didn't remember from where. Now I know she was Ginny's assistant. She offered me coffee and cookies that day I went into Ginny's office."

Malcolm came out of the room and closed the door behind him. "It's done. Both Lasher and Hailey are in custody. She's ready to talk, according to Baldwin, but she's been assigned a coven lawyer. He'll coach her on what to say and help her get the best deal possible. She was working with a serial killer."

"She's a good kid. She just got lost," Mia said, and the others nodded.

"Anyway, you're all free to go. And it's safe. From what we've found out from Henry, it was his uncle who was pushing them to get married at the school. So we had Silas go over to your house and check the wards. They were set to dissolve right after the wedding ceremony. Apparently, Lasher didn't much care for his relatives." Malcolm checked the paper he was reading from. "And we're handling settlements for Hetty and Theresa's families."

"Why would he do this?" Mia asked. The question of why kept bouncing around her head.

Malcolm shook his head. "Apparently, Ginny Willis had spurned his advances years ago. I guess he saw this as a way to burn her and the coven. He's been sanctioned several times for illegal use of magic. I guess he just wanted to take people out with him."

As they stood to leave, Mia stopped. "What about the ghosts from the cemetery? What are we going to do after the wards are reset?"

"The ghosts you were seeing were being controlled by Lasher. That graveyard was cleared of bodies when the school was built. Any additional issues were dealt with a few years later. Your school is clear." Malcolm nodded and then went back into the room.

Mia met Trent's gaze. "Why don't I totally believe him?"

"Because he's a politician and he's telling you what you want to hear?" Grans put her arm through Mia's. "Don't look a gift horse in the mouth. The school wards are reset and you got justice for two women. And you might have saved my life."

She turned to her grandmother. "What was that last one?"

"Don't push it. Stop at my house and let me get more food for Muffy and some additional clothes. I'm extending my stay with you for a few days until this all gets settled. I'll feel more comfortable knowing where you are."

Trent smiled over Grans's head at Mia. "You and Mia can ride with me. I'll get you back to the school."

"You're a good man." Grans turned to Trent and took his arm instead of Mia's. "Don't let that granddaughter of mine tell you any different."

Mia watched them walk away. "I'm standing right here."

Christina laughed and pulled Mia toward the

door. "Come on. We've got a wedding to prepare for."

"One without fireworks," Mia added as they made their way out of the building. "I'm wondering if we should only accept jobs from nonmagical people from now on. The last two weddings have been a bit of an issue."

"But you're so good at it." Abigail came up on the other side of Mia. "Besides, it's fun."

"Fun" was not a description of the last week or so, at least not in Mia's mind, but she did agree with Abigail. Working with this crew was fun and they were good at what they did. No matter what the circumstances. She'd worry about everything else tomorrow. Christina was right. Today, they had a wedding to plan.

The next morning, Christina and Mia were in the kitchen when the security monitor went off. A Land Rover pulled into the parking lot. Mia swore. "I bet that's one of the coven lawyers, here to take our statement. Malcolm said it would be this week, but he said he'd tell them to call first."

"That's not a lawyer." Christina stood and automatically smoothed her hair and clothes. "That's Mom."

"Your mother is here at nine in the morning? That's an hour drive from Boise." Mia glanced around the kitchen, which looked like a bomb had exploded because Levi and Trent had stayed over last night and they'd played a board game, trying to decompress from the crazy day. "We can host her in the living room downstairs. I'll go make coffee and get some cookies in the oven."

Christina shook her head. "No, we're not playing tea party with her. She's probably here to yell at me for something I took when we moved me out. I'll figure out what she wants and get it from the storage room. Then she can leave."

"Christina." Mia was about to say, *It's your mother,* but the look on her face told Mia she was barely hanging on. "Whatever you want, I'll support you."

"The keys are hanging by the door, right?"

"Yes. Call me if you need my help." Mia wanted to go stand by her friend, but Mother Adams hated Mia more than she did her youngest daughter. If she went down, the situation would just escalate.

Twenty minutes later, Mia saw the Land Rover leave. Christina was still downstairs. Mia hurried down the stairs to check on her.

She found her sitting on the couch, a necklace in her hand. She looked up at Mia with tears in her eyes. "Mom brought me Grandma's diamond necklace. The one she got from Grandpa when she was twenty-one?"

Mia sat down next to her. "That's lovely."

"She said she had it on the dining room table for me, but Isaac forgot to give it to me." She touched the large diamond, then closed the box. "She said she hated that we were fighting and invited me to dinner on Sunday. Everyone's going to be there."

"That's sweet. You should go." Mia didn't know Mother Adams had it in her, but something had triggered the woman to show some kindness to her only daughter.

"And she said there's a credit at the Land Rover dealership in Sun Valley. Mia, she bought me a car." Now Christina fell onto Mia's shoulder and started crying.

"Hey, now, this is a good thing, right?" Mia rubbed the top of Christina's head.

Christina sat up, controlling the tears. "Mom said she owed it to me as my high school graduation gift. That she'd bought one for Isaac and she thought it was only fair that I got one as well. I need to go call Levi so he can take me over to pick up my car before she changes her mind."

Mia watched as Christina sprinted up the stairs to get her cell. She sent a prayer to the Goddess that this wasn't a trick, but even if it was an attempt to win her daughter back to her, Mother Adams had finally stepped up in Mia's eyes.

Now they just needed to see what the cost of accepting the gift horse would be. And it would come with a price. Mia knew that. She just hoped Christina realized it as well.

RECIPE

Christina's Veggie Lasagna

Making lasagna is a time and ingredient commitment. And in my house, it means I'm going to have leftovers to freeze and eat later. I can't seem to make anything for two people, even though the Cowboy and I been empty nesters most of our married life. Although I love a good meat sauce, this veggie rich dish checks the box when I'm trying to increase my vegetables in my diet. This is a great way to use up the extra vegetables you grabbed at the farmer's market.

Heat oven to 350. Lightly spray oil a 13-inch by 9-inch baking dish

In a large pot, boil water, add salt and 12 lasagna noodles. Cook until al dente, then drain and rinse with cold water to stop the cooking process. Set aside.

In large deep skillet, add the following and sauté for five minutes:

> 2 tablespoons extra-virgin olive oil
> 1 cup (140 grams) chopped onion

Then add the following and cook until veggies are soft:

> 1 tablespoon minced garlic, 3 to 4
> cloves

⅛ teaspoon crushed red pepper flakes,
   or more to taste
2 medium chopped zucchini
2 medium chopped yellow squash
8 oz sliced fresh mushrooms
Salt and pepper to taste

Then add the following and cook until the sauce starts to thicken:

1 (28-ounce) can crushed tomatoes
Generous handful fresh basil leaves,
   chopped

Set aside.

In a large bowl, mix the following:

One (15-ounce) container ricotta
   cheese or cottage cheese
2 large eggs
½ tsp salt

In another bowl, gently mix the following:

⅔ cup grated parmesan cheese
2 cups of shredded mozzarella cheese

To assemble the lasagna:

Spoon 1 cup vegetable mixture into the baking dish to lightly cover the bottom. Set a layer of noodles, then a layer of veggies, a layer of ricotta (half), and a layer of cheese (⅓). Then repeat the layers starting with the noodles. The third layer only has noodles and the remaining vegetable sauce, finishing with the remaining cheese sprinkled over the top.

Bake covered with foil for 20 minutes, then bake uncovered for 15 minutes. Remove from oven and let set for 15 minutes.

Serve with garlic bread and a green salad.

Did you miss the first book in the Kitchen Witch mystery series? No worries! Keep reading to enjoy a sample chapter from *One Poison Pie*.
Available from Kensington Publishing Corp.

CHAPTER 1

Karma sucks.

Mia Malone slapped the roller filled with cottage yellow paint on the wall. She'd missed another spot. Her lack of attention was one more thing on the long list of karma credits she could blame on her ex, Isaac.

If karma didn't smack down the lowlife soon, she had several ideal spells just waiting to be used on the rat. Maybe he'd like to develop a rash? Or be turned into a toad to match his true personality? A line of yellow paint dripped off the roller and onto the scratched wood floor.

She set the roller in the paint pan and, with a rag, wiped up the paint before it could dry. Maybe a run would be more productive right now. She could burn off this pent-up energy tingling her fingers. Teasing her with all the curses she could inflict.

She took a deep, calming breath. Magic came back threefold. She needed to control her impulses, keeping her anger in check. As much as she wanted Isaac to pay for his betrayal, she didn't need any help in the bad luck department. Sighing, she sat cross-legged on the floor in the middle of the half-painted schoolroom and tried to envision her new life.

A noise echoed through the empty schoolhouse. *Had the door opened?*

"Mia," her grandmother called. "Are you here, dear?"

"To your left, Grans." Mia stood and dusted off the butt of her worn jeans, imagining dusting off Isaac and his bad energy at the same time. Keeping her karma clean seemed to be a full-time job since she'd left Boise.

Mary Alice Carpenter, tall and willowy, stood in the doorway to the foyer. The curl in her short, gray hair was the only physical trait Grans and Mia shared. Mia stood a good five inches shorter than the older woman, and Mia's curves would have made her prime model material, oh, about a hundred years ago.

Besides her curly hair, she'd inherited power from her maternal grandmother. While her mother had turned away from the lure of magic, choosing instead the life of a corporate lawyer's wife, Mia had embraced her heritage.

Her grandmother took one look at her and groaned. "I knew he wouldn't stay gone. That boy is worse than spilled milk. You just can't get rid of the smell."

"I can handle Isaac." Mia gave her grandmother a hug. "You don't worry about him."

Grans's eyebrows rose. "Are you sure, dear? I've

done a few transmutations in my time that may be quite appropriate."

Mia bit back a laugh and glanced around the large room. "Seriously, don't get involved. That part of my life is over. I've made a fresh start."

"You've bought a run-down money pit that's going to bankrupt you just trying to keep the place warm." A second woman followed her grandmother into the room, shoving a cell phone into her Coach bag. "Sorry, had to take that. Apparently, my long-lost nephew is gracing us with his presence at my birthday party. Probably needs money."

"Adele, so nice to see you," Mia managed to choke out after a death stare from her grandmother.

Adele Simpson stood next to Grans and glanced around the room, noticeable disgust covering her face. "Mary Alice, *this* is what you fought so hard with the board to save?"

"The building should be on the historic register. You and I both know it would have already been protected if it sat in the Sun Valley city limits. Magic Springs is always an afterthought with the historical commission." Grans slipped off the down coat that had made her look like a stuffed panda.

Mia watched the women bicker. Adele, the meanest woman in Magic Springs, was the dark to Grans's light and, for some unbeknownst reason, Grans's best friend. She was also Mia's first and only client for her new venture. *So far*, she amended.

Gritting her teeth, Mia forced her lips into what she hoped was a passable smile. "Ladies, welcome to Mia's Morsels." She glanced around the room, sweeping her arm as she turned. "Currently, you're in the reception area, where staff and students will gather before classes, and where we'll do most of the daily work scheduling. Here, customers will be able to sample dishes and peruse a weekly menu of available meals."

"You sound like a commercial," Grans chided. "It's just us. You don't have to put on the sales pitch."

Mia smiled. "Just trying it out. I've got a lot of work to do before I can even think about opening." She nodded to the half-painted wall. "Do you like the color?"

Her grandmother nodded. "It's friendly without being obnoxiously bright, like so many buildings. Day-care colors have swept through the decorating studios. I swear, the new crop of interior designers have no sense of style or class."

"Fredrick just did Helen Marcum's living room in pink." Adele sniffed. "The room looks like an antacid commercial. I swear, the woman shows her hillbilly roots every time she makes a decision."

"I don't believe Helen's Southern, dear." Grans focused back on Mia, closing her eyes for a second. "Color holds a lot of power. Pull out your books before you go too far. Although if I remember, yellow represents the digestive system."

Mia loved listening to her grandmother talk about the representations of power. Being kitchen witches was different from being Wiccan, or what normal people would think of when you said *witch*. They didn't wear black, pointy hats or fly around the moon. Mia's magic was more about the colors, the food, the process of making a house a home.

That was one of the reasons her career choice was such a natural extension of her life. Food made people happy. She liked being around happy people. Sometimes magic was that easy.

"You are not doing woo-woo magic stuff again, are you, Mary Alice?" Adele shook her head. "Next you'll be telling the girl to open on a full moon and wave around a dead cat."

Grans looked horrified at her friend. "I would never tell her to desecrate an animal that way. We've been friends for over forty years. You should know better."

"Oh, go fly your broomstick."

Grans and Adele had been the swing votes on the board, allowing Mia to purchase the property based on her pledge to save the building's history. The losing bidder had presented a plan to bulldoze the school and replace it with a high-end retail mall. Instead, Mia had a place to start over. Grans always said the best way to get a man out of your head was to change your routine.

Mia may have gone a little overboard.

Her arms and back ached from painting. Another two, three hours, the room would be done. Then she could move on to the kitchen, the heart of her dream. Right now, all she wanted was to clean up the paint supplies and return to her upstairs apartment for a long soak in the claw-foot tub. The unexpected visitors had her skin tingling, a sure sign nothing good was about to happen.

Catering Adele's birthday party had been an order more than a request, even though her business wouldn't be completely up and running for a month or so. The planning for the event had gone smoothly, like an aged Southern whiskey. The final prep list for Saturday's party sat finished on her kitchen table in the apartment. James, the chef at the Lodge, had allowed her time to prep in his kitchen tomorrow evening. By Sunday she'd have a successful reference in the books for Mia's Morsels. Now, without warning, the triumph she'd hoped for was slipping through her fingers.

"Add one, maybe two more, to the guest list. Who knows who he'll bring from Arizona to help me celebrate." Adele shoved a piece of paper toward her.

Mia glanced down. A name had been scrawled on the torn notepaper, William Danforth III. She hadn't known Adele had any living relatives, no less a nephew. "How nice. Are you close?"

A harsh laugh came from the woman. "Close? I wasn't kidding about the money. He's checking on his inheritance. I'm pretty sure he thought I'd be dead by now."

"Now, Adele, at least he's visiting." Grans picked up Mr. Darcy, Mia's gray cat, who'd wandered into the room. He'd probably been sleeping in one of the empty southern classrooms, where the afternoon sun warmed the wood floors. He curled into her neck and started purring. Loudly.

Unfortunately, during a late summer visit to Grans's house, Mr. Darcy had picked up a hitchhiker. The spirit of Dorian Alexander, who had been Grans's beau before his untimely death, had taken up residence with Mia's cat. A fact that weirded Mia out at times, especially at night, when Mr. Darcy slept on the foot of her bed. Mia really needed to get Grans focused on a reversal spell.

But this wasn't the time to be chatting about spells and power. Instead, she focused on Adele and her party.

"I'm sure he's . . ." Mia stopped. What had she been going to say? That Adele's nephew was nice? If the guy had any of Adele's temperament, the guy would be a royal jerk.

Adele waved away her words, her hands showing her impatience, "Let me worry about Billy. You're serving beef tomorrow." The words weren't a question.

"I'd planned to serve squab with raspberry sauce and wild rice for the main course." Mia held her breath. *Please no last minute changes—please.*

"That won't do at all." Adele watched as Mr. Darcy crawled up on Grans's shoulder. She reached out a hand to pet the cat, who hissed at her. Dropping her hand, she focused her glare on Mia. "My parents ran the Beef Council for years. You had to have known we had the largest cattle operation in the Challis area, maybe even the entire Magic Valley."

"I sent you the menu a week ago." Mia thought about the prep list she'd spent hours writing out last night. A list that would have to be completely revamped if Adele made this change in the menu. "I'm sure you responded."

"I've been busy. You should have called rather than sending paper." Adele stepped farther away from the hissing cat. "I don't remember everything. That's why I'm telling you now. Oh, and no cake; pie for dessert. Several different types, of course; you'll know which ones to serve with the beef. I've never liked cake."

"You already approved the menu," Mia repeated through clenched teeth. Apparently sensing her distress, Mr. Darcy jumped out of Grans's arms and walked over to Mia. He curled on her feet, watching the women.

"I doubt that. No matter, you need to serve beef. It's a tradition. I'm surprised you didn't know." Adele pulled out a beeping phone and, after glancing at the display, focused on Grans. "We need to leave now if we're going to keep our court time."

Mia sighed. Trying one more time to win a battle already lost, she asked, "Are you sure you don't want squab?"

"The homeless eat pigeon. Porterhouse. Or whatever cut you think is best. You're the expert." Adele turned toward the door, pulling Grans along with her.

That's what you keep saying. Mia said, "I'll try, but the party is this weekend."

"I'm sure you'll do your best." Grans shook off Adele's grip and turned back to Mia. She planted a kiss on her cheek.

Mia followed them to the front door. Daylight filtered through the dirt-covered windows. Another item for her to-do list: hire a window cleaner. Mr. Darcy's soft footsteps padded behind her. "Thanks for stopping in," she called as they left the building. After the door closed she added, hoping her grandmother wouldn't hear, "And ruining a perfectly good day."

If she was being honest, though, the ruination of her day had started with Isaac's call. She reached down to stroke Mr. Darcy. He meowed his wishes.

"Sorry, your dinner is going to have to wait. I've

got to get to Majors Grocery," Mia told the cat, who looked horrified at the thought. She hauled the painting supplies to the kitchen. Her mind whirled as water rinsed cheery yellow paint out of the roller and down the drain. Her detailed plan of attack for the event had disappeared with a flick of Adele's perfectly polished, bloodred nails.

Mr. Darcy wove through her legs as she stood at the sink. Finishing the cleanup, she laid the tools on a towel to dry and double-checked the lock on the back door. Then she climbed the two sets of stairs to the third floor and her apartment.

Christina Adams, the almost-twenty-year-old sister of her ex, jumped up from the couch when Mia entered the apartment. "I thought you were going to paint this afternoon?"

"I thought you were coming to help just as soon as you finished lunch?" Mia studied the girl. Last month Christina had returned to Magic Springs. She'd shown up on Mia's doorstep with a police escort. Mark Baldwin, the town's only officer, had found her loitering in the small downtown park. Her long, blond hair screamed cheerleader, but the bars in her eyebrow and her lip along with the row of piercings in her ear hardened the look.

Christina had been planning on starting college this semester after spending last year in Las Vegas, trying to make it as a dancer after some bad advice from her substitute dance coach. Now, after one more fight with the family, she'd tracked Mia down and asked if she could live with her for a while. Mia didn't have the heart to turn her away, even if Mia wouldn't be part of the Adams family, now or ever.

She had the decency to blush. "I'm not really

good at all that painting stuff. Maybe I could just help you with the cooking rather than the remodeling."

"Don't worry about it. I have a feeling we're going to have to pull an all-nighter if we want to finish prep before the party. And now we have to bake pies as well." She went into the kitchen to get her list. "I'm heading over to Majors. Be ready to work when I get back."

Mia heard the television come on as her only answer. Training Christina to be a sous chef might be harder than she'd imagined. Running her fingers over the cookbook she'd left out that morning with the prep list, she remembered Isaac's call. Could there be another reason Isaac's sister had come to live with Mia? She locked her cookbook in the safe in her room. She'd been stupid before. Today she'd take paranoid.

Where was she going to get thirty servings of steak by tomorrow evening? And the side dishes had to completely change. Adele was paying for both grocery orders, no matter what Grans said.

She hoped the small country store had enough meat on hand. Or an idea.

As she opened the front door, she tripped over an envelope. The delivery service must have dropped it off late yesterday. They'd been busy in the kitchen, doing a trial run-through of the menu. The return address on the top was smeared, but the envelope was clearly addressed to Christina. Mia shoved the envelope into her purse. She'd give it to her when she got back. Or after the party, when she wouldn't mind losing her apprentice.

A dusting of snow had fallen the night before, coating the town in white. Magic Springs looked like a Dickens-novel Christmas. The roads had been plowed. Someone had run a small blade—probably on the front of a four-wheeler—over the sidewalks in front of the school and down the two blocks toward Majors. Small towns, Mia mused. No way had the city paid for this type of service. It had to be one of the homeowners in the village who donated their early morning service for the pleasure of driving their toy around the snow-covered streets.

Mia took a deep breath, trying to focus on solving her menu problems rather than being filled with the quiet beauty of the town. Beef. Maybe a garlic mashed potato? Or a scalloped? Or would Adele consider the menu too homey for her party? Would there be any way Majors could pull off an order of fresh asparagus? It was April, even though the town wouldn't acknowledge spring for a few weeks at the earliest. There had to be asparagus ready to harvest somewhere.

Stomping the snow off her boots, she pushed open the glass grocery slider. A bell rang over the door, echoing in the seemingly empty store. No cashier stood at the register, no shoppers filled the aisles. Mia glanced at her watch: 5:15. The store closed early during the winter, but she'd just made it.

She grabbed a cart and headed to the butcher block in the back. The meat case stood empty and her heart sank. A bell sat on the top of the case and she rang it once. No one came through the doors. Maybe Adele would just have to suck it up and eat the food Mia had planned to serve.

Mia could see her grandmother's frown. Again, she banged on the bell, harder this time, picturing Adele's unsmiling face each time she hit the silver chime.

"Hold up," a man's voice called from the back. "I heard you the first twenty times. I have my hands full back here."

Mia jumped back from the meat case. Her hand still reached out in front of her. She called toward the door, "Okay, I'll wait here."

That was dumb. Of course she would wait. Now that she'd had some time to think, Mia pulled out a slip of paper and started making a quick shopping list. Peaches, asparagus, more butter, fresh horseradish, potatoes; she continued to write as she waited. Finally, she looked up from her list satisfied. She only needed to add thirty quality steaks. Maybe she should serve a soup too. That would give her more time to grill and prep the main course.

Loud voices were muffled by the swinging doors. Was that an argument? She inched closer, trying to see through the window in the door. Two men stood by a large metal table. One, dressed in a suit, shook a finger at the other. Now she could hear the actual words. "I'm not making this offer again. I'll wait and get the property for pennies when it goes to auction."

"I'm not losing this store. Majors has been in the family since the settlers came to Magic Springs. It's part of the community, the town's history. We're just going through a bad patch. Everyone is." The man dropped a box on the table. "I have a customer waiting for me. Unless you're here to shop, get the heck out of my store."

"You'll regret turning me down." The suit walked toward the door and caught sight of Mia watching. "Of course you'd be here. Are you trying to ruin all my business?"

"I'm sorry, do I know you?" Mia stood back, stunned at the man's outburst.

"Why would you?" The man glared at her, then stomped around the counter and almost ran from the store.

ACKNOWLEDGMENTS

As we start to venture out of our pandemic slow-down, it's been lovely to meet readers again who enjoy my characters and their antics as much as I do. Thanks to everyone who makes writing a fun endeavor.

Thanks go out to my buddy in crime, Laura Bradford, for her writing prompts at our Charleston retreat, which helped fix a plot hole I'd created without realizing it.

And, as always, thanks to my Kensington team, including Michaela Hamilton, my first editor, Esi Sogah, and my agent, Jill Marsal. I appreciate everything you do for me and my books.

Visit our website at
KensingtonBooks.com
to sign up for our newsletters, read
more from your favorite authors, see
books by series, view reading group
guides, and more!

Become a Part of Our
Between the Chapters Book Club
Community and Join the Conversation

Submit your book review for a chance to win exclusive
Between the Chapters swag you can't get anywhere else!
https://www.kensingtonbooks.com/pages/review/